A WILL TO SURVIVE

by John Jackson

◆ FriesenPress

Suite 300 - 990 Fort St
Victoria, BC, V8V 3K2
Canada

www.friesenpress.com

ISBN
978-1-4602-8167-3 (Hardcover)
978-1-4602-8168-0 (Paperback)
978-1-4602-8169-7 (eBook)

1. FICTION

Distributed to the trade by The Ingram Book Company

A Will To Survive

ONE

Tuesday May 22, 2001

Fred was already half awake when his alarm went off at six am. KJRL radio filled the room, slightly off station and fuzzy with static. Groaning, he stretched, then got up and stumbled down the hall to the bathroom. While he shaved and brushed his teeth, he listened to the local news and weather on the radio. The announcer's voice was artificially bright.

"Kenora weather for today, sunny with a high of ten. The temperature at the airport is currently a crisp minus five. Folks, yesterday there was a story in the *Miner and News*, I don't know if you saw it..."

Cool one for this time of year, Fred thought as he climbed into the shower.

Like most bush pilots, he was fit—no room in a small Cessna floatplane for a large man. Sleepy as he was, he was excited too.

Today would be the first flight on floats of the season. The ice had been off the lakes for a couple of weeks now, but Fred's plane had been in the hangar getting the skis removed and the floats reinstalled. While the mechanics had been conducting the annual maintenance check up, they had found a few other problems that had to be addressed. The plane was in great shape now, but the delay had cost him a couple of weeks work. No work, of course, meant no pay, so he was eager to get back at it.

Getting out of the shower, he dressed warmly in long wool underwear, denim shirt, jeans, wool socks and a hooded pullover. As he dressed, Fred thought about his buddy Tim. He and Tim Wagner had been friends since their student pilot days, fifteen years earlier. Tim was a go-getter, always on the lookout for the next big deal. He had stayed in Calgary after they finished their flight training and jumped into the oil patch, flying everyone from rig pigs to oil execs. Now Tim was the chief pilot in charge of hiring at a charter company. Tim had phoned him last night. He wanted Fred to come back to Alberta and pilot a plane for him. The oil patch was booming and the demand for charter plane pilots was crazy.

"It's time to grow up and get a real job," Tim had said. "Put down some roots and, what the hell, get some *furniture* for God's sakes!"

The last time Tim had visited, Fred had had four folding camp chairs and a second hand coffee table for living room furniture. As a matter of fact, as he looked around, it was still his living room furniture.

Maybe I should move on. This bush flying is getting a little old.

He pulled on his well-worn leather flight jacket and hunted through the closet for his hiking boots.

I'm sure not getting rich here.

He would be turning thirty-six soon. Maybe it was time to give up the simple life and join the rat race, but the thought of moving back to Calgary really didn't appeal to him. He hadn't liked it when he lived there all those years ago, and he could only imagine what the traffic would be like now.

He picked up his favourite Cessna hat and pushed it onto the back of his head—he'd bought that hat in Calgary the same day he had bought the flight jacket. Both were a graduation present he had treated himself to after achieving his private pilot's license. He patted the inside pocket to make sure his sunglasses were there. The hat hadn't held up as well as the jacket had. The once bright red hat was now a faded pink with a frayed brim. He checked himself out in the hall mirror. He looked sharp with his fresh haircut. The ball cap hid the annoying little bald spot that had just appeared this year. Over the winter he had put on a bit of weight, and it bugged him that he had to go up a size in jeans.

Gettin' old.

After a quick stop for a coffee and a breakfast sandwich to go, Fred drove down to the floatplane dock at Morgan's Bay and parked his old Chevy. He sauntered down the stairs the dock to prepare the plane for the flight ahead.

—

Mike woke to the buzzer of a clock radio in his Kenora hotel room. He sat up in bed and stabbed at the buttons until it shut off. Then he lay back down and waited for the room to stop spinning. Finally his desperate need to pee and brush his teeth won over. Last night's scotch binge had some lasting after effects.

Yesterday he had taken a taxi from his home in Oakville to Pearson International a full two hours before his flight north to Thunder Bay. Mike was a careful man and didn't like upsets to his plans by being late for anything. After he checked in and made his way through the security check line, he stopped at a bookstore to grab some reading material. He had purposely left his laptop and cellphone at home. This was, after all, supposed to be a vacation. After a quick browse he grabbed two Michael Crichton paperbacks, a Robin Cook he hadn't read yet, and a copy of the *National Post*.

That should be enough for a week, he thought.

As he stood waiting for his turn at the checkout counter, he spotted a harmonica and book combination set. The book cover promised that even the rankest beginner would be playing within hours. Mike had always wanted to play some kind of musical instrument but had never been willing to put in the time to learn. This looked like it would be relatively easy. Impulsively Mike put the harmonica on the counter with the rest of his purchases.

With an hour to kill he wandered down toward his gate. He stopped at a pub and took a stool at the bar. After he perused the menu he called down to the bartender.

"I'll take a cheese and mushroom burger and a pint of dark ale."

He studied the harmonica book while waiting for his burger. It looked so easy that he had an urge to blow a few notes right then and there but resisted. He would have plenty of opportunities to play with this new toy in the coming week.

Mike was on his way to a fly-in fishing lodge on Trout Lake—but not the Trout Lake near North Bay, no *this* Trout Lake was about four hundred clicks northwest of Thunder Bay near the Manitoba border and was only accessible by plane. He had liked the sound of that when he and two of his friends had booked this trip last fall on a whim. Of course, Mike could only get a week off work this time of year, but his buddies had gone ahead to the lodge last week. They had phoned him yesterday just before he left for the airport: they were out of liquor and were having a blast. Laughing, Mike promised to restock before arriving. The week promised to be a lot of fun.

Once his plane landed in Thunder Bay, Mike picked up his rented car and made his way out of town on Highway 17 for the two hour or so drive west to Kenora. He arrived in town with only minutes to spare before the government liquor store closed for the night. Keeping his floatplane luggage weight limit in mind, he got as much hard liquor and wine as he thought he could get away with. He grabbed an extra mickey of scotch for the hotel room that night. Before he went back to his hotel, he got directions to the floatplane dock and drove over there to make sure he would be able to find it in the morning without any trouble.

Back in his hotel room, he drank up the entire mickey of scotch while he tried to teach himself the harmonica, playing until his neighbour in the next room started banging on the wall. Out of scotch anyway, he took the hint, went to bed and passed out.

Now his head hurt like hell, but he felt he had accomplished quite a bit towards teaching himself to play the harmonica.

I'll have a concert for Cathy and the kids when I get back.

His son Tyler had been taking guitar lessons for the last year. *Who knows,* he thought, *maybe this will give Tyler and me something to do together.*

Mike showered, dressed and packed up his suitcases. A free continental breakfast later and he was on his way to the dock. *Vacation time!* he thought, humming tunelessly as he pulled into the parking lot. He beeped the horn, looking for the luggage valet service.

—

Ruth woke to an automated telephone wake-up call. For a moment she was completely disoriented. As soon as she realized where she was, however, a big smile crossed her face. Today she was going home for the summer. Home for Ruth was a fishing lodge that her parents owned on Trout Lake in Northern Ontario. Ruth had grown up at the Trout Lake Lodge and had loved it there.

She had made a decision to quit her job in Thunder Bay a month ago and had phoned her mother to tell her the news.

"What are you going to do for a job?" The first thing out of Anne Denver's mouth.

"Nothing! First I am going to take a relaxing Mexican holiday, and then I'll face reality when I get back."

"Well why don't you come home for the season? You can work at the lodge until you get things sorted out."

Ruth only had to think about it for a moment. "Thanks, Mom. I'd love to."

A flurry of emails later and they had all the details worked out. They had a guest and one of their own fishing guides flying in to the lodge around the same time that Ruth was getting back from her holiday. She could catch a lift in the floatplane leaving from Kenora for free. Ruth *loved* flying in small planes, which was a good thing, for it was the only way to get to Trout Lake. And getting there directly from Kenora rather than making the tortuous drive up to Red Lake sounded just fine to her.

Ruth had arrived back in Thunder Bay from her trip to Mexico the day before yesterday. She called home to see if her parents wanted anything from the city. It was her dad who answered.

"You bet," he said. "Got a pen?"

Five minutes later Ruth hung up shaking her head in disbelief with a huge shopping list in hand. Her dad loved cooking ethnic food and had a wish list as long as her arm.

A couple of hours and a lot of stores later, Ruth got out of the city and headed west to Kenora. When she arrived in town, she had a late lunch with a couple of high school friends who had moved there from Red Lake. Both were married now with the requisite two kids each. After a two-hour lunch, listening to her friends bragging about kids and getting grilled on her nonexistent love life, she was ready for a summer in the bush. Although the ribbing she took on her single status hit home, she knew her friends meant well. One of them had volunteered to pick her car up from the floatplane dock the next day and store it at her house for the summer. To perk herself up after the girls' lunch, she found a hair salon/spa and got the works, a manicure, pedicure, facial and haircut. That night as she turned in, she felt like a million bucks.

The first thing she did once she got out of bed was set up the coffeemaker. With that done, she hit the bathroom for a hot shower. When she stepped out again, she wiped the steam from the mirror and looked at herself for a moment.

Not bad for thirty-one, she thought, recalling the concerns of girlfriends from yesterday. She decided she'd wear the tight sweater and form-fitting jeans today. They went well with the faded blue jean jacket.

One never knows who might be staying at the lodge. When she was a kid it seemed like there was nothing but middle-aged men staying there—and that was exactly what she was hoping for now.

She put on her hiking boots and grabbed her overnight bag. A frosty morning greeted her when she stepped outside. She opened the trunk to stash her overnight bag in the big duffel with her summer's worth of supplies. Her excitement at the prospect of going home stayed with her all the way to the floatplane dock at Morgan's Bay.

—

It was the smell of fried bacon and coffee that drew George from sleep. He dressed and went down to the kitchen. He would miss these meals. No one could cook like his Mavis. George and Mavis had been married for thirty-five years and were still the best of friends and very much in love.

He was leaving today for the lodge at Trout Lake. George had spent the last six summers there, working as a fishing guide for the Denver family. Both he and Mavis hated being apart for that long, but the money was good, and it gave him something to do between trapping seasons. Before he landed this job, he used to work the summers on a highway paving crew. The work had been hard and the hours long, and at fifty-five, George just couldn't abuse his body like that anymore. Used to the fresh clean air of the bush, the stink of the hot asphalt made him feel ill.

He liked working up at the lodge. He felt comfortable there in a way he never could in the towns. The base pay wasn't great, but the *tips* were, and he liked the family that owned and ran the place. Anne and Kevin were a laid back couple who were almost as bush savvy as he was.

An Anishinaabe, he'd grown up in the Red Lake area and had hunted and fished up there all of his childhood years. He had only moved to the Kenora area after he met Mavis. She was a townie and had convinced him, in her quiet way, to stay in Kenora close to her large extended family. They had done quite well here, so he couldn't complain.

In their early years together, before the kids, they managed to buy a trapline of their own. He taught Mavis the ways of the bush, and to his surprise, Mavis loved living in the little trapper's cabin. It only had water access, and the feeling of solitude was wonderful. As the kids starting appearing, it was a wonderful life. The kids ran free, exploring their world far from the dangers of a town. No traffic, no television. It was only when they approached school age that she quietly manoeuvred George into the idea of buying a house in town for her and the kids to live in during the school term.

The kids were grown and gone now, with kids of their own. They had kept the place in town, but spent as much time as they could at their trapline cabin. It was their *real* home. George ate his hearty breakfast and lingered over one last cup of his wife's coffee. With a big sigh, he rose and picked up his gear.

"Guess we better get going Mavis, my girl."

Mavis put on her jacket and followed him out to their rusty old pickup. They drove hand in hand over to the floatplane dock in silence. At the dock, Mavis leaned over and kissed George softly.

"Be safe," she whispered.

He squeezed her hand and slid out of the truck. He picked his gear out of the back of the truck and, with a quick wave, disappeared down the stairs to the dock.

Mavis watched him go. It would be a long, long summer without him. Mavis put the old truck into gear and headed back home, her cheeks wet with tears. It wasn't just for her that she cried. It was hard on their children and grandchildren as well. George was a big part of all their lives.

TWO

When he got to the dock, Fred saw that the shore end was covered in frost as were the wings of his Cessna 206, so he untied the little craft and towed it almost silently down the side of the dock and out into the morning sunshine.

That should melt it, he thought.

Frost was something you didn't mess with. Like ice, frost changes the airflow pattern over the wing. It could alter the speed at which the wing stalls dramatically. The next chore was pumping out the float compartments with the hand bilge pump. Fred was fanatical about checking for water in the floats before each takeoff. At ten pounds per gallon, water in the float compartments could seriously affect the lifting capacity of the plane, as well as the weight and balance characteristics.

His planned flight for today would take him to a remote fishing lodge on Trout Lake, forty kilometres or so northeast of the town of Red Lake in the heart of the Canadian bush country. Red Lake was approximately two hundred kilometres, as the crow flies, northeast of Kenora. Fred had flown up to this particular lodge numerous times while he had been working for Bud Morgan, so he was quite familiar with the general area.

Hearing footsteps on the dock, he turned to see Bud's wife and business partner. She was carrying a big stainless steel thermos of coffee and a brown paper bag in her hands.

"Hi Mary."

"Morning Fred." She handed him the thermos and the bag lunch she'd made him. "Bud just phoned the lodge. They've checked the local weather. There are a few squalls in the area, but Bud figures it's nothing you can't go around."

Fred nodded. He'd also checked the en route weather this morning before he left home and felt the same way.

"Be careful, and we'll see you tonight. I'm making a roast chicken and an apple pie for dessert, so plan to stay for dinner. Bud will be down to help you load once your guests have arrived."

"Sounds good."

Fred hopped up on the floats to stow the food away in the plane.

Having no kids of their own, Mary and Bud had really taken to Fred. He had boarded with them for the first few weeks when he first came to Kenora and began working for them as a pilot. They had really got to know one another. Fred had quite happily let Mary mother him. Her home cooking was something he just couldn't get enough of. He was a frequent guest for meals at Bud and Mary's. The promise of a chicken dinner sent his mouth watering. It would be a lot more pleasant than the leftover pizza he had planned on having for dinner tonight.

He stepped back onto the dock. "Who's on board today, Mary?"

"Well, let's see, there's George White. You should know him, the fishing guide. He's worked up there at the lodge for the last few years."

"Oh yeah, I remember George. He's a pretty nice guy. He's awfully quiet though."

"That's George alright," she said. "You also have a doctor from Toronto by the name of Michael Cleveland. His friends have been up at Trout Lake Lodge all week, and he's flying up to join them. Your third passenger is Mrs. Denver's daughter Ruth. She is going up to help her mother cook and clean at the lodge for the season." Mary smiled and shook her head. "I haven't seen her in years. I think she's living in Thunder Bay these days. I'm not sure. Anyway I should see what's keeping Bud. You take care, Fred."

"You know it."

As the sun warmed the wings of his Cessna, dispelling the frost, Fred looked to the sky and took a deep breath.

The first of the passengers to arrive was George White, the fishing guide. He was First Nations with a face weathered from years of being outdoors and strong fit frame, making his age was hard to pin down. But Fred knew he had grown kids and grand-children, so he was likely older than he looked. George knew the area up there like the back of his hand and was known as an expert fisherman with the uncanny ability at finding the fishing hotspots. It was very unusual for one of his clients to come back skunked after a day of fishing with George, and as often as not they would come back with their legal limit.

George was friendly but a bit of a loner. Once the fishing was over for the day, he was done socializing with the guests and the other guides and would disappear to a private cabin tucked into the woods behind the lodge and spend his evenings reading and going over his fishing gear. He was also an accomplished small engine repairman and spent some of his spare time keeping the lodge's fleet of outboard engines operational.

The other guides that Fred had met at the lodge were quite a bit younger than George, and they usually hung around together at night in the big bunkhouse, smoking pot or drinking and gam-bling away their tip money. George did not fit in at all with this younger crowd, so it was no wonder that he stuck to himself. The clients, however, loved George. A lot of the regulars would try to book him as their personal guide before they left the lodge.

George nodded a greeting to Fred as he set down his gear on the dock. This consisted of a medium sized red backpack—the back to school type with a broken strap—a big arctic sleeping bag, a tackle box, and a very expensive rod case. Fred knew that a satisfied American customer had given the rod and case to him after George had a guided the fellow for a week last year.

"Fred," he said.

"Howdy, George."

The guide looked to the sky. "Good day for it, you think?"

"I'll get us there."

George nodded then quietly walked down to the end of the dock and sat down with his feet dangling over the edge of the dock. Then he took out his pipe and lit it.

A few minutes later, Bud Morgan came puffing down the steps carrying several plastic grocery bags. Behind him came a rather attractive blonde, half carrying, half dragging an army-style duffle bag. Seeing Fred eyeing up the luggage, she smiled.

"You must be the pilot. Sorry about the size of my bag, but I'm staying the whole season, and my dad asked me to pick up a few things they can't get in Red Lake."

Bud placed four plastic grocery bags on the dock beside the duffle bag.

"Fred Henderson," he said.

"Hi. I'm Ruth." She stuck out her hand and smiled at him.

Fred took her hand and shook it maybe two seconds too long and could feel his ears starting to burn. *Smooth, Fred, real smooth.*

"Well let's see what we have here."

Fred picked up the duffle bag and attempted to estimate the weight.

Probably eighty pounds including the groceries...

He surreptitiously checked her out while she looked out over the lake and introduced herself to George.

One twenty-five to one thirty maybe.

Bush pilots know better than to ask a woman what she weighs. Bud always said they lie by at least ten pounds anyway. A horn blew up top at the parking lot.

"That must be the doctor," said Bud and hobbled back up the stairs to greet him.

Fred knew that Bud's arthritis flared up on these chilly mornings but that he would get prickly if Fred offered to carry for him.

When he looked back, Fred saw that Ruth was looking at him. She gave him a nervous smile.

"So how long have you been flying for, Fred?"

"Since eighty-five," he said, thinking that she really was quite striking and feeling foolish for some reason he couldn't put his finger on. Luckily he was saved further small talk when Bud arrived at the top of the stairs with the next load of luggage and saved him.

Bud had a big soft-sided suitcase in each hand and they looked heavy by the way his neck muscles bulged.

"Hey, remember your heart, you crazy old fool," Mary called from the deck.

Fred took that as his cue and bounded up the stairs to take the bags from Bud.

"Thanks Fred," he said with relief.

Doctor Michael Cleveland descended the stairs like a paunchy monarch. He carried two rod cases and an oversized tackle box. His hat had hand-tied flies neatly arranged around the brim. Fred stole a glance at George who had stood up now that the last passenger had arrived. He saw a tiny smirk cross the guide's face before he turned and purposely filled his pipe. George knew Fred wouldn't let him smoke on board so he was building up his nicotine reserves.

The newcomer was about to introduce himself when Bud spoke up from behind him.

"Everyone this is Doctor Michael Cleveland."

Cleveland looked confused for a moment.

"I uh. Mike is fine," he said. "Really."

He nodded to George and turned to offer Fred, who was closer, his hand. Fred took it and gave it a quick shake.

"Fred Henderson, welcome. This is George White, a fishing guide at the lodge." He motioned to George with his chin. "And this is Ruth uh... *Denver,* I think."

Ruth nodded and shot them both a bright smile.

"Hi Mike," she said. "Where are you from?"

"Toronto. Oakville actually, but it's part of the GTA."

"Right, yeah. I know where it is."

"Alrighty folks," said Fred. "Give Bud and I a few minutes here and we'll be on our way."

With that Bud and Fred finished loading the luggage into the back of the little Cessna, tying it in securely with the cargo net. When they were done, Fred climbed up on the step for one last check of the wings. The frost was completely melted now.

Okay, he thought, *here we go.*

THREE

"Okay," said Fred. "I have completed the weight and balance calculations. George, please take the seat behind me. Doc, you're in the other back seat—"

"It's just Mike."

"—and Ruth, please take the co-pilot seat."

The three passengers climbed up into the plane and got themselves settled. Fred thought the doctor looked put out to have paid good money to end up crammed in the back seat, but he didn't really care.

Although the plane had just been fully inspected, Fred took no chances. He had checked the oil and fuel levels himself, and now after checking that all gauges, controls, and switches were operational, he nodded out the window to Bud. Bud hand turned the plane towards open water and pushed him off. Once clear of the dock, Fred started the engine and taxied out to the centre of the bay to do a quick engine run up.

His next task was to brief the passengers on the location of the safety and survival gear.

"It's a little over a hundred and eighty clicks to the lodge, so we should be in the air for an hour fifteen to an hour and a half depending on the weather." It looked like Doctor Cleveland was perhaps going to ask about the weather, but Fred kept talking. "I only have one spare headset, and I'm going to have to give it to

Ruth here as the co-pilot. But I have foam earplugs for you two. These small planes can be pretty loud."

He handed back two small packets of plugs. Again he thought he caught a flash of annoyance from the doc. He gave Ruth the spare headset.

With the airplane run up checklist completed, Fred pointed the nose of the plane into the wind. He raised the water rudders, dropped the flaps ten degrees, and smoothly pushed in the throttle. There was a deafening roar as the engine in the little Cessna came to life.

Fred kept one practiced hand on the yoke while the other stayed firmly on the throttle handle. Within a minute the plane was up on the step. With one eye on the airspeed indicator, he gently lifted one float out of the water, then the other. The Cessna 206 staggered into the air.

"I am amazed that these things can fly," said Ruth over the intercom.

"So am I," said Fred. "So am I."

He watched the airspeed indicator hovering just barely above the wing stall speed. He knew they were well over the recommended load weight limit for this plane, but he had learned long ago that leaving valuable fuel behind to compensate for extra weight was just foolhardy in the remote areas he flew. Morgan's Bay was quite large, so he stayed low over the water using what pilots call ground effect to pick up airspeed before he began his climb out. He knew he would burn off enough fuel on the trip up to the lodge to get the weight down for a safe landing.

Ten minutes later, they were clear of Kenora airspace and cruising at a comfortable two thousand feet. Fred started to relax. He turned his head and spoke loud enough for George to hear."George," he said, "there's some coffee cups tucked into the seat pocket in front of you and a thermos right behind the back seat.

George nodded, and with the doctor's help, set to work pouring coffee for all.

"Would you like to try flying this thing for a minute Ruth?" asked Fred.

"I would *love* to." A big beaming smile lit her face.

The Cessna was equipped with side by side dual controls so Fred had no problem letting a green person fly. Besides, being a commercial pilot, he was also a licensed instructor.

"Okay good. I want you to keep the top of the cowl level with the far shore of that big lake over there, and keep the nose of the prop right down the centre of it. It's sort of like driving a car, but in three dimensions," he said. "When you want to make the nose turn to the right, turn the yoke right. When you want to go up, pull back on the yoke. When you want to go down, push forward. This here is the altimeter—keep the needle on 3,500 feet. I've set the trim already, so it should fly pretty steady."

"What are *you* going to do?"

"Take a nap." He smiled.

Actually what he *wanted* to do was adjust their course to account for the winds aloft. At different elevations the wind can blow from a completely different direction and speed from those on the ground. If they are not accounted for, they can cause an aircraft to drift off course. He had plotted their course the night before on the map. This morning, he had called flight services at the airport and asked them for the winds aloft. Once he added this additional information into his flight calculator it provided him with a true heading. Flying by dead reckoning alone was dangerous in the north as all the lakes could look alike, and there were few other landmarks to go by.

When he had been flying on Vancouver Island, it had been easy to find your way around as there were lots of little communities scattered around to use as landmarks. During his flight training in Calgary, as long as you could see the mountains, you knew which way was west. Here in northwestern Ontario, most of the local pilots had memorized the close in landmarks. However, their course today would take them over territory that Fred only flew a few times a month—and not since last year.

Once he had the course plotted on the map, he took control of the plane again and adjusted their heading using the directional gyro as the primary instrument. He had set the gyro to the airplane's main compass while they were still at the dock.

"Could I try flying again, Fred?" Ruth asked.

"Sure you can."

He showed her how to steer a direct heading. They were humming along with lake after lake sprawling below them. He traced their progress on the chart to be sure they were on the right route.

Both George and the doctor had finished their coffee and had dozed off. The drone of the big Continental engine had that effect on a lot of people. Fred was glad they were back there and that his pretty co-pilot was awake and engaged in what she was doing. He recalled the time a client fell asleep in the co-pilot seat and suddenly jammed his foot onto one of the rudder pedals. It had been a very tense situation for a few seconds while he had wrestled the plane back under control.

"So tell me about yourself," said Fred. "Mary says you were living in Thunder Bay."

"Well, I grew up at Trout Lake Lodge. Mom home schooled my brother and I until it was time for us to go to high school. It was great. We got to play outside all the time. It's funny, we really didn't miss having other kids to play with when we were little, but by the time we were teenagers we were ready to have some friends. Mom and Dad rented a little place in Red Lake, and we would stay with my aunt and uncle until the fall season was over and Mom and Dad came to town. Then we'd move into the little house. When they left for the spring season, we'd go back to Auntie Lynne's place until school was out again. Then it was back to the lodge for the summer.

"You know, now I love staying at the lodge, but back then, in my teenage years, I couldn't wait to get away. When I graduated from high school, I wanted to get away from Red Lake and the lodge and the bush and the bugs so I could see the world. My mom didn't want me to go. She was afraid I'd end up living somewhere far away like my brother. He went to college in the west and stayed. He has a high tech job in Calgary now. My folks are lucky to see him more than once a year."

"Right," said Fred. "So *did* you—see the world I mean?"

"A bit. I talked a high school girlfriend into going with me, and we took the bus down to Toronto right after graduation. To us, Toronto sounded like it was the end of the earth. It took us two full days of travel to get there. Those buses stop at every wide spot on the highway to pick up or drop off passengers."

Fred laughed out loud at the thought.

"We got off the bus near Union Station," said Ruth. "Do you know where that is?"

"No. Y'know what, I've never been right into Toronto," he said. "I have relatives down in the London area, but whenever I go down south, I make a habit of skirting around the big city."

She nodded as though that made good sense. "Well Union Station is right downtown near Yonge Street. I got a job as a chambermaid at the Royal York Hotel, and my friend Betty got on as a waitress at the Hard Rock Café just down the street. We stayed at the YWCA. It was a lot of fun living right in the heart of a big city like that when you're that age. The trouble was we couldn't save enough money to get an apartment anywhere.

"Luckily, we could use the computers at the Y, so I started looking at college courses and found an interesting environmental course at Lambden College in London. It was a lot smaller college than what Toronto had, and I figured I could afford an apartment in a smaller town like London. Mom and Dad helped me with the tuition, and I got a part time job. Managed to graduate without too much in student loans."

While Ruth was talking, Fred was watching a big snow squall that was cutting across their path.

"I had better take it back now," he said, keeping his voice calm.

Ruth took her hands and feet off the controls. The little plane was soon bouncing in the turbulence. Before long it was rough enough to wake up both back seat passengers.

"What's happening?" asked the doctor, rubbing his eyes.

"No problem," replied Fred. "Just a little bit of weather. We'll swing around west for a few minutes and let it pass by us."

George looked relatively unphased, but Ruth had gone a little pale.

Left aileron... left rudder... raise the nose and add a bit of power.

It was all automatic to him. Instinctual. They flew west for fifteen minutes or so until they were well past the squall. Then Fred swung back north.

Except, as he made the turn and put his hand on the throttle to add power, he felt the throttle lever slam to a sudden stop.

The engine cut back to an idle.

A glance at the tachometer was all he needed. He was pretty damn sure the throttle cable had snapped.

Shit!

FOUR

Fred had a couple of emergency landings under his belt, but that was on the flat prairies of Alberta. This was different. This area contained an endless sea of trees. For an instant he felt panic threaten to overwhelm him. He took a couple of deep breaths and forced himself to calm down. His mind automatically recalled the drill that every student pilot was compelled to practice over and over again until it became second nature.

He quickly raised the nose and set the trim wheel to hold the plane at the best angle of descent. He scanned the horizon looking for the best possible landing spot. There was only one patch of blue in their glide path. It was a little lake due west of them. It was their only hope. He did a quick coordinated turn and aimed the nose of the plane at it. Now that they were on course for a landing, he turned his attention to the radio and dialled in 121.5, the emergency frequency. He pushed the talk button on the yoke.

"Mayday... mayday... mayday! This is Golf Yankee Bravo Golf. We are a blue and white Cessna 206 on floats. We are approximately forty miles south-southwest of Red Lake, attempting an emergency landing on a pothole lake."

There was no answer.

Ruth was listening to his one-sided conversation through the intercom. She looked over at him with a concerned look on

her face. She realized they were in trouble. Fred saw the look on
her face.

"I think the throttle cable snapped," he said. "I'm going to have
to put her down."

Ruth didn't reply, but he could tell by the look in her eyes that
she scared stiff.

Three minutes to touchdown, no more than that.

He tried the throttle again, but the lever flopped uselessly
back and forth in his hand. The engine was still idling, so he tried
adjusting the mixture control to see if he could get any more
power out of it. There was no significant difference.

*Might as well shut everything down. Fuel off... ignition off... leave
the electrical master-switch on so we can keep trying the radio.*

"Ruth," he said with calm authority, "I want you to push the
talk button on the yoke and call Mayday, Mayday, Mayday until
you get a response."

She nodded back at him.

He turned his head around and motioned to the back seat
passengers to remove their earplugs. He spoke loud enough that
they could hear him.

"Doc, George we are going to be making an emergency lake
landing. I want you to take off your watches, rings, belts and your
sunglasses. Take your jackets off and put them in a ball in front of
your faces. Doc, take off that hat and stow it under the seat."

They nodded grimly. George gave Fred a long look and then,
an encouraging smile.

"Try and pick a lake with fish in it," he said with a grin.

Fred couldn't help but grin back.

Ruth was frantically trying to raise someone on the radio. She
was shouting into the mike on her headset.

"Mayday! Mayday! Mayday!" She repeated it over and
over again.

With less than a minute to touch down, Fred spoke urgently
through the headset.

"Ruth, I have control of the radio! I want you to do the same as the others. Take off your jacket and put it in front of your face. Also put that headset under your seat. One more thing I want you to do," he said. "Just before we touchdown, unlatch your door so it doesn't jam if we hit hard."

He turned to look at his backseat passengers. He couldn't see their faces as they were covered with the jackets, but he guessed they were as scared as he was. He took off his own headset and sunglasses and stowed them under the seat.

He'd known the lake he was attempting to land on was small from when he first picked it as their landing spot. It was only as they neared that he fully appreciated just how small it was. Fred pulled up hard on the yoke to bleed off some airspeed, and then, as soon as the indicator dropped below 80 knots, dropped full flaps.

The plane slowed to a crawl, but even at this speed he judged they would touch down somewhere in the middle of the little lake. That would not give them anywhere near the distance they needed to stop before hitting the tree-lined shore at the far side. As soon as they crossed over the treetops and were over open water Fred tried one last ditch trick.

Cessna would not approve of this, he thought as he cranked the yoke hard to the left at the same time he applied full right rudder. Cessna had a warning against this sideslip maneuver with full flaps down, but it was their only hope. The little plane dropped out of the sky like a piano falling from the heavens. Five feet off the surface, he stomped the opposite rudder pedal to straighten the plane out and eased back the yoke to flare in for a landing.

They hit the water with a smack that rattled his teeth. They were still hurtling towards the opposite shore. With no way of braking, all he could do was watch the approaching trees.

"Shit, shit, shit!" he said.

He switched off the master electrical switch and unlatched his door. He hoped Ruth had remembered to do the same. She now had her face covered with her jacket.

Fred waited for the plane to slow before he made any directional changes. At this speed, if he made any huge corrections, the plane would catapult. To the left of their path was a little swampy area with a few smaller trees growing right out of the shallow water. As the plane began to slow, he dropped the water rudders. He eased the rudder left and almost immediately they were mowing down the little swamp trees. This slowed the plane down quickly. There was a bang as they hit the shore and stopped. The silence was deafening.

"Jesus," said the doctor.

"Holy shit," said George.

Fred and Ruth said nothing.

Almost a full minute passed before Fred turned around.

"Is everyone okay?"

They all nodded and began taking off their seat belts. They opened the doors and clambered out and onto the shore.

FIVE

The black flies were ferocious, but no one took notice. They were alive, and that was, for the first time in a long time, something they could not take for granted. George walked up and down the little shore, puffing furiously on his pipe.

"Holy shit, hol-leee shit."

Mike Cleveland was bleeding from a small split on his forehead and kept putting his hand to the wound as if to double and triple check the fact.

"What happened?" she said. "I mean, what did you—"

"I looked up," he said. "Last second, I couldn't help it. I looked up and clocked myself on the back of your seat. Jesus that hurts."

Ruth got out the plane's first aid kit. She handed Mike an alcohol wipe and, as he cleaned up his forehead, searched for an appropriate Band-Aid.

Fred checked the plane over. He first checked the emergency locator transmitter. It had not gone off although he felt they hit hard enough to set it off. He flicked it to manual and listened to the radio for the telltale beeping that meant it was operational. There was no response.

Goddammit, why'd those idiots not checked it when it was in for service?

Next he tried the radio.

"Mayday, Mayday, Mayday."

Nothing.

He walked around the front of the plane looking for damage. The prop was fine. One float had a visible six-inch gash in the front. Both wings had big dents where they had taken out small trees, but he'd seen worse on planes still in service.

George knocked the ash from his pipe into the water. He took a deep breath and went over to the plane.

"What do you think, Fred?"

"Not too much damage. I can hire one of those big Sikorsky helicopters and have her airlifted out."

Fred climbed up into the plane again and emerged with a can of insect repellent and a brown lunch bag. They all took turns spraying themselves down with repellent. When they were done, Fred washed his hands in the lake, sat down on the shore, and opened the bag. He shared out two ham and cheese sandwiches and some of homemade oatmeal cookies that George assumed came from Mary. Half a sandwich and a cookie each.

George brought out the coffee thermos. "Still a bit left," he said.

"Now what?" asked the doctor munching his sandwich.

"Well," said Fred, glancing up at the sky. "Now we wait for help to arrive. After lunch, why don't you and George see if there are any fish in that lake?"

The doctor dug into one of his suitcases and came out with a bug jacket. Grabbing his fly fishing rod, he stomped off to a little clearing further down the lake. After watching this little display of temper, George shook his head then took his spinning rod and went off in the opposite direction.

While the other two fished, Fred got Ruth to help him haul the luggage out of the plane and set up a temporary camp. It was already close to noon, and they both agreed they would probably have to spend the night before help arrived.

Fred and Ruth pulled out the plane's mandatory emergency equipment duffle bag and inventoried what it contained:

2 tube tents

mosquito netting

2 pump bottles of musk oil insect repellent

1 four-season sleeping bag

3 wool blankets

1 space blanket

1 US Henry 22 caliber survival rifle

1 brick of 22 shells (500 rounds)

1 folding buck saw and two spare blades

1 axe

1 hatchet

1 whet stone for sharpening

1 roll duct tape

2 rolls black electrical tape

1 spool of fishing line and a package of hooks

1 emergency stove with 2 candles

1 small pot

6 packs waterproof matches

1 five-gallon, collapsible water jug

water purification tablets

1 flashlight with 2 D cell batteries

1 compass

1 signal mirror

4 plastic ponchos

1 sewing kit

1 pair leather work gloves

2 rolls toilet paper

2 pencils

1 notepad

100 feet nylon cord

20 feet nylon rope

5 packs chicken noodle soup

50 tea bags
2 chocolate bars
1 heavy plastic garbage bag

From under the seats, they pulled four inflatable life vests. In addition to the emergency gear, was a little red plastic toolbox with some hand mechanical tools and miscellaneous hardware bits. There was also the plane's first aid kit.

"Wow, you pack a lot of survival gear," she said. "I feel better already."

"Well we pilots are compelled by aviation rules to carry the basics up here, and I like to have a few extra things on board. I've never had to use anything before though."

The two of them cleared out some brush with the axe and set up the tube tents. A tube tent is basically an emergency plastic pup tent without poles. It has no ends to it. A cord is supplied to suspend the top of the tent between two trees. The ground close to the lake edge was pretty spongy, so they cut some boughs to keep folks from sinking into damp furrows while they slept.

"You take the sleeping bag," said Fred. "George has his own sleeping bag. The doc and I can share the blankets."

Ruth took out a Mexican blanket from her duffle bag. It had been intended as a gift for her father. She handed it to Fred.

"Here, this might help keep you warm tonight."

Fred took the gift from her with a warm smile.

"Thanks."

They unfolded the little foil survival blanket and cut it into two pieces. They tied the pieces over one end of each of the tents. Next they unrolled the mosquito netting and cut it into two pieces and tied one over the other end of each of the tents.

"Well," he said. "I'm afraid that will have to do. The men will share the tents, and you can sleep in the plane."

"It's just one night. I'll be fine," Ruth said—however, she didn't really believe it. Growing up in the bush, she had heard plenty of stories of people in the bush for extended stretches of time, some of whom were never found.

They removed the back seat and pushed the front seats forward as far as they would go to provide Ruth with a sleeping space. They took George's sleeping bag and put it in one of the tents. Then Fred laid out two of the plane's three blankets for Dr. Cleveland in the other tent and kept one wool blanket and the little Mexican blanket for himself. They blew up the life jackets to use as pillows. They decided that George and Fred would share one of the little tents, and give the doctor one to himself.

George and the doctor arrived back from fishing around five o'clock. George had caught three rainbow trout, and Mike had a sucker and a rainbow. Dinner would be a rainbow each roasted over the fire.

George cleaned the fish and sunk the sucker into the lake with rocks to keep from attracting any bears. It would be breakfast. They roasted the fish on green sticks over the fire. Mike produced a bottle of very expensive white wine from his luggage, and they filled their paper coffee cups to toast their survival.

Ruth raised her cup in a toast.

"Here's to life! It's great to be alive," she said. "Nice landing, Fred."

The men grunted their appreciation in return and Fred nodded.

"So what the hell happened anyway?" Mike asked.

He'd had time while he was fishing to get over the shock. Now he was really mad, the wine was setting in, and he wanted an explanation of why his vacation had been interrupted. On some level he knew he was being unreasonable, but he had a hard time keeping it out of his voice.

"I think the throttle cable snapped. I'll look over the plane in the light tomorrow while we're waiting to be rescued."

"And when do you think *that* will happen? I paid good money for this fishing trip, and the brochure definitely included a lodge."

Mike was working himself into a full blown snit, and George was not interested. He got up, left the fire, and went to bed. Unsocial at the best of times, he had no use for city slicker complainers.

Guy's alive; some pilots might not have pulled off even that much.

Back at the fire he could hear Fred's patient (if somewhat strained) response.

"Search and Rescue will be starting to look at first light. It shouldn't take them long to find us. I'm sure Bud's insurance company will compensate you for your trip if that's a concern at this point."

George wondered if the doctor knew he was being snowed about the S&R. Not that he blamed Fred for doing it. They'd veered west off the flight plan and hadn't managed radio contact before going down. George wasn't an expert, but he knew enough to know that they would be outside the initial search area.

SIX

Wednesday May 23, 2001

At first light, Fred awoke. The previous day's events flooded his mind for a moment. He tried to organize his thoughts. *First things first,* he thought.

He desperately had to pee.

After a few agonizing minutes, he managed to unroll himself from his cocoon of blankets without waking George and get out of the tent. He was cold and stiff from lying on the ground. He had finished relieving himself behind the tent and was just zipping up when he saw her.

Ruth had been bathing in the lake not a hundred feet from him, but she hadn't seen him climb out of the tent. He ducked down and tried not to look as she waded out of the lake but he couldn't help himself.

She was gorgeous. Perfectly formed breasts, firm buttocks, and a nice flat stomach.

She must be a lot tougher than I thought swimming in that ice cold water, he thought.

Embarrassed, he hid behind the tent until she was out of sight then quickly slipped into the back of the tent through the foil blanket and climbed under his blankets. Thirty minutes later he emerged from the tent, yawning, pretending to have just woken. Ruth was dressed and was busy making tea for everyone.

Breakfast was boiled sucker mixed with a package of chicken noodle soup. It wasn't the tastiest dish, but they all choked it back. Mike was still in a foul mood.

"I didn't sleep all night. Those blankets aren't any good. You should have to keep more of those down sleeping bags in your survival gear, not these cheesy blankets! I bloody well froze to death."

If only, Fred thought. *At least your fat ass provided some cushioning.*

All day they took turns in the plane calling out 'maydays' sitting at the ready with the signal mirror or fishing. By late afternoon Ruth announced that the battery in the plane was dead. This news brought a feeling of desperation to the camp. Even George was starting to look worried. They decided to have a formal meeting to discuss their options.

George and Fred had taken the engine cowling off during the afternoon and had located the source of their troubles. As Fred suspected, the throttle cable had indeed broken. Lucky for them, the break was quite close to the end where it attached to the carburetor. They came up with a plan—by re-routing the throttle cable they could shorten it and eliminate the broken piece.

The major problem they faced now was one of geography—the little lake didn't provide a long enough runway to take off with all of them on board. After a long discussion it was decided, in order to keep the weight down to a minimum, only Fred would attempt to fly out. The rest would have to stay and hope he made it safely out to civilization to find help.

"So long as you don't forget where we are," Ruth said with tentative smile.

For some reason she felt quite safe with Fred there. Being the pilot had, of course, made him in charge so far. They were conditioned to follow his instructions. Without Fred, she wasn't sure how they would get along. Mike kind of gave her the creeps. She had seen his type way too many times at the lodge. He would be ordering her around and treating George like shit the minute Fred took off.

The second night was a repeat of the first. Cold, uncomfortable and long. First thing Thursday morning, Fred got them all up and outlined the work duties for the day. A lot of repair had to be done to the plane before Fred could attempt a take-off.

The first problem, the rerouting of the throttle cable, was fairly simple. Fred figured the dents on the wing were so close to the fuselage that they would not seriously affect the lift action. Next on the list was the gash on the float. A section of the space blanket big enough to fill the gash was cut and stuffed in. Next five layers of duct tape were laid crisscross to cover the gap. The floats were then pumped out with the hand bilge pump to remove as much water as they possibly could.

The final problem was turning the plane around and getting her off the beach. By this time darkness was approaching, so they decided they would have to wait for morning for the takeoff attempt. They were wet, dirty, hungry and exhausted. Twice during the day, they heard the engine of a plane, but both times it was too far away to for them to signal it.

For the third night in a row, trout was on the menu. They had caught five rainbow trout over the course of the day. Dinner was a more festive event than the previous night. All the work of the day had kept their minds off the situation, and by dinnertime they were joking and laughing, so tired they were giddy. They no longer felt helpless. They were taking control of their own rescue.

Mike produced another bottle of white wine from his luggage.

"Holy crap, Mike, did you bring any clothes?" Ruth asked.

Mike laughed. With rescue so close at hand, this was starting to feel more like an adventure than a disaster. He could hardly wait to get to the lodge so he could tell his buddies all about it

On Friday morning, after a quick cup of tea, the project of turning the plane around began. A few of the swamp trees had to be cut a good two feet below the water surface so that the pontoon floats could clear them. The three men took turns diving below the water to saw as much of the tree trunks as they could before they ran out of air. Ruth took over the fishing duties. She was the only one who didn't mind the cold water, but she wasn't strong enough to be effective at sawing underwater.

By early evening they had cut a path large enough to turn the plane around. They decided not to turn it that night as they felt their duct tape patch might leak. Ruth had caught three rainbow trout and a sucker. At the doctor's suggestion, they drew for them. Ruth drew the sucker. Fred offered to switch, and they quietly agreed to share.

Fred awoke on Saturday. He had to pee and hoped Ruth would be still asleep. She was, so he relieved himself behind a tree and started the morning fire. As he sat feeding the fire, he pondered the plan they had devised around the fire last night. It was a dangerous maneuver, but they had seen very few planes searching this area. And those they did see were miles away.

Fred still privately thought that there was a good chance this lake would not be included in the search area at all. Certainly they would not include this area in the *initial* search. After looking at his map, he thought that in trying to avoid the storm, they had veered off course by at least thirty miles. Standard searches were usually conducted five miles on either side of the flight path. He also knew, from past experience, that with every passing day the searchers would be fewer and fewer. He kept this information to himself, not wishing to alarm his passengers further. If it were not for this fact, he would never even think about trying to takeoff on such a tiny lake.

After breakfast, they went to work on their plan.

First, because the battery was dead, they would have to "hand prop" the plane. This in itself would be a dangerous maneuver.

Once the engine was started they would have to be very careful of the rotating propeller. They would have to turn the plane around so that it was facing the lake. The problem was it would be facing downwind. Fred would have to taxi the plane to the opposite end of the lake and turn it around so it was heading upwind. His helpers would have to wade or swim from shore and tow the plane back close to the shore and tie it to a stout tree.

The plan was, once the engine had reached full throttle, George would cut the rope with the axe. They all hoped that would give Fred enough space and energy to lift off the lake and clear the trees. They would have to move quickly and precisely once they started. Everyone thought the patch on the pontoon would be the weak link so they spent a few minutes adding yet another layer of duct tape as insurance.

The first chore was to remove any unnecessary equipment, including the co-pilot's seat, from the plane. Fred calculated his fuel reserves and even with the mandatory thirty-minute fuel reserve, he would easily reach floatplane dock at Red Lake. He decided to drain out five gallons. Five gallons was fifty pounds. He decided to use the water container to collect the gas. He reasoned this was the only way he could accurately measure what he was taking out even though it would render it useless as a future water container.

Next came the radio equipment.

That's probably twenty-five pounds, he thought as he passed the radio stack down to George.

He took out every other unnecessary piece of equipment, including the fire extinguisher and his flight bag. With Fred yelling instructions to George, it took less than a minute to hand prop the plane. Within five minutes the plane was turned around. George jumped on the pontoon and they taxied across the lake.

George had already jumped off the pontoon and had swum to shore with the rope by the time Fred got the plane turned around again to face upwind. George waded back out and attached one end of the rope onto the tie down loop below the tail of the plane.

He waded back to shore where he tied the other end of the rope around a stout black spruce. Ruth and Mike had caught up to them now and Mike handed George the axe.

When Fred looked across the lake, he had his doubts.

Just because this has to work doesn't mean it will.

There was a nervous flutter in his stomach. He knew he owed it to everyone to try.

"Ready?" yelled Fred, out the side window.

George gave him the thumbs up response.

"Wait until she just about pulls that goddamned tree over before you cut her loose." Fred could barely be heard above the noise of the engine.

George gave the thumbs up again. He understood the task. He stood back, axe held firmly in both hands, focused on the straining rope. He waited, waited, waited, and only when he felt he was in the middle of a hurricane did he strike.

The rope snapped—almost taking George's head off in the process—and the plane left the shore like a rocket.

The little Cessna was airborne by the time she was halfway across the little lake.

"Come on baby," urged Fred as he pulled back on the yoke. "Come on you sonofa—"

With the stall horn screaming, he helplessly watched the treetops approach. In desperation he aimed the windshield between two big spruce trees with one final hope of brushing past.

Then everything went black.

SEVEN

Ruth, George and the doctor watched excitedly as the little plane staggered off the water, each thinking of home. Laughing and jumping they were slapping each other on the back when they suddenly realized the Cessna would not clear the trees at the far side of the lake.

As they watched, both wings and the floats sheared off when the battered plane hit the trees. The fuselage carried on further into the bush. They all started to run towards the crash site. Ruth and George were the first there. The doctor was a good five minutes behind them. They found the fuselage laying right side up in some brush. Some smaller trees had broken its fall, and it was actually suspended on thick layer of brush a few feet off the ground

George yanked the door open and began examining Fred—he had a pulse, but he was unconscious.

"Don't move him until Mike gets here, in case we make it worse," said Ruth.

When he finally puffed up a few minutes later, out of breath and red faced, Ruth was really upset.

"Mike, quick," she said. "Fred is hurt bad. You need to help him!"

"What? Why me?"

"Well, you're the doctor," Ruth said, exasperated.

"Oh Christ," he said. "I'm not a *medical* doctor. I have a PhD in chemistry for crying out loud. I teach chemistry at the university."

Quietly George stepped forward and took control of the situation.

"Maybe I can help."

Slowly Fred began to regain consciousness. He became aware that someone was checking him over for broken bones. He felt gentle hands examining his limbs one by one. He struggled with his memory trying to piece together where he was and how he got there.

Then it came to him.

His last memories were of the two big spruce trees that he knew he wouldn't be able to clear. As his mind cleared and he opened his eyes, he realized it was George examining him. He also realized his left leg hurt like hell.

"Well, George," he asked. "Am I dead?"

George snorted and shook his head, smirking.

"No I guess not, but maybe you should let me finish the examination before you move. I think you may have broken that leg."

After fifteen minutes of careful checking, George decided that, apart from the broken leg, the only other thing wrong with Fred was the knot on his forehead where he had whacked the yoke. With a lot yelping in pain from Fred, his passengers eased him out of the wreck and onto a sleeping bag.

Fred stared over at the damage. It was obvious to him that his beloved Cessna would never fly again. Tears started to well up in his eyes, and he turned his head to the group. He stared at the plane for a couple of minutes. Finally he dried his eyes on the cuff of his jacket and turned to face the rest of the group.

"Well, we had better figure out what to do now," he said.

"First let's get some painkillers into you and splint up that leg," said George.

Mike took the cue and pulled a bottle of scotch out of his luggage.

"Here, take a few pulls of this," he said.

Fred obliged him. Once the whiskey had kicked in, George set the leg with one quick snap. Whiskey or no, the pain was so sharp that Fred passed out.

George set to work cutting saplings and fashioning a splint for the leg. This was not the first time George had performed this procedure. Once it had been a brother's leg, and once one of his own boys had broken his arm horse playing at the trapper's cabin.

While Fred slept, the others examined the wreckage. The fuselage was damaged but was still usable as sleeping quarters. They decided that where it sat was less than ideal for a camping site, and George deemed it too heavy to move.

"Hell, the engine alone's probably five hundred pounds."

When Fred woke up, they decided to move him back to their last night's camp, using the sleeping bag as a stretcher.

EIGHT

At the camp, the four of them were quiet, each lost in their own thoughts. There was no wind whatsoever, and the water on the little lake was glassy smooth. Black flies swarmed around their heads like dark private fears, and though they had a fire going, the smoke did little to dissuade them. It was Ruth who broke the silence.

"I've been thinking," she said. "We've been here for almost a week without even a hint of rescue. Now we've lost the plane. It might be weeks or even months before someone stumbles across us."

"*What?*" said Mike. "Are you kidding me? No. No, no, that can't—"

"Unfortunately, I agree," said Fred. "The snow squall pushed us off course. We were turning *back* when the cable snapped, and at that point we were maybe thirty miles from any logical flight path. That's pretty far afield for search and rescue teams."

He could tell that none of this came as news to George or Ruth, for they grew up out here. Mike, however, was another matter. Fred glanced over at him. He'd been pretty quiet since the accident—and since admitting he wasn't a real doctor—and Fred could tell that he was cooking something up in his head. He told himself that he'd have to try not to take what the guy said personally, no matter how pig-ignorant it sounded.

We're stuck here together, don't forget that.

But what Mike said next surprised him.

"Why don't we build a big fire?"

Everyone was quite for a few beats.

"Sure. Well what we'd need is a *smoky* fire more than a big fire," said Fred. "But even that might not get the attention of the search crews unless they are fairly close to us. I've done search and rescue, and the spotters in the back of the plane are trained to concentrate their vision on just the couple of miles on either side of the plane. The problem is that it's too easy to start scanning all over creation. The best chance of seeing something is if it's close, and you risk missing even that if you start sightseeing." Fred sighed and tried to readjust himself to get comfortable. "Looking for a lost plane in this bush country is like trying to find a needle in a haystack. The bush has a way of swallowing them up."

"You've *done* search and rescue," Mike said, a statement rather than a question.

"Yeah."

"In your own plane?"

Fred nodded.

"How many?"

Fred held up four fingers but didn't say anything.

"Right, and so how many were successful?"

Fred closed his eyes and curled his fingers around to form a circle with thumb. None.

Ten seconds of silence.

"Maybe a couple of us should try to walk out," Mike said.

Fred shook his head. He asked Ruth to get him his flight bag so he could retrieve his map and when she returned with it he spread it out for all to see. Between where they thought they were located and the highway, the map showed hundreds of lakes and swamps but there were no roads or towns anywhere in the area.

"...and the swamps that are marked are only the really big ones," said Fred.

"Makes no difference anyway," said George. "Fred is not going anywhere for the next six weeks unless they find us."

"Look folks," said Fred, "the book says stay where you are and let help come to you. Here we have food and shelter. I say we stay put and wait. Besides, there aren't any roads within miles of here."

Ruth and George nodded in agreement.

"We need to stay together as a group," said George with authority. "If we make this our main camp, I can scout around to see if there is any sign of trapping or fishing camps in the area."

More nods from the group.

"If we are going to be here awhile, we need more food and proper shelter," said Ruth. "Let's take an inventory of what we have left in our bags."

Rising, she walked over beside the tent and picked up the four grocery bags she had brought with her.

"This isn't going to help us much. Most of this is gourmet food and spices."She dumped the contents onto the ground and started to go through it. The bags contained a mixture of strange foods.

"Dad watches those cooking shows now that they have satellite television at the lodge."

There were four packages of Tom Yum soup mix, two cans of coconut milk, a jar of vindaloo paste, and a small bag of sushi rice...

"God, I wish I had bought the bigger bag of rice now, but I was worried about weight."

There were also two packages of seaweed wrap, a can of wasabi mustard powder, two small jars of pickled ginger, a bottle of extra virgin olive oil, a bottle of cranberry vinegar, a box of green tea and another of lemon tea, and a bottle of saki rice wine. Finally there were two boxes of medium Ziploc bags.

Next she dragged her big duffle bag over and unzipped it. It contained a lot of frilly undergarments and enough menstrual supplies for the summer, which she quickly stashed out of sight. Her clothing was obviously chosen for a combination of lodge duties as well as lounging on the dock. She had jeans and tee shirts, sweatshirts, and a jean jacket mixed in with a couple of bikinis. Besides the hiking boots she was wearing, she also had a pair of sandals and a pair of running shoes. She had brought along a couple of Janet Evanovich novels and a copy of *Vogue*. At this point in time, the boys were more interested in survival gear. Finally she produced a bottle of tequila wrapped in a sweater.

"Yes!" They all cheered at once and then laughed.

She also had a couple of tubes of suntan lotion, some hand lotion, shampoo and conditioner, her toothbrush and a part tube of toothpaste.

She dumped out her handbag onto the ground. She had a small leather wallet with a snap that held all her credit cards and money. There was a bottle of perfume, a variety of makeup items, gum, sunglasses, a huge Swiss army knife as well as a new deck of playing cards.

The men took a lot of interest in the knife. It got passed around from hand to hand. It was the most deluxe version any of them had ever seen. There were scissors and a magnifying glass as well as any number of knife blades, sewing awls and wood saws. George wondered aloud if he couldn't build an entire cabin with this one tool alone.

Once Ruth was done displaying all her worldly possession, George quietly got up and picked up his pack. The first thing he pulled out was an old Colt 45 semi-automatic pistol and a box of shells.

"Jesus," said Mike. "Is that thing even legal?"

George shrugged. "I don't know. I've had this pistol for over thirty years. In ninety-one I heard they were going to clamp down on things, so I stocked up on ammunition. I gather I need some sort of permit for the thing, but I figure they have to catch me with it. Besides," he added with a grin, "I'm a native, and we can do whatever we want."

"How often do you use it?"

"No more than I need to," he said. "Put down animals in traps if they're still alive. Scare off bears from time to time."

At the mention of bears, Ruth shrank a bit. "Well, I'm glad we have it and the rifle from the plane."

"Well it ain't as accurate as the rifle, of course, but it packs a lot more punch."

He also had a large hunting knife with a tooled leather sheath, two cans of pipe tobacco, two large boxes of strike anywhere matches, a couple of Bic lighters, two rolls of toilet paper, four pairs of wool socks, a new pair of work gloves, a pair of green twill pants and matching work shirt, a pair of long underwear, six pairs of briefs, three tee-shirts, and a shaving kit with a toothbrush, two tubes of toothpaste, six razors, shaving cream, a comb, and a bottle of shampoo.

There was his fishing gear, his well-stocked tackle box and his fishing rod. In addition to the fishing lures the tackle box had a filleting knife, a bottle of liquid insect repellent, a couple of packages of paper matches and a pair of sunglasses.

"Most of my stuff is up there in the cabin already," he explained.

They all turned then and silently looked at Mike, who got up without a word and grabbed the larger of his two suitcases. He brought it over beside the fire and set it down. He opened it and began to take out the most amazing stuff. His shaving kit was bulging with insect repellent, painkillers, soap and shampoo. He had two rolls of toilet paper. There was a big fluffy terry towel bathrobe with the now part bottle of scotch and one of bourbon rolled up into it. He had a rain suit, a bug jacket, rubber boots, sandals, the three paperbacks he'd picked up at the airport, a flashlight, sunglasses, four pairs of pants, five shirts and a wool sweater with a bottle of rum rolled into it.

Bag number two was also packed. It had two bottles of merlot wrapped in long underwear, a bag of Twizzlers liquorice, Liquorice Allsorts, six pair of socks, seven pair of briefs, five tee shirts, two belts, a toque, lined work gloves, a fishing vest with tons of pockets, a portable fish finder, a new deck of cards and two pairs of folding reading glasses. The others were speechless at the amount of gear he packed for a one-week stay.

His big tackle box was the most amazing thing they had ever seen. He had every lure one could imagine. In addition there was an array of filleting knives and sharpening stones. He also had two more cans of spray insect repellent.

When he pulled out the the harmonica, George picked it up and looked at it with interest.

"Can you play this thing?" he asked.

"No," replied Mike. "Sadly I only picked it up in the Thunder Bay airport."

"Well, you've all seen what I have," said Fred. "I also have *this*."

He reached into his pants pocket and pulled out a butane lighter and a much smaller version of a Swiss army knife. From his jacket pockets he produced a pair of aviator sunglasses and a very worn wallet.

"I think I *might* have ten bucks in here," he joked. "Oh, and I also have my flying bag."

He grabbed his daypack and dumped it out. It contained a can of bug spray, five pens, a couple of pencils, several maps, a few airsick barf bags, a flight calculator, six packs of paper matches, a little flashlight with a red lens and a variety of protractors and straight edges.

Mike picked up the flashlight and stared at the red lens with a curious look on his face.

"It's so you can read your map at night without screwing up your night vision," said Fred.

"Cool."

There were also a couple of flying magazines and of course the now useless manual for the defunct 206.

There was a little shaving kit—the kind the airline people give you to appease you when they have lost your luggage. Fred opened it and passed it to Ruth. She dumped the contents of it onto the top of her duffle bag. They all laughed. There was a tiny fold up toothbrush in a case that also contained a tube of toothpaste large enough for maybe two brushings, a comb, a nail file, a tiny bottle of shampoo and one of conditioner. There was also a hotel-sized bar of soap. And a little sewing kit with one needle.

"Wow," Ruth said. "That should certainly last you awhile."

Fred chuckled. "I only carry that in case I have to stay over at one of the lodges because of bad weather. I had never thought of being away from civilization for more than one night.

"Well George," said Fred after they finished repacking their gear. "You guys better get busy and build us another shelter for the night. Ruth doesn't have a place to sleep now that her bedroom has crashed into the trees."

"True enough," George said. "Come on, Mike, you can help."

While George expertly cut spruce boughs with the axe from the plane, Fred directed from his bed while Ruth and the doctor lashed a pole between two trees. They then cut down some poplar saplings and laid out a lean-to. Next they wove the spruce boughs through the saplings and placed another layer on top. They used the rest of the boughs for a bed inside.

"This will have to do," said Fred. "We can do something more permanent in the morning."

While the men were building the shelter, Ruth made dinner. Ruth would take one tent George and Mike would have the other. Fred decided it was a clear night, so he would sleep in the shelter. Mike and George helped him over to it and made him as comfortable as they could.

"Thanks for the boughs, George," Ruth called and crawled in to rearrange her bed.

The last five nights were horrible sleeping in the airplane with just the sleeping bag between her and the cold hard floor. With the front seats still in there was not quite enough room in the back of the plane to fully stretch out so it had been rather uncomfortable. The tent and the spruce boughs would make a huge difference.

Tomorrow I'll see about fixing this place up.

She thought about joining the men at the fire, but she was just too tired. She took off her hiking boots, put on an extra pair of socks and a sweater, crawled into her sleeping bag and was soon fast asleep.

NINE

Sunday May 27, 2001

Ruth awoke at dawn and crawled out of the tent. She was surprised to see that George had a nice big fire going already and was busy going over his fishing gear. He looked up at her and smiled.

"I found some grubs in a rotten stump last night, so I thought I'd tease those trout a bit. I made some tea," he said. "It's in the pot."

"Thanks, George."

After a trip to the bushes, she found her paper cup and poured some hot tea into it. She wondered what they would use for cups once the paper cups were gone. She walked down to the shore to watch George fish. He was already reeling in the first one of the day when she arrived.

"Boy, they like these things," he said.

He fed another grub carefully onto his hook and cast it out a few feet off shore.

He was rewarded almost immediately with another strike. He reeled in another little trout. He expertly fed the stringer through the fish's gill opening and out the fish's mouth. He put the stringer back into the water to keep the fish alive as long as possible.

"What can we make some cups out of?" asked Ruth.

"I've been thinking about that," he said. "At first I was thinking birch bark, but this morning I had a better idea. Why not make them out of aluminum? We have lots of it right over there in the bush."

"But how will we cut it and form it?"

"Well, it's real soft. If we take my big knife and tap it with the hatchet it should cut pretty easy. To form it, we can try using a small sapling stump as a form. The cups would be crude but they would be good enough to drink tea out of."

"That's a great idea," said Ruth. "I'm going over there right now."

"Hang on a minute," said George. "I'll go with you. Mike can take over the fishing here. I see he and Fred are out and about. I want to take the guns in case we see some game."

While George was off getting his pistol and the little rifle, Ruth told Fred of their plan.

"Well," he said. "Go ahead and cut up the wings, but I do have a plan for the fuselage. Doc and I will be over to help you after we catch a few more fish for breaky."

Fred was the only one who still called him Doc, but he was able to get away with it, thought Ruth, because there was no malice in it at all. Mike never called him on it either. It was just one of those things.

George and Ruth headed for the plane. Ruth carried the hatchet and Fred's little toolbox. As they neared the fuselage, George grabbed Ruth's arm and silently pointed ahead. Right beside the plane was a huge black bear maybe twenty paces away. Standing erect on its back legs, sniffing at the wreck, it was over six feet tall. It probably weighed four hundred pounds, maybe more. It pushed at the fuselage and it shifted slightly. It let out a grunt and pushed again. It hadn't seen them yet.

George handed Ruth the rifle and pulled the big pistol out of his belt. Ruth was frightened, but stood her ground. It wasn't the first time in her life she had come upon a bear in the woods, and she knew that a .22 calibre rifle would only annoy it.

The bear heard the pistol cock but still couldn't make out what kind of strange creatures these were. It took two steps forward on its hind legs trying to get their scent. George raised the pistol. The bear took another lumbering step and gave George a clear shot. He put a bullet in its skull just above the eyes. The bear staggered backwards then collapsed. The sound it made when it hit the ground was like a tree being felled.

"*Christ*, George! I thought you were going to scare it off."

"No point in that. We aren't going anywhere and it would come back, and it'd be less scared next time."

"And what if you hadn't managed to kill it with one shot?"

"I woulda shot again, I suppose," he said, a satisfied smile on his face.

Ruth felt weak in the knees. *I was going to come here alone.*

"Besides," George said, "a black, even a big boar like this sonofagun, he'd a run off injured. No grizzlies up here."

"Well, good shooting. I'm glad I had you with me."

"Me too," he said. "I was getting sick of trout."

The sound of the gunshot brought Mike running.

"Is everyone okay we heard a—*Holy shit!* That's a big bear." It seemed almost impossibly massive to him. "Are we *sure* it's dead."

"He's dead," said George.

Everyone was quiet for a moment. Then Mike spoke up.

"So whaddaya think, can we eat it?"

"Oh you bet. Give me a hand," said George. "Let's get him cleaned."

Ruth paled at the thought of what was about to happen.

"I'm going to go let Fred know that everyone's okay."

It was over two hours later that George and Mike arrived carrying a hindquarter of the bear lashed to a pole between them using wiring from the plane. Mike looked a little green after his first skinning and butchering experience.

"We need to build a smoke rack," said George. "We need to lay out the meat over a smoke rack to keep the flies away. They will try to lay their eggs in it unless we work fast."

Ruth and Mike went to work on that project and soon had a suitable rack made from green poplar saplings. While George expertly butchered the first quarter, they went back to the plane crash site to haul back another.

Ruth and Mike hauled the rest of the bear meat and the hide back to the camp. George set up the smoke rack, built a big smoky fire under it and began laying thin strips of meat over the rack. He stretched the hide between two nearby trees so it could start to cure.

The others sat by the fire cutting the meat into more and more thin strips—it was a huge job. Fred propped himself up and tirelessly took the lead in that project. While they worked by the fire, George began scraping bits of flesh from the hide with his big knife.

"So Fred, was the plane paid off yet?"

"It was," he said. "But not that long ago."

"Insured?" asked Mike.

Fred took a deep breath and blew it out between his lips.

"Yes, but God only knows if I'm covered now. After the first crash maybe, *probably* even. But after that second one, I kind of doubt it."

There was a general silence while that sunk in.

"But that's okay," he said. "It was worth a shot. And given the same opportunity I'd do it again, though I'd probably take a few days and fell those two trees and a couple more beyond them. I'm just sorry I couldn't pull it off."

"Don't you *dare* be sorry," said Ruth. "We're alive because of you, and you could've been killed."

"We'll be fine," said George. "Might be a long haul, but we'll get out of this."

Mike said nothing.

Later, they built up their cooking fire and roasted some of the bear meat on green sticks cut from the willow bushes. Ruth kept turning the meat so it wouldn't burn while George and Mike packaged up the remainder of the bear carcass that hadn't been smoked into the black plastic garbage bag that Fred had as part of his survival gear. It was a thick construction grade bag and perfect for the job.

George threw a rope over a tree branch about fifteen feet up. It took a couple of tries, but he got it over. Then he tied on the bag containing the meat and hauled on the other end of the rope until the bag was high in the air. He tied the rope off to the tree.

"That should keep it safe overnight until we get it all smoked," George said. "I'll sleep with my guns nearby tonight in case I hear anything sniffing around. Better give me one of those flashlights too."

By then dinner was ready.

"Come and get it," Ruth said. "I hope you like it. I grilled some of it plain and some with a tiny bit of my vindaloo paste as a marinade. You know, I hear bear meat is best served with white wine." She smiled at Mike and batted her eyelids.

Mike laughed. "Okay, I get it." He got a bottle from his baggage. "Just a small glass each though. We're running low."

He poured the wine out into their paper coffee cups.

"We're going to have to get back to the cup project tomorrow too. These cups have just about had it."

Mike took the first bite of the bear meat. The others watched for his reaction. Bear meat tends to be an acquired taste. He wolfed it down and reached for another.

"This is *great.*"

"Try one of the spicy ones too," Ruth said and handed them around.

George raised his eyebrow but picked one up.

"Hey, not bad," he said. "We should put that on everything."

"This is a special treat to celebrate that we're not eating fish tonight! I'm going to try and make it last as long as possible, so it's going back in the bag after this," Ruth said. "But thanks for the compliment."

They sat around the fire, eating the greasy bear meat and chatting about the day. For the first time it felt like a group of friends, not four strangers stuck together. Knowing they now had enough food to keep them going for a while had relaxed everyone.

Before going to bed, George showed them how to rake the fire to keep the coals going all night.

"This way we can just feed the coals in the morning to get the fire going again. We can't keep using our matches all the time or we'll run out in no time."

TEN

Monday May 28, 2001

In the morning, they all awoke feeling positive and eager to get to work. They all pitched in and finished cutting the remaining bear meat into strips and smoking it.

"Now we have meat, and soon we'll have some wild vegetables," said George. "This afternoon, I'll go on a hunt to see what I can find. Ruth and Doc you can come with me, and I'll show you how to collect fiddleheads. They should be up now. If we stock up, they will keep us going until the berries are ripe."

They left poor Fred behind with the little .22 for protection and a Michael Crichton novel to read, but try as he might, he couldn't concentrate on it. He wondered how Bud and Mary were coping. His guess was *not well*. When he'd taken the job with Bud a couple of years back, Fred was stepping into a role left vacant when a previous pilot went down.

It was a couple of months before Fred arrived. The pilot's name was Chris Rivers—young, funny and full of life, he was flying solo en route to pick up some fisherman and simply disappeared. After a frantic weeklong search, it was presumed that the missing plane was at the bottom of one of the thousand lakes in the area. Rivers had left behind a pretty young wife and a toddler in Kenora, neither of whom Fred had met. Rivers' death had also cast a long shadow over Morgan's Bay, and both Mary and Bud were still grieving him when they practically adopted Fred.

Apart from Bud and Mary, Fred was not leaving much behind, and he couldn't tell if that was a blessing or a curse all things considered. He had a few friends, sure, and a sister and a brother with whom he had a strained long-distance relationship, but the only serious relationship in his life had dropped out of the sky as surely as his beloved Cessna had. Only *that* had been due to money and a failure to communicate and perhaps different fundamental values and expectations—certainly nothing as straightforward as a throttle cable. His marriage to Amanda had lasted less than a year and the last time he'd seen her was when he climbed into his plane and flown east from Vancouver Island bound for Kenora.

—

As Ruth scanned the bush for fiddleheads, her heart was racing. But it wasn't fear that gripped her, for Ruth was someone for whom the wilderness held no particular terrors. She respected it, of course, and knew enough to know that they were lucky to have George—and to a lesser extent Fred—with them. The four of them simply needed to hang in there and survive until they were rescued. But how likely was that? Their chances were good, weren't they? It was just a matter of time.

Time. *This* is when dread crept into the scenario. What were her parents going through up at the lodge? She could not even imagine. Ruth was haunted by the fact that she had been thinking of asking her mother to spend the summer at the lodge even *before* she'd been invited. She'd been considering it hadn't she? Now she wished she had asked, or at least admitted to Mom that she was hoping to have been invited.

She knew her mother well enough to know that she would be lost in a fog of corrosive self-recrimination for having invited Ruth up to the lodge in the first place—as though this were somehow her fault. She was not someone who handled grief well. And her father was prone to depressive episodes—if he fell into one of his funks... well and then there were still the guests to think about, the lodge was booked solid straight through the summer, and they couldn't afford to cancel bookings, not with the recent repairs on the roof and the new propane furnace that they had just put in.

———

Mike had stumbled across a patch of fiddleheads tucked in the partial shadow of a big spruce and had got down to start picking them the damp ground soaking his left knee.

Terrific.

Not a man who was comfortable with unknowns, it unsettled him not to be where he was supposed to be, and to not have a way to get there was maddening. In fact, there were altogether too many unknowns here, and too many unknowns were a problem, for it made any equation difficult to solve. Sometimes impossible. He got the sense that Fred was not being entirely candid about their situation. George too, for that matter, though the old guide was harder to read.

What was Cathy thinking right now? What about the kids? The kids would want answers and assurances. Was Cathy keeping things together? Then there was Cathy's parents; her mother would be all over the crisis and not making it any better.

How long before Cathy started giving up on him? Not yet surely; it hadn't even been a week for Christ's sake. What about after two weeks? How long before she started adjusting herself by small degrees to the idea of life without him.

And why were they still out here coming up to a week anyway? What would it mean if they were here after another week? How many folks were looking for them? When would that number start trailing off? Was there was some sort of law of diminishing returns when it came to search and rescue? He suspected there was.

How long before they should realistically give up on the idea of rescue and try walking out? How long until Fred could attempt something like that? His guess was that the former would come a long before the latter, and he wondered how *that* would end up playing out.

—

George looked up at the sky as though trying to tally something in the clouds while, across the lake, a small band of ravens were raising a ruckus over something, a fish maybe or an eagle. He was torn. He knew Mavis would be worried, and of course, that grieved him. He knew his kids and grandkids would be worried too, and he hated the idea of casting a long shadow across so many sunny young lives.

He knew they were lucky to have come through things as unscathed as they had and that he should be grateful for that—and he *was* grateful—and that the smart move was to stay put and wait for rescue.

But George was torn because he knew that, before long, once the chance of rescue withered, it would chafe him to stay put when he knew damn well that, on his own, he could walk out in a month, maybe less. The problem was he wasn't on his own, and he'd never be able to bring the other three out in that kind of time, if at all. Their chances of surviving would drop without him around, and there was a chance that once he got out that he wouldn't be able to locate them again for rescuers.

ELEVEN

Tuesday May 29, 2001

On day eight, Fred woke to the sound of an airplane. He scrambled out of the lean-to and tried to signal it with the mirror, but it was too far away. They talked again over morning tea.

"I'm sure someone will find us," said George. "We just need to survive until they do."

Fred had a different opinion, and he had planned to hold his tongue, but Mike had other ideas—he saw the hesitation to speak written all over Fred's face.

"Fred, I need your honest opinion. *Are* these guys going to find us?"

Fred hesitated for a moment before he spoke.

"Hand me that map," he said.

He spread the map out on the ground for all to see. He pointed out the pencil line he had drawn the night before they left on their flight.

"This is the route I filed in my flight plan. They will be searching five miles on either side of that line in the initial concentrated search. Depending on the number of planes that show up. It probably will take them a week to search that area. I think we are way over here in one of these little pothole lakes."

He pointed to a couple of dots on the map thirty miles or so west of their intended route.

"In the initial search, they will be listening for the beeping of the ELT. Of course, they won't hear it, and the most logical conclusion to draw from that is that we crash landed on a lake and sank."

"What does that mean for us?" Mike asked.

"What it means, Doc, is that they will likely be searching the lakes for debris a *way* over yonder." He pointed east with his finger.

"What it means," he said, "is that we have to build a better shelter. The tents are fairly waterproof, but if it rains hard, I am going to get soaked sleeping out here. I think you guys should go back over, recover the fuselage and drag it back here."

"George, didn't you say it was too heavy?" asked Ruth.

"Oh you'll have to strip it down," said Fred. "You can take the front cowl off, drop the engine, and remove the instrument panels. Heck, we could even strip off the tail section—well, *you* could I'm kinda useless at the moment. All that would be left then is an aluminium cone. It wouldn't weigh more than a couple of hundred pounds. I bet if you all work at it, you could have it here by lunch. Take your gun, George. God knows what's feeding on that gut pile."

Five or six overstuffed ravens flopped into the air from a pile of bear guts crawling with flies and carrion beetles. A couple of jays sat in the nearby trees waiting for their turn at a meal. The smell was god-awful. Mike saw that Ruth almost lost her breakfast as she walked past. He also noticed that she eyed the woods warily.

"I'll work on the engine with George," she said.

"Well first there is the cowl," George said. "And it might be a bit of a job; it looks a little mangled."

"Right," said Mike. "Well, I'll try to get the tail off. If there's one thing we chemistry profs are used to it's dealing with strong smells." Though he didn't look anywhere near as confident as he sounded.

He tried breathing mostly through his mouth, but after choking on the third blackfly he just grit his teeth and suffered with the stink.

A couple of hours later they heard a plane approaching fast and low from the north. They ran to the lake shore, and it screamed over them at no more than five hundred feet above the trees almost directly above them.

———

Back at camp Fred heard it too and scrambled to grab up a signal mirror, only to realize that it had grown overcast. He wasn't going to be able to jump up and down, but he could wave his arms. The blanket draped over his legs was bright enough, and so he grabbed it up. It was hard to judge exactly where it was coming from but he had a good general sense. North. When it broke into view, Fred waved the blanket—throwing himself a little off balance and tweaking his leg. It was a small Cessna 185 and though it was too high to make out the call letters without binoculars, Fred recognized the plane nonetheless.

It's Danny, he thought. *Come on Danny. Come on...*

———

"We're saved!" The three of them jumped up and down, waving their arms.

"Hey, over here," George yelled.

"Down here. Hey hey..."

They watched in shock as the little plane didn't bank, just stayed the course and disappeared behind the trees the sound of its engine diminishing.

"Fuck!"

———

Well, at least Bud's guys are still looking for us, thought Fred.

He turned to see Mike stomping along the shore. He looked pissed, and Fred guessed he could understand why.

"What the hell?" he said. "How could that guy have missed us? He could hardly have been closer without crashing into the same goddamned lake."

"I dunno, Doc. Maybe he didn't have a spotter with him. He was directly overhead meaning that once he passed overhead we were in a bit of a blind spot. Who knows. He might have been dead tired too. Shit happens."

Fred didn't offer the fact that he probably knew the pilot. He didn't want to hear Mike trash talk a buddy of his. He was also haunted by the thought that he himself, on one of his search and rescue missions, may have flown over a survivor and missed them. *Shit happens.*

By noon the fuselage was back at camp and levelled out on some strategically placed logs. They spent the next couple of hours plugging holes in the firewall with bits of moss so the bugs couldn't get in. Once it was relatively bug proof, they moved Ruth's things into it. With all the seats removed it was quite a roomy home for one person. George cut her some fresh boughs for bedding so it even smelled nice in there. Mike and George took over her tent. They gave Fred the other one to himself because of his broken leg. They moved both the tents into the lean-to to provide shelter from the winds and rain.

For the rest of the day, Ruth stayed close to camp so she could feed the smoke fire and turn the meat. She built up the fire every so often and added green wood to the smouldering coals. In between tending to the fire and turning the meat strips, she chatted with Fred and collected wild edibles. George took the little rifle and his pistol and went hunting. Mike took his fishing rod down to the lake to fish—though in truth he was brooding more than fishing.

PART 2

SUMMER

TWELVE

June 2001

June came and went slowly. They were really glad they had their rainproof shelters, as it was a very wet month. Because of the almost constant overcast skies, the flying activity in the area was almost nonexistent. They neither saw nor heard a single airplane for the entire month.

George had been expanding his knowledge of the area on the few dry days that they did have. On one of his journeys, he discovered another slightly larger lake a couple of miles to the west of their camp. After a bit of experimentation, he discovered this lake also had trout in it. Mike and Ruth hiked over to the new lake to inspect it and they discussed the idea of moving camp. After all it was a bigger lake. In the end, they decided it would be too much work to relocate. Instead they would stay put where they were and make fishing expeditions over to this new lake from time to time.

They had managed to salvage the less bent of the two wings from the crash site and were now using it as the roof of the camp kitchen. This new roof was making the cool rainy days a lot more bearable. Ruth and George salvaged some aluminum from the other wing and had created a whole set of camp dishes. George carved some crude wooden forks. Ruth, Mike and Fred all had acquired skill with chopsticks from their city years and preferred their homemade chopsticks to George's implements.

Near the end of the month, George began construction on a log picnic table. With Mike's help they felled a couple of spruce trees about six inches in diameter and sawed them into six-foot lengths. Using the hatchet, George cut a groove down the length of the first log. The others sat back and watched with interest. Once the initial groove was cut he deepened it by chopping away with the hatchet. Now he took his knife and carved a few wooden wedges about three inches wide and six inches long. Next he took the hatchet and placed it in the groove about a foot from one end. He tapped the hatchet into the wood using the back of the axe as a hammer. The log started to split and he inserted one of the wedges into the split and tapped it tight with the axe. He moved the hatchet up the groove a couple of feet and again tapped it into the log until the log started to split. He inserted another wedge. He continued this process until he reached the end of the log. Now he went back to the other end and placed the hatchet in the groove between the first two wedges. He tapped the back of the hatchet with the axe until the split widened. He then tapped the wedges in further to hold the split open. He removed the hatchet and placed it between the next two wedges and continued the process. It took about an hour from start to finish but in the end the log fell apart neatly in half.Mike was quite impressed and decided to try the next one himself. George went to work smoothing the flat surface of the first two half logs with his knife. Even Fred got involved by whittling the wedges. By the end of the afternoon, they had all of the components for the table cut.

Over the next couple of days, George worked on the frame of the table. With limited tools at his disposal, it was a slow process to notch the pieces and tie them together with wire. He wanted to use wooden pegs to fasten the seat and the top to the frame, but in order to do so he needed some way to bore holes in the wood. He got the toolbox and hiked over to the crash site to see what he could salvage. After an hour of searching, he decided that the best thing available was a bolt that was about a half an inch in diameter and around four inches long. He took it back to camp and began the slow process of filing the end into a point.

"The problem is," he told Fred, "the threads are too fine. They might not bite into the wood."

It was a slow process, but after about an hour of work he managed to use a combination of techniques to make his first hole. He would tap the point of the bolt deep into the wood and then use a wrench to turn it to widen the hole. Once the hole was widened he would pound the bolt in deeper and repeat the process. Once George had perfected the technique, Fred and Doc took over while George began whittling the pegs to hold all the pieces together. Ruth got out her big Swiss army knife and pitched in on that part of the project. The end result was a very solid table.

More importantly, however, it had kept them all occupied

By July, Mike was growing increasingly restless.

He was the kind of person who needed to be busy all the time, but unfortunately had very few practical skills. He had read all three of his novels plus the two Ruth had brought along—deeming them fluff but reading them anyway. He paced the campsite relentlessly and lately had been dressing up in his rain gear and rubber boots and going for walks around the lake. Once he was out of earshot of the camp he would pull out his harmonica, find a log to sit on, and practice for a while.

He still felt a bit bashful to play it in front of the others. Whenever he did go out on his solo walks, he would collect a bit of firewood and birch bark. The other thing he searched for was fiddlehead ferns, wild onions, Indian cucumber and leeks. George had shown them these delicacies during their first days here. The fiddleheads could be boiled like spinach, but in truth they becoming hard to find now as most of the ferns were maturing. He would sometimes find a few in very shady areas where the lack of sun had retarded their growth. They were quite delicious.

The other green food source George had shown them was the young willow leaves. They were quite bitter but they forced themselves to eat some of them. George also knew which mushrooms were safe to eat and which of them were poisonous, so they left the task of gathering those to him. By early July, their diet of smoked bear meat and fish was already getting old. George would eat most grubs and insects he could catch, but the others were too squeamish to try. He was also good at finding and raiding bird nests for eggs. These were welcome additions to the soups.

One day, however, Mike had an inspiration. They had been playing card games for weeks to kill the time whenever it was too rainy to venture out. The trouble was the games they all knew were quite juvenile. Mike had grown up on the game of cribbage and so had Fred. Mike borrowed Ruth's big Swiss army knife and began the process of creating a crib board from a piece of birch that he saved from the woodpile. Because Fred too had played crib, Mike enlisted his opinion on the design of the board. They both agreed that the design should have one hundred pairs of holes plus a finish hole.

Mike worked on his piece of birch in his spare time for a solid week, first with a knife and then a file and finally with sand from the beach until the surface was flat and smooth. Working carefully, he laid out the peg hole patterns with a pencil. Now using the awl from Ruth's big army knife, he drilled out each of the holes. By the end of the second week, he had finished the board.

Doc and Fred taught the other two how to play the game. To keep things fair the two experienced players put themselves on opposite teams—Fred of course selected Ruth for his partner. They invented numerous competitions. The losers would have to cook dinner or haul water and firewood the next day. It was a fun diversion, especially on rainy days. The rainy days were a problem for everyone. At first, the few books they had brought with them kept them amused. Then the card games took over. After a while even that got old. They all hated the bad weather.

By mid-July, the little group of survivors had all but given up hope of rescue.

The bear meat was gone. The last of it had spoiled in the summer heat. They seemed to be catching enough fish to get by, and George would shoot a grouse or a rabbit every once in a while for variety. The blueberries were out everywhere. Any spare time they had was spent picking berries and George crafted some crude birch bark baskets to collect them in. They were full to the brim almost every day.

They ate some of the berries fresh, but there were always a lot left over. They decided to dry the surplus for future survival. George showed them how his ancestors had accomplished this. He boiled the berries until they were the consistency of mush, then he hand-packed this mush into patties. Once the patties were formed, they had to be dried in the sun. Drying the patties took up all the space on the top of their wing roof—and someone had to stand guard to keep the birds away. Scarecrow, that was Fred's job.

His leg was healing nicely, and he was able to hobble around camp on a pair of homemade crutches. He still did not dare to put any weight on it. The others realized that it would be a while yet before Fred was strong enough to attempt a walk out with them.

Doc and George had started work on building a crude out-house. They dug the hole with a homemade spade that George fashioned from parts off one of the airplane's water rudders. It was not easy work. First they had to cut through a thick layer of roots with the hatchet. The soil was quite rocky, so digging was quite slow. A lively discussion took place as to how deep the hole ought be. Mike opted for just a couple of feet, where the more practical George insisted on a good five feet. Mike for his part kept digging, albeit begrudgingly.

The walls of the outhouse were built from notched poplar logs that they painstakingly felled and dragged to the building site. When they got to the roof, another debate ensued. George wanted to use aluminum, but Fred wanted to conserve the aluminum for a more worthy project.

"What about birch bark and spruce gum?" he suggested.

George agreed to give it a try. He and Mike sliced sections of bark from the trees and laid them out on the roof, using logs to weigh them down and to help flatten them. Sitting around the fire one night, George announced he thought they had better start working on a more permanent structure to live in.

"Winter can sneak up on a guy," he said with his quiet matter-of-fact tone.

Silently he was wondering about Fred's ability to walk out before the snow flew—he was still using one crutch and heavily favoured his good leg.

All agreed that a cabin sounded like a good idea, and a discussion as to what it should look like began. Mike however was growing increasingly uneasy at how complacent the others seemed when it came to spending the winter. To his mind it sounded like madness.

"It should have a cold room in the floor," said Ruth. "It's like a well where you keep your meat. It's below the frost line so they don't freeze, but cool enough so they keep until the really cold weather sets in. I remember my grandmother having one in her house in Red Lake when I was a little girl."

"Sure," said Mike, "and what about a stove?"

"I've been thinking about that," said Fred. "Nothing on the airplane makes sense to me. The settlers used rock to build fireplaces. But I have no clue how to go about it."

"There are lots of rocks in the creek," said Mike.

Ruth nodded. "How tough could it be?"

"The problem is chinking the chimney well enough with mud so the cabin doesn't burn down," said George. "You also have to create a shelf of some kind so that the smoke gets out but the heat stays in. I saw it in a book once. I'll start working on a design."

"How should we build the cabin?" asked Fred. "We don't have a lot of big trees here. Let me throw out an idea, and you guys can tell me if I'm nuts or not. I've been laying awake nights over this. Do you see that stand of poplar over there? They aren't huge, but look how straight they are. I normally would not use poplar because it shrinks so badly, but this cabin will be used for one winter only. Believe me, if I'm still here next spring, I'm getting out of here even if I have to crawl out."

If any of us survive a winter out here, it'll be a miracle, Mike thought.

"I agree," said George. "But let's use those two big spruce there for the sill logs. They are close, and we can use the boughs for fresh bedding."

And so it was that for the next few weeks the group was consumed with building the cabin. George and Mike went to work felling the trees they would need for the construction. They decided on a twelve by sixteen structure give or take an inch. As they did not have nails everything had to be notched at the corners to hold it together. The few nails they needed for the window and door bucks were fashioned from bolts salvaged from the plane.

One morning, while Fred was stripping down the engine for bolts, Ruth walked over to see what he was doing. He had just pulled off the oil pan and was pouring the oil into a homemade aluminium pot.

"What do you want that for?" she asked.

"I really don't know, but I would hate myself if I just threw it out. We also have a little less than half a tank of gasoline left in this wing tank, plus the five gallons in the water jug, George wants to experiment with mixing the two to make lamp oil."

"What is he going to use for a lamp?"

"He was talking about using one of Doc's wine bottles and some kind of homemade wick."

"Sounds like a Molotov cocktail to me," she said.

"I thought that too, but he says he thinks it will work."

"What about that?" Ruth asked, pointing to the oil pan.

"It's the oil pan," he said.

"I know that, I want to know if I can have it," she said, smiling and batting her eyes at him.

"Of course," said Fred, smiling back.

To Fred it was an oil pan. To Ruth, however, it was a pot—and a better pot than the little one she had been using up until now. That night after the others had gone to bed, Ruth built the fire back up. Once she had it burning bright and hot, she placed the oil pan on the flames face down to burn off the residual oil. In the morning, she woke early with the project on her mind. She went down to the beach and rubbed sand and gravel onto the inside of the pan until it shone like chrome.

When the guys saw the new pot they were quite impressed.

"I'll go over and salvage something to make handles for you," said Fred.

"Thanks Fred," said Ruth with her best smile. "That would be nice."

Fred found a couple of pieces of aluminium, and spent a lot of effort bending them so they were almost perfect. He bolted them onto the top lip of the oil pan, using four of their valuable bolts and nuts.

Over the course of the summer, Ruth manoeuvred herself ever so quietly to work on whatever project Fred was on—and vice versa. Mike and George would poke each other whenever it became too obvious.

THIRTEEN

Late summer 2001

The cabin was taking shape. They had felled the two big spruce trees, and using "arm strong" labour they managed to pry, pull, and push the sill logs into place. The foundation logs were squared the best they could using marked fishing line as a tape measure. They decided a dirt floor would be quite adequate considering this would be a temporary shelter. Layer by layer the logs for the walls were laid, notching them carefully at the corners until they reached about seven feet high. Then they started on the rafters.

Fred and George had painstakingly filed points on the ends of the bolts salvaged from the engine. Only twenty or so were long enough to be useful as building spikes. The rest of the construction was a hodgepodge affair, using whatever they could scrounge. Rafter poles were tied on with aircraft cable and wiring. George's homemade willow rope was also incorporated into the design.

The roof was a shed style. Both George and Fred would have liked to have a peaked roof, but in the end both agreed they did not have enough improvised nails or wire to pull it off. The shingles that they had cut from the other wing and one of the pontoons were laid out on the roof and tacked with small-sharpened bolts. They got about half the roof finished before they ran out. Now they had to make a decision. They could dismantle the kitchen and take down the wing to cut up or they could cut up the fuselage. George wanted to keep the one pontoon intact for a future project.

"I say the fuselage," said George. "We could take the windows out of the doors and cut window bucks into the logs and make them part of the cabin. It would be really nice to have some light in here."

They all agreed, so the process of cutting the fuselage into aluminum shingles began. Fred and George moved into the unfinished cabin and gave Ruth their tent.

George found a boggy area on the other side of the lake that had a large area of thick moss. Using Ruth's spade, he and Mike cut out large sections of moss. They built a pole stretcher to carry the moss back to the cabin. They laid the moss out over the shingles. This would act as both an insulator and a waterproofing layer.

Mike had also been busy, collecting rocks from around the lake. He had quite a pile at the back of the cabin where the fireplace was to be built. They dug a footing for the fireplace and filled it back in with smaller rocks. George figured this way it might not shift and heave as much with the winter frost. Ruth collected the moss and clay for use as chinking between the logs and the fireplace rocks. She found a little clay bank on one of the creeks and enlisted Mike to help her dig it out and haul the clay back to the cabin. She couldn't help but squirrel a little bit away for a future project.

It was now the middle of August, and the little cabin was all but finished. George went back to his *real* skill, hunting. He carried both guns with him. The .22 was great for rabbits and grouse. A few times now he had managed to take down grouse with just a rock after they had flown onto a low branch. This saved valuable ammunition but also honed his rock throwing skills.

"When we were kids," George said, on a day when he had managed to stone three grouse to death, "we didn't own any guns, so we carried a pocket full of throwing rocks with us everywhere we went just in case we saw some game. Some guys were pretty good at throwing knives and hatchets. They could even take down bigger game like deer. I lost my knife when I threw it at a rabbit and missed. The knife landed in the river. I never found it, so I went back to throwing rocks."

Early one morning, George came across a big whitetail buck drinking at the water's edge. He pulled out the big .45 Colt and aimed. The first shot hit the deer in the shoulder and the buck whirled, stumbled and started to run. In a panic, George squeezed off four more shots before it fell. When the others showed up he was already gutting it.

"Nice work," said Fred.

But George was upset.

"It took me five shots to drop it. At this rate we'll be out of bullets in no time."

That night he counted the shells: there were still 344 shells left for the rifle and 43 left for the Colt.

We still need a lot of meat to get us through the winter, he thought.

That night George began working on a bow and arrows. Mike sat beside him and watched with interest. He had spent a lot of time selecting this particular piece of willow for the project. He spent two entire evenings carving out the handle and shaping the bow itself. When it was done it was a work of art. He then started work on the arrows. They were also created with the care of a true craftsman. Each arrow was fitted with grouse feather flights. George used a variety of materials all salvaged from the wreck to fashion the arrowheads. While he worked, he told Mike stories of his ancestors that had been passed down to him by his grandfather.

"If we really look at our situation here, we have a lot more materials to work with than my people had only a few hundred years ago. Back then we only had flint arrowheads and flint knives to work with. We didn't have rifles or axes or steel knives. With these simple tools my people survived thousands of years in this land. When the white man got here, we started to get spoiled. Now because we can just go down to the store and buy what we need, we have forgotten most of the skills our ancestors had mastered."

Once his bow was finished, George carried it with him in place of the little rifle. He managed to bag a quite a few rabbits, squirrels and grouse with it.

George decided to take a day off from building the cabin. They had enough food, so he felt he didn't really have to go hunting either. George had a plan. He had been over at the crash site yesterday salvaging aluminum for shingles. One of the floats had been badly damaged in the crash, but the other one that they had already patched once didn't look too bad.

"I want to build a boat today," he told Fred.

Fred was a little sceptical.

"The lake is not that big" he said.

"I know," said George. "But if I had a boat, I could troll in the deeper water. There might be more fish out there."

"Won't that thing will be pretty top heavy and roll with you sitting up there?"

"I thought about that too," said George. "I'm going to make some outriggers for it out of logs."

Fred held up his hands in surrender.

"Get Doc to help you drag it down to the water," he said with a sigh. "I can help once it's there."

He had planned to go close in berry picking with Ruth today. Pushing and pulling, the three able-bodied people—and Fred helping where he could—managed to get the pontoon down to the water's edge. Ruth and Fred left George to his work and went off in search of blueberries.

George removed all the mangled struts and spreader bars from the float and then rolled it over to inspect the damage. Their quick patch had been intended as a onetime use kind of repair. He needed to think of something more permanent. He walked over to the camp to look around.

Plastic, he thought. *I could melt plastic and pour it into that gash to seal it.*

Out of a little piece of aluminum he fashioned a pot. He had hauled over one of the plastic door panels from the plane. With his knife he sliced off slivers of plastic from this and put them into the pot. He built a little fire on the beach to melt the plastic with. While he waited for the plastic to melt, he removed the old makeshift patch. With the needle nose pliers he had borrowed from Fred's toolbox, he carefully unrolled the aluminum in the gash and tried to work it back into place closing the gap to within a quarter of an inch in most places.

Working slowly, he formed an aluminum patch slightly larger than the damaged area. He poured the molten plastic around the gap and spread it with a stick. This was his gasket. Now he pushed the patch into the soft plastic and taped it temporarily in place with duct tape. He melted two more pots of the plastic goop and spread them over the patch. It seemed secure, but he added a couple of layers of duct tape over the patch just to be sure.

Now he went looking for the outrigger hardware. He found a nice straight spruce with a butt diameter of about six inches. He felled the tree with the axe and cut two eight-foot sections from it. These would be the floats for the outriggers. He spent most of the afternoon scrounging wire and fasteners from the wreck in order to lash two birch poles onto each log float and then onto his new boat. Finally, by around four in the afternoon, he was ready to launch. He got the paddle and his fishing gear and, as a precaution, put on one of the life jackets from the plane. As a last minute thing, he went back and grabbed the bilge pump and duct taped it onto one of the birch poles.

She was a fine craft, a little hard to steer with the outriggers on, but she floated beautifully. He put a spinner to the swivel and tossed the line overboard. He was rewarded within five minutes with a two-pound rainbow trout. After he landed two more, he turned and paddled back to camp. Fred met him at the shore.

"Nice boat."

"It's not bad," said George. "I got three fish with it. Now I can go to where they are."

Fred took Ruth for a romantic evening paddle around the little lake in the new boat. He was quite impressed with how stable the little craft was.

By the time they got back to shore, George had come up with yet another idea.

"I could make a second outrigger for it and leave it over at the other lake. That way if we wanted to fish over there we could portage this thing over."

That seemed like an awful lot of work to Fred, so he said nothing to encourage it.

Mike thought the little boat was wonderful. Whenever it was free, he took his fly rod out and was able to cast without the worry over getting snagged in the brush. While George was the master hunter, Mike was the fisherman of the group.

In his travels, George had discovered several little trout streams in the area around their camp. He showed these to Mike, who spent all of his free time alone down by one of the lakes or creeks with either his fly rod or his spinning rod in hand. He seldom came home empty-handed. He was picky now, only keeping the trout.

FOURTEEN

After the first let down of not being rescued, Mike perked up for a month or so. Over the early part of the summer, it seemed to him like he was almost on vacation. He had books to read, fish to catch, and his harmonica to keep him amused. He did, however, miss his family terribly. Worse still, the thought of being given up for dead by a grieving wife who was preparing to move on gave him an anxious flutter in his chest that was not easy to still.

August had been warm and sunny, so he had spent many pleasant days down by the two lakes fishing and playing his harmonica. He had mastered all twenty-four songs in the book but would only play the harmonica when he was alone. The harmonica was in the key of C and that limited the songs one could play on it. He'd made up a couple of reels himself to add to the songs in the book.

Now, with September approaching and faced with the prospects of spending a winter in the wilderness, his depression and anxiety were beginning to set in again. He found himself becoming increasingly moody. He avoided the others every chance he got. For their part, they seemed to almost relish the winter preparation chores. True, he didn't know what was going on in their heads—perhaps they were simply better at putting on brave faces than he was—but their earnest industry only made him feel more isolated. Weeks before he admitted it to himself, he knew he would not be able to stay the winter while his family back in Oakville moved on with their lives.

Early on the morning of September third, he lay in his bed after the others were up and having their morning meal and thought about what he should do. Finally he made his decision.

Today is the day, he thought. He had been daydreaming about this for weeks now; he would walk out. Michael James Cleveland would be a hero. He would walk out to the highway, flag down a passing car, and hitch a ride to town. He would then send help back for the others.

He knew Fred had a map of the area neatly folded in his flight bag. He needed to study that map. He stalled around the camp that morning waiting for the others to leave on their daily routines. George left soon on a hunting mission. Fred and Ruth set off soon after with their berry picking bowls in hand, trying to harvest the last of the blueberries and raspberries.

And whatever else they get up to out there, he thought.

He offered to stay behind to clean up the dishes before he went fishing.

As soon as he had the camp to himself, he walked back to the tent and retrieved Fred's little daypack and took it up to the cabin. He opened Fred's pack and got out the map to study. He spread it out on the table and put on a pair of his reading glasses.

According to the map, highway 105 from Kenora to Red Lake was close to fifty kilometres east of where Fred figured they went down. Their particular little lake was not on the map, but Fred and George had circled the area they thought they were in. The map was littered with big lakes and swamps on his route, but he figured he should be able to skirt them. The route would, obviously, be a lot more than the fifty kilometres as the crow flies.

The main highway was due east. North-northeast was the town of Red Lake. The route to Red Lake looked to be rough with a lot more lakes and swamps. Kenora was more or less due south of his location. This route looked a little less rugged on the map, but there didn't appear to be any roads until one reached the Trans-Canada Highway. Fred and George had both agreed that the terrain on the south route was a lot more boggy than the map showed. They had planned on the east route if and when they went. Mike had his doubts as to whether they could leave anytime soon. Fred was still limping badly and, before long, the approach of winter would close off their options.

To the southeast there was a labyrinth of logging roads that eventually connected to the highway 105. He decided that finding the main highway to Red Lake was his best bet.

He glanced back out the open door. He could see Fred and Ruth bent down picking berries on a rock outcrop on the other side of the lake. This was his chance. The weather looked good with no sign of rain. He would have to move quickly. He went back into the cabin and dumped out Fred's duffle bag onto the dirt floor. He sorted out the little stove and the two candles, two boxes of matches, the water purification tablets and a roll of black tape. He threw the map on the pile. He felt guilty about taking anything that wasn't his but *especially* the map. He had agonized over whether he should take it over his last few days of planning. Now he had made his final decision. Fred and George as a team could find their way out map or no map. He'd need it more they would.

I'll need something to put this stuff in, he thought.

George had repaired the broken strap of his pack with some seatbelt webbing. He went over, picked it up and brought it over to the open door where he could see. Other than the pack itself, George didn't really have anything useful. He laid George's possessions in a neat little pile on one of the airplane seats against the wall and went back over to pick up his treasures. He agonized over the compass and finally decided to take it—for without it, the map would be all but useless.

Besides, Fred has the big compass from the plane.

Next he crossed over to the kitchen. He took the little pot and a couple of George's homemade utensils.

Next was the food cache. As requested by Ruth, they had dug a food well in one corner of the cabin to store meat and wild vegetables. He pulled up one of her crude homemade birch bark baskets full of dried venison. There was a second basket that contained the dried berry cakes. He quickly split off a share of the meat for himself but left the berry cakes. Berries, he reasoned, he could pick fresh in his travels.

He slipped over to Ruth's fuselage. She still had some of her gourmet food left. She had been rationing it out a bit at a time. He grabbed two of the plastic grocery bags and dumped the contents on the ground outside, making sure he was out of sight of the two berry pickers. He selected two packs of tom yum soup mix, the unopened jar of pickled ginger and the rest of the lemon tea.

About thirty bags left, he noted. He put the remaining items back into the bags and returned them to where he found them in the fuselage.

Once back in the cabin, he packed everything into George's pack. He opened up his own suitcases. The scotch had one last mouthful in it and the bourbon was half full. He slugged down the last of the scotch and packed the bourbon into the pack. He walked to the door and glanced over to where Ruth and Fred were sitting on the rock, close together in deep conversation.

A little too close, thought Doc with a grin.

With a pack full with supplies, he realized he had no room for clothes. Going through his suitcases he selected his wardrobe with care. He went through his shaving kit and selected only the useful items. The aspirin and insect repellent got jammed into the pack along with three of the plastic Ziploc bags.

He laid out his two wool blankets and put his jacket and rain suit into it. He agonized over the big terry cloth bathrobe, and decided to take it. Next came the long underwear and the toque. His work gloves would come in handy and so would that sweater and a couple of pairs of socks he thought. He decided the jeans he was wearing were the best, but put another long sleeved shirt into the pile. He decided to wear the bug jacket and the fishing vest. He laid out his spinning rod into the middle of the pile. He opened his tackle box and selected a couple of lures and two rolls of fishing line. These he slipped into his vest pockets. He already had most of his favourite lures stashed in various pockets of his fishing vest. He left the fly rod behind. Fly rods were more for sport. The spinning rod was more reliable for catching food. He bundled his clothes, the spinning rod and the blankets into a roll and wrapped one of the plastic ponchos around the whole works and tied the bundle up with cord.

While he was getting the cord out of Fred's duffel bag, he found the leather sheath for the hatchet. *They have the axe and the saw...* and went to the kitchen and found the hatchet. He picked his filleting knife out of the tackle box and strapped both onto his belt.

One more thing.

He went into the outhouse and selected the larger of his two remaining novels. They had run out of their meagre supply of toilet paper after only a few weeks. No one thought of rationing. Lately they had been rationing Mike's novels and Ruth's two trashy paperbacks for toilet paper. They had all read them at least twice anyway. Even so Mike had always made a habit of reading the page he was about to use one last time. He often thought of the newspaper he had so carelessly left behind in the motel room the day they had left. How many days of toilet paper would *that* had provided.

He was leaving them one and a half novels plus the two paperbacks. He knew Fred still had some technical manuals and a couple of flying magazines in his flight bag.

They have lots.

He tucked the novel into one of his oversized vest pockets. This trip couldn't possibly take more than a couple of weeks at most. Doc looked over at the two tiny figures on the rock. They were still deep in conversation.

He tidied up the survival gear duffle bag and wrote a quick note of explanation. He pocketed the pencil and a few sheets of notepaper and left the note along with his last bottle of merlot on one of the airplane seats. He changed out of his Clark walking shoes into his rubber boots, putting the shoes over onto George's pile. George's cheap running shoes were shot from all the hunting he had been doing.

Trade for the pack, he thought.

He tied the bedroll onto the top of the pack and hoisted the load onto his shoulders, and left the cabin. He wanted to put a few miles between himself and the camp before darkness fell.

As he slipped away from the camp, he paused for just a moment to admire it. It was a tidy little place. The cabin was almost finished except for the fireplace that Fred and George were slowly building. They were all always looking for the right rocks around the lake and in the creek. Ruth was chinking the rocks with clay as they went. The outdoor kitchen had a home feel to it. All of their worldly possessions had a place on a peg or a shelf.

He looked wistfully at his tent but decided against taking it. Fred and Ruth would surely spot him taking it down from their vantage point across the lake, and in the end would be too awkward to carry. He turned, and slipped into the woods at the back of the cabin. He sighed and began his long solo journey.

—

Hi Gang,

> *I've decided to walk out and get help. Sorry, I just can't see voluntarily spending a winter out here in hopes of being in better shape come the spring. I just don't see it. I borrowed a few things for my journey. I wish you folks well, I really do. Wish me*

some luck in return. I will send help. I have the map with the best guess as to location of the camp.

Help yourself to any of my stuff in return. Enjoy the wine.

Best regards,
Mike

PART 3
FALL

FIFTEEN

Fred had been trying to find the courage to grill Ruth about her personal life for months. Every time he mustered up the courage to do it, there was someone within earshot. At last today they were alone. George had gone hunting, and he could see Mike over at the camp bustling around on a project of his own.

"So is there a man in your life, Ruth?" They were busy picking berries just a few feet from one another.

"Oh there have been a couple of men in my life, but none at the moment." She stopped picking berries and looked over at him. "Why do you ask?"

"Oh just curious." Fred started feverishly picking berries with his head down so she couldn't see his red face.

"Well let's see. I had a serious boyfriend when I was in college," she said. "We ended up living together our last year in our last semester."

"What happened to him?" he asked.

"Well, you know it's funny. I thought I was in love with him and wanted to settle down in suburbia with a couple of babies, but the longer I lived with him, the more trapped I felt. When we graduated, he went home to Montréal for a visit. He called me a few times the first week he was there and then he called me the next week asking me to move there. His father owned a neighbourhood pub and had asked him to stay home and help run it."

"So did you go?"

"Yes I did," she said. "I had a yard sale and sold all of our furniture, gave the rest that didn't sell to the thrift shop, and took the bus to Montréal."

"Wow."

"Yeah, and when I got there we lived with his parents," she said. "It was horrible. French was their mother tongue. I couldn't understand anything they said. My high school French didn't cut it. I can barely order a couple of eggs and a cup of coffee in a restaurant."

"I'm no better," said Fred. "And I grew up close to the Quebec border."

"Where abouts?"

"Kirkland Lake."

"Oh, I drove by there once when the south highway was closed. I never actually went into town though."

"Most people don't," said Fred. "So what happened in Montréal?"

"Well the French thing was driving me nuts, so I asked Andre to speak English when I was in the room. The whole family was *completely* bilingual, you understand. He would try, but his mother would always answer in French. I don't think she approved of me. One morning I just packed my suitcases while they were all down at the pub getting ready to open. I took a taxi to the Greyhound station and left."

"Where did you go?" he asked

"I went where every girl goes when their first love affair ends." She smiled then. "I went home to visit my mommy."

"So that was it," said Fred. "It was over?"

"Pretty much. He called me at the lodge a few times whenever he'd had a few beers asking me to come back. He said he could rent our own place so we didn't have to live with his parents. But I was never going back there. The phone calls just stopped after a couple of months. I figure he had met someone new, some nice francophone his mom approved of."

"His loss," he said, then blushed despite himself.

"So is there a girlfriend for you back in Kenora?" Ruth asked.

"Nothing serious. There are a few girls around town who chase me from time to time, usually once all the cottagers have gone home after the summer and the pickings are a little slim. Most times it's the waitresses. They like the catch and release way of doing things. I was married for a few months when I lived on the Vancouver Island, but it didn't work out."

"Oh yeah, how come?"

He dragged a hand through his hair. "Amanda and I didn't see eye to eye, about a lot of things. When the flight school I was working at went belly up, the owner decided to unload his Cessna, and I decided to cough up a down payment for it, which was a big commitment we really couldn't afford. But I saw it as my best chance to secure a future. Unfortunately, when money got tight, which it did almost right away, she wanted to know when I would get a real job."

"Ouch."

"It pretty much went downhill from there. When the opportunity with Bud came up in Kenora, I jumped at it even though I knew that would pretty much be it between me and Amanda—maybe *because* I knew."

"And was it."

"Oh yeah. We spent around the same amount of time getting divorced as we spent being married from beginning to end the whole trip took less than a year."

"And I suppose the Cessna in question..." She trailed off.

Fred nodded and gave her a wry smile.

"Uh huh. Stripped down for wire, parts, and aluminum while we brace for winter."

"I'm really sorry, Fred."

"Don't be," he said. *It's how I met you.*

"I was married once too," said Ruth, a faraway look in her eyes. "It's been over for a while as well."

"Who was he?"

"His name is Desmond Sykes, but everyone just calls him Dizzy, even his parents. He was tall, good looking and rich. His Dad owned Sykes Motors, the biggest Ford dealership in Thunder Bay."

"Where did you meet him?" Fred asked.

"Well after my healing summer at the lodge, I got offered a job in Thunder Bay and decided to take it. I needed a car, so I treated myself to a used Ford Mustang. When I took it in for its first service, there was Dizzy. He was quite charming and asked me out. I think I was just happy to have someone in my life other than workmates.

"Anyway over the next few months, we became an item. He would stay over at my place a couple of times a week. I never stayed at his place. He had these two macho roommates who spent most of their waking hours drinking beer and watching sports on TV. It was awkward for me to be over there at his house period, let alone spend the night.

"One night he completely surprised me by asking me to marry him. It was something I had just not expected. I was confused, but it all sounded so wonderful, almost like a fairy tale. He promised we would go downtown shopping for a ring at the fanciest of jewellery stores. We would go on a tropical honeymoon—I had but to name the destination. He already had more than enough money for a downpayment, and between our two jobs, we could live like royalty."

"Certainly *sounds* like a good deal," he said. *A lot more than I could offer.*

"No kidding, right? Well, how could I refuse? And so the whirlwind engagement began.

"His parents threw a huge party at their house the very next weekend. The who's who of Thunder Bay attended. Even Bill Jessup, the mayor, came for a while. The old lecher had the cheek to pinch my ass when I danced with him. Mrs. Sykes just took over the wedding plans. She booked everything, the hall, the band, and the caterers. I had absolutely no say in the matter.

"My mother was quite hurt I think. She and Dad would have liked to have hosted and paid for the wedding. 'Imagine hiring a band,' Mom whispered to me as we watched models parade wedding dresses before us at the spring bridal fair. She came down from Red Lake to help me pick out a dress.

"I was really starting to get cold feet but just didn't know how to make it all stop. Gifts were arriving daily at the Sykes residence for us from relatives of theirs I didn't even know. There were showers for me on a weekly basis. The weekend of Dizzy's stag, he left on Friday, and I didn't see him again until Sunday night. He smelt like a brewery when he got home.

"Our wedding day was a blur of people rushing around the Sykes household trying to get ready. Finally around noon I snapped at Dizzy. 'You can have that effing limo pick me up at my apartment. I'll get ready there' I said, and I just walked out. I drove home and poured myself a tub. I cried for an hour. Finally I pulled myself together and when the Limo driver rang I was ready.

"I barely remember the ceremony. Ditto the reception. I think that was because of the double gin and tonic I had poured myself just before the Limo driver got there. I barely remember the trip back to the hotel after the reception.

"The next day there was a huge gift opening ceremony at the Sykes's. The same people from the day before started arriving at one o'clock, and at two we began opening gifts. There was so much stuff it was unbelievable. It was actually a little obscene.

"That night we took a plane to Toronto and stayed overnight at a hotel near the airport. In the morning we caught our charter flight down to Cuba."

"Wow, so how was that?" asked Fred. "I hear Cuba is pretty nice."

"Oh it is. We stayed at an adult only all inclusive resort on the Veradero Peninsula. They had everything. It had three or four restaurants, as well as bars and clubs. And the beach was to die for. The first week was fun. We lazed around on the beach all day reading books and swimming. At night after dinner we would go dancing at one of the clubs."

Fred felt jealous despite himself. "So you had a good time."

"Well it was nice for the *first* week," she replied.

"What happened after that?"

"Dysentery for one thing," she said. "Not the most romantic thing to happen on your honeymoon. I couldn't leave the toilet for more than ten minutes. It was coming out both ends. Dizzy was sympathetic the first day and hung around the condo all day. Finally he phoned for a doctor whose best guess was dysentery.

"The next day he was up and gone before I even woke up. I had no idea where he went until about four o'clock when I looked out the living room window and saw him sitting at the pool bar chatting up two bikini-clad beauties from Vancouver we had met on the airport shuttle bus the week before."

Fred winced. "Yikes."

"Oh yeah. I pretended to be asleep when he stumbled in at two or three in the morning reeking of booze and perfume. And I didn't say anything, but he knew by my tone at breakfast I was pissed at him. He spent the rest of the holiday trying to make up to me. When I finally confronted him with my suspicions, he tried to tell me that he had simply gone dancing with them. I didn't believe him, but what was I going to to? So I let it go."

"Not a great start," Fred said.

"Once we got back to Canada, we started looking for a house. I wanted a little starter house in one of those new subdivisions, but Dizzy wouldn't hear of it. There was a new golf club community in town, and he was fixated on the idea. That afternoon we put a down payment on a new house. It had four bedrooms with three full bathrooms and a triple car garage. The down payment Dizzy had promised was the bare minimum. That night I realized almost three quarters of our take home pay was going towards that mortgage.

"Dizzy's parents had given us a brand new Explorer for our wedding gift. It was a loaded XLT with leather seats. Dizzy announced this was my car. I was really happy until he traded my old school mustang in on a black mustang GT convertible for himself. I drove the Explorer."

"Wow!" said Fred.

"Oh it gets worse," said Ruth. "Once we moved into the new house, the parties started. At first I didn't mind, they were civilized dinner parties with bonafide clients, but then they deteriorated to boys' parties. That was about the time we got the pool table."

"Why didn't you put your foot down?" asked Fred.

"I did," she said, her mouth hard. "I told him I didn't want any more parties."

"What did he say?" asked Fred.

"Not much," she said. "He stopped having parties and also stopped coming home on weekends. They just changed the venue to someone else's house."

"Jesus. So how long did you hang in for?"

"Oh another couple of years. I didn't seem to have anything better on the horizon. Dizzy and his buddies would have a million plans that didn't include me. I was developing my own hobbies."

"Like what?" Fred asked.

"Well I made friends with a girl at work, and she and I took a few night classes together. You know, pottery, stained glass, watercolour painting and that sort of thing. Dizzy had moved over to take the sales manager job. This gave him plenty of reasons to be away from home. 'I won't be home until late tonight,' he'd say. 'Got to take so-and-so out for dinner. We're trying to get their fleet business.'

"One night when I had night school, he was supposed to be taking a client out for dinner, a guy names Frank Chapman if I remember correctly. On my way home, I saw the GT parked in front of East Side Mario's, a chain restaurant in Thunder Bay. I don't know why, but I decided to stop. Instinct I suppose."

"Oh yeah..." Fred had a pretty good idea where this story was headed.

"Well, I pulled the Explorer to the back of the parking lot and waited. About half an hour later, out he comes. Frank Chapman turned out to be a tall redhead in a dress so tight that her boobs were hanging half out. He didn't notice the Explore because he was all over her and she was all over him."

"Did you follow?" he asked.

"No, I didn't need anymore proof. I just went home, packed some suitcases and left. I checked myself into a cheap motel and drank red wine until I passed out. The next day I asked my boss for a leave of absence from my job. I called Dizzy at work and asked him to meet me for lunch. Over lunch I quietly told him I wanted a divorce."

"What did he say?" asked Fred.

"The bastard didn't even ask why. He didn't even flinch. He just nodded and told me to set it up. I couldn't believe it. I went over that day and hired a sharp female lawyer whose ad said she *specialized* in divorces. She drew everything up and we were legally separated.

"I left for London, England, a few days later. I didn't want much of the furniture. The house was sold a few weeks later, and the lawyer wired me my share of the money. I had sold the Explorer to a used car dealer before I left. He ripped me off big time, but he had a certified cheque for me the same day."

"How was London?" asked Fred.

"It was very expensive. When I arrived, I had no clue where to stay. The cab driver recommended a Holiday Inn close to Hyde Park. I checked in for one night, but it was over one hundred and fifty Canadian dollars a night. At breakfast the next day, I was chatting to a young Australian couple. He was there on business. His wife had come along for the week as a sort of vacation. We talked about the prices in London, and she told me about a little bed and breakfast in Bloomsbury that they usually stayed at when the company wasn't picking up the tab. I found the address in the phone book and called them. They had a weekly rate that was much cheaper. So I moved over there."

"How long did you stay?" asked Fred.

"About a month," she said. "I used it as a base to take day trips from."

"So where did you go?" he asked.

"Well I met a bartender in London who was working his way around the world."

"And..." said Fred, raising his eyebrows.

"Well if you must know, we had a little fling. I spent the next two months travelling around England, Scotland, Wales and Ireland with him. We bought a rail pass."

"But it didn't work out," he said, wanting to skip ahead somewhat.

"Well, it was what it was. But then Sean wanted me to go back to New Zealand with him. He wanted me to meet his folks. It was moving way too fast for me. So I told him I was heading back to Canada because I had a job waiting. It never would have worked with him. He was way too needy."

"So you came back to Canada," he said.

"Yes," she said, smiling and gesturing across the lake to the camp. "Back to Canada and all of this."

"And did you have a job waiting or were you just saying that to put off uh whathisname."

"Sean," she said. "No I—"

Fred leaned over then and kissed her softly on the lips. She kissed him back, then pulled back smiling.

"That was nice," she said.

"It was."

"What was I saying?"

"Your job I think."

"Oh yeah," She was blushing. "No I really did have a job lined up. I worked for the Ministry of Environment, looking after a fleet of ambient trailers."

He looked at her for a second. "I have no idea what that is."

"Oh right. Well an ambient trailer is sort of like a camper trailer without windows," she said. "You install instruments inside and monitor the outside ambient air for things like sulphur dioxide or methane or oxides of nitrogen. The government collects this data and looks for high readings or trends in the data."

"Sounds interesting," he said.

"It was for a while," she said. "My job was to keep the systems going, repair and calibrate the analyzers. The problem was twenty-year-old gear and no budget to replace anything. I decided to look for something else to do. I thought a season at the lodge would do me good. Besides I had to leave Thunder Bay— every time I went anywhere in that town, there was Dizzy with yet another bimbo."

"I bet you wish you caught a different flight, huh?"

She gave him a long hard look as if trying to read something in his eyes.

"That," she said, "requires a complicated answer, and there are still berries to pick."

SIXTEEN

George felt good, walking back to camp. It had been one of the most successful days hunting he'd had in a while. He'd shot a ruffed grouse, two rabbits and a mallard, which would have been illegal in another place and time, for it had been swimming when he shot it and it was out of season.

Not that I have a hunting license anyway, he'd thought as he took aim. Now his clothing was soaked because he had to wade out almost to his chest to get it. *Next time I crash, I'm bringing a dog.*

Fred spotted him walking around the lake and hobbled down to meet him. George held up the catch, and Fred nodded his approval, but George could tell something was up.

"So what's happened, Fred?"

"It's Doc; he's gone. Cobbled together some gear and left a note, says he's going to try to walk out."

"Hmmm," said George and shook his head. He was not really surprised. "That's pretty rough country out there, and winter's coming. I sure wouldn't try that right now. Maybe if we had left early in the summer and stuck together we might have had a chance. Did he say which way he was going?"

Before Fred could answer, Ruth caught up with them. She seemed out of sorts.

"Did you tell him, Fred?"

"Yep," said Fred. "I did."

"Do you think we should look for him, George?" she said.

"We don't know which way he went," said Fred.

"Right, but this is serious, guys."

George took a second before responding.

"It'll be dark soon," he said. "I'll get up early tomorrow and poke around to see if I can find his trail. It'll be pretty hard though. I'm a decent hunter, but I'm not much of a tracker, and we've all tramped around the camp so much in search of berries and firewood and fiddleheads and rocks that I honestly don't know what I'm going to pick up."

"He's going to die out there, George."

"Come on, we don't know that," said Fred. "Give the guy a little credit."

"Wait, *you* think he's actually going to be able to walk out?"

"Hey, I didn't say—"

"Because that's the only other plausible scenario. You get that, right?" There was an edge of genuine panic in her voice. "What's he got with him?" asked George hoping to deflect the conversation a bit.

"He took your pack," said Fred.

"And the hatchet," said Ruth.

"I liked that pack," said George.

"He left you his shoes," said Ruth. "Put them right on your pile of stuff."

"Good trade, I guess," said George, looking down at his dilapidated running shoes. "What else did he take?"

"Some food," she said. "Plus the compass *and* the map."

"Damn," said George.

"He also has his blankets and whatever else of his own stuff as well," said Fred. "Some of his fishing gear."

"Sounds like we'll manage," said George.

"It's not *us* I am worried about," said Ruth. "Dammit we agreed to hunker down and walk out in the spring."

"He didn't agree," said George. "Not really. Whenever he said anything it was about risking the hike rather than waiting. When we *agreed*, he mostly stayed quiet. He wanted to get back to his wife and kids."

"We *all* have folks we want to get back to," Ruth said. "I certainly do."

"Sure," said George. "Me too."

"Do you want me to go with you tomorrow to look for him?" asked Fred.

"No, you should stay here," said George. "If your leg was up to *that*, then we all would have walked out weeks ago."

That annoyed Fred somehow.

"My leg wasn't as *good* as it is now weeks ago." He sounded slightly pissed.

It was Ruth's turn to deflect things.

"Look maybe he changes his mind and turns around, right?"

"Could be," said George.

"I doubt it," said Fred. "He seems pretty bullheaded."

"Probably better if he *didn't* turn around, actually."

Ruth couldn't believe what she was hearing. "What?"

"Well, the way I see it," said George. "If he gets even a few hours beyond where he's scouted before, especially if he gets turned around at all, his chance of finding us again are pretty slim. The road, whichever one he's headed toward is a line drawn through the wilderness, this lake's only a point."

Silence.

"Yeah, you're right," said Fred.

"Shit," said Ruth. *What the hell have you got yourself into, Mike?*

That evening, back at the camp, George took down the big bear hide from the rack on which it had been spread. And after he did so, he walked over and handed it to Ruth.

"It's a housewarming gift from me."

She smiled at him, bundled it up in her arms and took it into the cabin.

When they were about to retired at dusk, both men were surprised when Ruth handed George the Mexican blanket as a gift.

"Fred and I will be sharing the bearskin."

Inside the cabin, she had spread Fred's wool blanket over the hide and opened the sleeping bag up as a quilt. Fred was quite embarrassed, but George didn't let on there was anything odd about the situation at all.

"Goodnight, folks," was all he said.

SEVENTEEN

September 3, 2001

Mike headed north from the camp, for had seen George hunting on the south side of the lake in the morning, and he didn't want to run in to him in the bush and have to explain his actions. After about an hour of traveling north, he took out the compass and headed due east. He was making good time he thought. He wandered in an easterly direction for the rest of the afternoon. Toward evening he came across a large beaver pond and marsh. He had no choice. He had to change directions. To the north stretched a huge marsh. The route south seemed easier so he headed in that direction.

A deep creek fed the beaver pond. The creek was too deep to wade and far too wide to jump. He could have swam it but doubted he would be able to throw the heavy pack across. He sat down and rested. He could try the marsh but that was definitely the wrong way.

Dark soon, he thought. *Tomorrow I'll figure out what to do. Better find a place to spend the night.*

He found a big poplar tree close by that had rotted at the stump and had fallen over onto a hillside. It was positioned so that there was a four or five foot space under the trunk. He started piling deadfall logs against this to make a crude lean-to. Next he cut spruce boughs with the hatchet. He wove some onto the roof but saved the smallest limbs for his bed. He smiled, knowing that he had learned a *few* tricks over the summer. He collected a pile of deadfall for firewood along with some kindling and a bit of birch bark.

It was getting cool at night, these last couple of weeks as fall neared. He lit the fire, making sure to use only one match. He carefully put the matches back into the plastic baggie. He then laid out his bedroll, and put a couple of more logs on the fire to build it up. He took off his jeans, bug jacket and vest. He pulled on his long underwear, a second pair of socks and his big plush terrycloth housecoat, and rolled himself up into the blankets, using his rolled up jeans as a pillow.

It could be worse, he thought. *Least I'm somewhat prepared.*

Doc slept fitfully. He dreamed of Cathy and the kids as he often had over the course of the summer. Several times the dreams were so vivid during the night that he sat bolt upright expecting to see them. He fed sticks into the fire all night, whenever the dreams awoke him. At dawn he gave up trying to sleep. He needed desperately to pee, and so rolled out of his little cocoon.

He had run out of razors months ago. Shampoo and soap too were also a distant memory, and he hadn't tasted toothpaste since the middle of July. They had been so convinced of rescue at first that no one had thought to ration toiletries. It was the paperbacks and novels for toilet paper now. He had tried a big leaf once when he had been too far from camp to make it back but had been rewarded with a rash for his troubles.

The fire was cold, and he decided not to waste a match, making tea. He risked drinking a pot of water from the creek, choosing to save the purification tablets for later. He packed his gear, stopped at a berry patch to eat a couple of handfuls for breakfast, and set out following the creek.

Around mid-morning he found a big bush full of ripe chokecherries. He ate them until his mouth was so puckered up he couldn't eat another. He pulled out one of his plastic baggies, filled it half full and stuffed it into one of his big vest pockets. *Handy*, he thought as he peeled off some birch bark from a dead log. It would be the starter for that night's fire.

He had been following the creek all day. It ran in a southwest direction. At one point it was shallow enough to cross. He did cross it but still followed it. He was still reluctant to leave his only source of fresh water. His dreams of Cathy and the kids had been haunting him all day. He wondered how they were making out. He had a bit of life insurance but doubted the insurance company would be in a big hurry to pay out the claim without proof of death. Cathy had only been working part time as a dental assistant while the kids were growing up. It would be tough to pay the bills on her meagre salary.

Their house was almost paid for, and her car was fully paid. His Jeep Cherokee was leased, but she'd take that back. He had been fretting over their finances for the last couple of months. With the growing kids, they had very little in savings. They had preferred to spend the money on fun family vacations. Last year they had taken the kids to the Caribbean on a cruise. The year before it had been Disney World. His position at the university was still on contract, so he was doubtful any money would come from there. In truth he didn't know how she'd manage.

Late in the afternoon he came across a large spruce with big overhanging branches that formed a big dry shelter at the base. He was starving. Besides the chokecherries, he had only found a few handfuls of blueberries, six wild onions, and four rosehips. Two he had eaten and two he had saved. He had also pulled out some cattails and saved the roots.

For the next hour he collected boughs and firewood. A fire in his shelter would not be a good idea, so he walked back over to the creek to build it there. Not wanting to use the stove, he collected rocks to balance the pot on and built the fire partially under and against one side of the pot. The water came to a boil much faster that way.

He unwrapped the dried meat and selected a strip. He cut it into a few bite-sized pieces and threw them into the pot. Next he cut up two of the four cattail roots, the wild onions and a handful of chokecherries and the few blueberries he hadn't already eaten. After dinner, he treated himself to a cup of tea, carefully saving the used tea bag in his last plastic bag. Since he was close to the creek, he built the fire up and sat up close drinking his tea. He played a few tunes on his harmonica then rolled into his blankets at dusk and slept soundly.

He awoke at dawn to the sound of rain. It was pouring, yet he was perfectly dry in the shelter of the big spruce. He dressed in his sweater and rain suit and went outside to pee.

In the morning after he had eaten, he walked down to the clearing by the creek and looked at the sky. It showed no sign of letting up. He decided he might not find a better shelter and that he should just stay put. Besides, he had an idea. He would use this down day to make a bow and some arrows. He took the hatchet over and cut some likely looking willow saplings. Back under the big spruce he spent the morning shaping a bow and sharpening six of his straightest arrows. He used fishing line for string. It was not nearly as nice as the one George had crafted, but it looked like it would function fine.

Once I get a fire going I'll harden those arrow tips, he thought.

George had taught him that trick. All day it rained hard. He knew he couldn't sustain a fire for cooking, so he just gave up and ate a few berries for dinner. He washed the meal down with a good slug of bourbon. It was still raining when he rolled up in his blankets at dusk.

He awoke on the fourth day to a bright dawn. Because he knew the bush would still be soaking wet, he put on his rain suit before packing his gear.

If I don't find a route through this maze of swamps soon, I'll never get out of here.

He tried striking out in an easterly direction but the bush was so thick he got all turned around, and by late afternoon he realized the sun, where it broke through the trees, was in his eyes. He was walking west.

He checked the compass to be sure.

Yessiree, sun setting in the west. Goddammit.

He hadn't had much luck foraging for food this day. He started looking for a shelter. He found a rock outcropping with a little overhang. He laid four deadfall logs against it and cut spruce boughs to lay on top the ground for his bed.

This is getting old, Mike thought. He was still angry with himself for ending up walking in the wrong direction all day. He was really hungry because hadn't eaten properly for a couple of days. He eyed the bourbon bottle. There was still a good quarter of a bottle left in it, but tomorrow he was going to strike due east and he needed that bottle to carry the water in.

Ah the shame of it, he thought as he took a swig from the bottle.

The next morning Mike awoke with a bit of a headache and a dry throat. He sought out his extra strength Tylenols, grabbed the empty bourbon bottle and headed for a nearby creek. Once there he drank his fill then filled the bottle with water for the trek ahead. He packed his gear and left without breakfast. He was careful now to check his compass every hour or so to make sure he was still headed on an easterly course. It was more of an easterly meander as there was no clear trail to follow. He had to steer around several swampy areas that were just impassable.

The next two days were hot and sunny. His progress was painfully slow. Mike had found a little spring at the edge of a swamp and had filled his water bottle there. He had drunk from the spring until he could drink no more before moving on. Now he had to ration the water, choosing to keep it for the hottest part of the day.

Early the following morning he awoke and climbed a little hill to look around and was rewarded by the sight of a beaver pond about a mile northeast (according to the compass) of where he stood. He took a compass sighting and set out. He was almost at the dam when he scared up three fat grouse. They flew into the *safety* of a nearby spruce tree.

Mike dropped his pack and untied the bow and arrows. He bent the bow and slipped the noose of the bowstring into the notch. He took careful aim at the closest one and let fly. The arrow went wide, and the grouse just stared at him. He fired a second arrow. This one was closer, but still a foot off target. The third shot hit the tree right beside the grouse and it flapped off into another nearby spruce.

"Shit!"

He turned his attention to the other two. He could just make out one of them through the boughs. The other one had to be there *somewhere*. It was just camouflaged too well. He took aim at the one he could see and shot.

The arrow was deflected by the branches and missed by a good margin.

He fit his last arrow into the bow and moved around to get a better shot. The grouse had had enough of this game and took wing. Mike crept around further and finally spotted the third grouse. He took aim with his last arrow and shot. Not even close. He threw the bow down in disgust. He looked up at the grouse as it walked further out onto the bough as if taunting him.

Looking down Mike saw several good sized throwing rocks on the forest floor. He picked one up and threw it at the bird with all his might—and nailed it right in the head. It fell out of the branch and lay flapping around on the ground.

He knew it was only stunned, so he ran over and threw himself on it before it could recover. He stuck a hand under his stomach and managed to grab a hold of both of its feet. He got up and swung its head into the nearest tree trunk. It lay still.

He picked up more rocks and went after the other two. They were both really spooked and wouldn't let him close enough for a clean throw. Finally he gave up and collected his prize. He hunted around and found most of his arrows and the bow. He picked up the rest of his gear, and headed for the beaver pond.

He found a nice camp spot and so decided to stay there for the night. He built a fire and began boiling water to replenish his drinking water supply. While the first pot of water was heating, he set about cleaning the grouse. George had taught him a neat trick for cleaning grouse. Step on their wings and pull their feet; the breast pops right out.

Normally recovering the rest of the meat would not be worth the effort, but today he took the time to pluck the feathers off the legs and saved the tiny heart and the gizzard for tonight's soup. Mike took the meat down to the pond to clean it. The rest of the bird he took a few hundred yards from his camp and threw it up into a spruce tree.

Those jays will make short work of that, he thought.

Two of them had been watching him carefully the whole time he was cleaning the grouse. Mike had grown quite fond of these comical birds over the summer. George called them Whiskey Jacks and camp robbers, but Ruth had told him they were actually Canada Jays.

Once the water had boiled and cooled a bit, Mike poured it into the bourbon bottle and filled up the pot again. He built up his fire and dug out his fishing rod, wondering if the beaver pond held any fish. He tried a few casts with a spinner but without any luck, so he decided to get on with other chores.

He turned over a few rocks looking for bait and found what he was looking for, a big fat earthworm. He selected a hook from his tackle and added a stick for a float to the line and tossed it out onto the pond. He propped the rod over a log with a big rock on the handle to secure it, and went off to collect materials for tonight's shelter.

On one of his trips back to the shore he saw the bobber down and ran down to reel in the fish. It was a sucker.

A fish is a fish.

He baited the hook again and set about cleaning the thing. The jays made short work of the fish guts as well. Mike was careful to guard the fish and the grouse or else the jays would steal them right out from under his nose.

He skewered the fish and started roasting it over the fire. He was beside himself with hunger. It was fishy tasting mush, but it was food. The grouse, he thought, would make up for this. That night he roasted the grouse over the coals until it was golden brown and ate it.He knew that he'd better find the highway soon or he'd be in trouble. He spent the rest of the evening fashioning flights for his arrows from grouse feathers. He still was not willing to give up on this tool.

The next day he carried on with his eastern wandering. He slept out under the stars beside the campfire that night. He just didn't have the energy to build a shelter. He was losing track of time. How long had it been since he left? A week, maybe ten days, he just wasn't sure.

He woke the next morning at dawn. He was cold and jumped up and down to warm himself. Finally he felt warm enough to leave. He packed his meagre belongings and set out on his quest for the road.

At midmorning he found himself at the edge of a huge swamp. It was impossible to cross through this marshy mess, so he turned south in an attempt to find his way around. By dusk he was still picking his way along the swamp's western edge. As darkness fell, he had resigned himself to the fact that he was going to spend another night without shelter. He found a spruce tree, leaned the pack against the trunk, and untied his bedroll.

He nodded off, and when he awoke sometime in the night, it was raining. The blankets were already wet, but he wasn't yet.

Quickly he pulled on his rain suit and just sat there until dawn, cold and miserable.

He packed his gear. The blankets were now soaked. He tried to get anything that was dry into the backpack and tied the now tattered rain poncho over it. The blankets couldn't get much wetter he thought as he hoisted the pack onto his back. It seemed to him it was twenty pounds heavier today with those wet blankets.

It rained hard all morning. The going was slow because everything was wet and slippery. By noon, the sun had began to peek through the clouds and by around three it was out in full glory. He found a big rock outcropping, spread the blankets out on it to dry and went exploring and located a big spruce with a huge overhang of boughs that he could use for a shelter.

He dropped his pack and went searching for food and water, making sure he kept the outcrop in sight at all times. He knew he wouldn't stand a chance of surviving if he lost his gear. He heard running water and walked toward the sound. It was a little creek.

As he cut through the brush to retrieve the water bottle, he caught sight of a cow moose with her calf not fifty feet from him. As they ambled off he thought of the other survivors.

George would have had one or both of those moose down in a New York minute, he thought. He had a brief thought of shooting an arrow at the calf but in the end decided all he would manage to do would be to wound it. And the cow would give him a lot worse than he gave her calf.

He found an uprooted tree stump with some big fat white grubs in it, and after a moment of hesitation, popped one into his mouth. He had a moment of nausea that passed and he soon found himself devouring every one he could find. George had told them all they should eat any insects they could find as they have a high fat content, but he had not been desperate enough until this very moment. Now he couldn't find enough to satisfy his hunger.

He spent the evening practicing with his bow shooting at a chosen spot. Satisfied he could hit the target at least once in a while, he put the bow away for the night and wrapped himself in his still damp blankets. He decided to sleep in his rain suit again that night.

At dawn, using some birch bark and a few dead branches from the big spruce, he soon had a blazing fire going. He decided to spend the morning foraging for food before he moved on. As usual he was really hungry. He found a couple of likely looking trees and tied his cord across them. He then draped the blankets over the cord hoping that the morning sun would dry them.

He found some blueberry bushes with a few berries still hanging. After an hour he had collected a full baggie load—not to mention the thirty or forty he ate on the spot. By noon he decided to move on. The morning sun had worked its magic, and the blankets were dry. Mike packed up camp.

Again he pushed eastward. A few hours later he paused to look around. He was looking for a spot to build a shelter. He was walking toward what he thought was a big clearing when he saw blue water and realized it was a lake. He ran forward, stumbling as he did, and fell flat on his face winding himself in the process.

Once he caught his breath, he stumbled the last hundred yards to the lake. He walked down the shore until he came to a point that jutted out into the lake. He walked out to the end of the point and stood up on a big rock that offered him a pretty good view up and down the lake. From his vantage point, he judged it was a pretty big lake. He could see about a mile roughly north and about two miles to the south. There were two good size islands to the south and a small one to the north.

He sat down on the rock and took out the map. He got out his reading glasses and studied it intently. After about fifteen minutes of staring at it, by process of elimination, he located the lake. The map showed a lake with two big islands north and one small one south.

If I'm right, we're looking at Big Buck Lake and I'm right about here. He pointed with his finger to a lake on the map. It was one of the few lakes in the area that was actually named on the chart.

Where he was, according to the map, was just about the centre of the lake. The lake was close to ten miles long so, no matter which way he turned, he had about a five-mile hike just to get to the end. According to the map, the lake was fed by a big river.

Doc looked at where he was compared to where he had started. He was about twelve miles south and about ten miles east. It had taken him ten days to travel ten miles east. He had forty more miles to go. Maybe.

He began to cry.

At first it was a mist at the eye and then full fledge tears. Finally he was sobbing uncontrollably hugging the base of a poplar at the shore of the lake. He had very little food left, and he was really growing tired of all this.

I never should have left on this foolhardy mission.

He was really stuck now. He had to press on. Even with the map and the compass, there would be very little chance of his finding his way back the little lake and the others. The highway was his only hope, he just had to keep going east. Sooner or later he would have to cross it.

Mike stared at the map. If he went south, he might not be able to cross the river at the end of the lake. If he went north, he would be backtracking *again*. The north route at least showed a very narrow creek leading out.

A creek is something I can cross, he thought. *Probably.*

But north would be generally going the wrong way so, in spite of the river hazard, in the end he finally decided on the south.

He was hungry again so he decided to try fishing. He tried all of his usual trout lures without success. Finally he switched to a big red and white spoon, and on his second cast with *that*, he got a hit.

Whatever it is, he thought, working it to shore, *it's big.*

It turned out to be northern pike as long as his arm. A fierce thing with a lot of fight. Mike guessed it weighed around ten pounds. Under other circumstances he'd have considered mounting it but it wasn't trophies he was fishing for today. He gutted it and then built a fire. As the fish cooked he tried a few more casts and got a second pike, not nearly as big, maybe five pounds.

Mike made a decision. He would stay put for a day or two to build up his food reserves before moving on. He feasted on the big pike that day and started smoking the other one. Pike he discovered is bony with lots of scales, so he filleted the second one before putting it on his little smoke rack.

He went to work building a lean-to. He took a little more care with this one as he thought he might use it for at least a couple of nights. He wove spruce boughs carefully through the poles then added a couple of more layers on top as waterproofing. It wouldn't be completely waterproof in a downpour, but would work for light rain. Some boughs for a bed and he was done.

Now back to fishing, he thought.

He caught another pike and a large walleye that afternoon and added the fillets to the smoke rack. He smoked them until dusk and then put them into the plastic bags and wrapped the bags up in his bug jacket. He tied one end of the cord around the bundle and a rock to the other end. Then he threw the rock over a big limb on a poplar. He pulled the fish up and suspended it well out of bear reach.

At first light he was up and built up his smoke fire. He set up the smoke rack and again laid out the fish fillets from the bug jacket onto it. He walked down to the lake and began fishing. By noon he had caught two walleye and a decent sized perch. He added the fillets to the smoke rack and roasted the remainder of the fish for today's meals. Two more of the pike were added to the smoke rack that afternoon.

It was a beautiful warm afternoon. Mike decided he was going to take a bath and while he was at it, *what the heck*, he might as well rinse out his clothes. He walked down to the lake dressed in his terry cloth dressing robe, laughing out loud at the luxury of it all.

I'm lost, he thought, *and winter's closing in, but I have one hell of a nice dressing gown.* He dropped the robe and walked down to the little beach.

The water was dead calm. When he saw his reflection he was startled. The man before him bore no resemblance to the fat professor he once was less than four months ago. Gone was the fatso. In his place was a well-muscled man with long hair and a beard. His stomach was flat, and his arm muscles bulged. He fancied he looked rather like Jesus on the cross from those Sunday school books he had read when he was a kid.

Ah! If only Cathy could see me now, he thought. She had been quite critical of his weight these last few years.

Just before he had left for holidays he had visited his family doctor.

"You are killing yourself, Mike," the doctor had said. "You are probably fifty pounds overweight for a man of your height."

It was all the fast food he lived on. He knew it too, but it was just too hard to resist.

Mike guessed he was down to one sixty-five now. *Diet and exercise*, he thought. He slowly turned around noting that even his legs and his bum were firm.

If I get out of here, I'm going to get a float plane tattooed on my ass.

He thought for a moment then changed that:

When I get out of here. When, not if.

He had a nice long swim. It was only once he got out that he realized his body was covered in little brown leaches. He had to sit on a rock and carefully pluck them off one by one. That task done, he rinsed out his clothes and hung them up on tree limbs to dry. He stretched out naked on the rock outcropping, and in the warm sun, was soon fast asleep. When he awoke from his nap a couple of hours later, his clothes were pretty much dry. He dressed and then tried his hand at fishing again.

The rhythm of casting out and reeling in felt good and natural. Second nature. He decided that he would break camp the next day and try to make his way around the lake. He had enough food now to last him a few days if he rationed it. Besides the dried fish, he had a bit of the pickled ginger and two Tom Yum soup mixes. He also had some tea.

He was determined to get around Big Buck Lake in the next few days. He had studied the map. It showed some small pothole lakes east of this one—that usually indicated some pretty swampy country. He figured he might have to walk all the way around to the south end of the lake then figure out how to cross the river before he could head east again.

At least I know where I am for once, he thought. *Not that that'll be much comfort if winter catches me.*

He left when the sun came up in the morning. It was slow going, picking his way along the shore. He tried going inland a bit and followed a game trail that seemed to parallel the lake but was forced to go back to the shore because of deadfall across the trail.

It has to be mid to late September by now, he thought. The leaves were turning colour. Twice he came upon creeks leading into the lake that were too deep to wade and had to waste hours following them upstream before he found a place to cross. When he had the lake in sight again, he decided to make camp for the night.

Mike was walking down towards the lake looking for a campsite when something red caught his eye. It was a pop can. He picked it up like it was gold. Someone had been here. Looking around, he found a faded cigarette package and the remains of a campfire. Someone had been there for sure! He didn't know why, but this leftover human litter gave him hope. From then on whenever he set up camp he put the pop can and the cigarette package on display like they were national art treasures. They just made him feel good.

EIGHTEEN

About a week after Mike's disappearance, Ruth was up early and trying to get the fire going in the stone fireplace. The coals had been banked the night before as George had shown her, and she was trying to coax some new tinder alight by with careful steady breaths.

She thought about Fred, still asleep in their bed behind her. She decided that she really did love him—even if she had a thousand men to choose from she would pick Fred. And Fred, she knew, felt the same about her. He wanted her desperately and the feeling was mutual. They talked about it and agreed that sex was not a good idea right now. Apart from wanting more privacy than the cabin could ever hope offer—and respecting the fact that George might be made uncomfortable—the possible consequences of an unplanned pregnancy in the wild was simply not something either of them wanted to contemplate.

Which isn't to say they didn't give each other a great deal of pleasure whenever they could, only that—as she put it—they were leaving themselves a lot to look forward to.

The tinder was going and she was feeding small twigs into the fire when something pulled from her revery. She thought she heard something behind her. She turned and looked but both men were snoring. She listened and she heard it again. Something large was moving around just outside the door.

Mike?

It was an odd thought and she realized it right away and shook her head. Still there was *something* out there. She tiptoed over and gently shook George by his shoulder.

"George," she whispered. "There is something outside."

George's eyes snapped open. He reached over between the wall and his sleeping bag and pulled out his pistol and cocked it. Still just wearing long underwear bottoms and one of Mike's ill fitting golf shirts he tiptoed across the dirt floor and eased open the door.

Their dried fish cache was suspended between two trees in the airplane cargo net. Up one of the trees was a fat old black bear trying to figure out how to capitalize on his newfound treasure.

Two shots later, the bear was dead on the ground.

Fred stumbled out of the cabin dressed only in his long johns to see what the commotion was about. Ruth looked them both up and down.

"Nice look boys!" was all she said as she turned to go back into the cabin. Fred looked at George and grinned.

After breakfast they went to work skinning and cleaning the bear. They set up the smoke rack and began the tedious process of smoking the meat. That night they celebrated the bear kill and the newly finished fireplace with bear steaks and Mike's gift of the Merlot.

Ruth actually toasted him.

"Here's to Mike wherever he is. Stay safe."

"I'll drink to that," said George.

"Me too," said Fred.

The next day, Ruth and George came up with a plan for soap. They rendered down as much of the bear fat as possible in their oil pan pot and mixed it with ashes. Then they packed it into cakes. It was a slow process. Ruth mixed in a little of her precious perfume into a few of the bars and put them aside in zip lock bags.

"This is my girl soap," she said in a tone that brooked no discussion.

George held up his hands. "Don't worry. I won't touch it."

That night after supper, Ruth handed each one of the men a bar of soap.

"Bath night," she said. "and when you are done with that come on back here for a haircut. I'll keep my back turned."

She had raided Mike's suitcases and handed each of them a clean change of clothes. "And wash your clothes while you're at it."

When they returned, she burst out laughing. They both looked like boys dressed up in their fathers' clothes. The pants were so big on George he had to hold them up when he walked. She dragged out one of the airplane seats from the cabin.

"Sit," she ordered George.

With the scissors on her big Swiss army knife, she hacked away at George's thick black hair until he looked like he had just arrived in an army boot camp.

"You're next," she said to Fred when she caught him smirking. She went to work chopping off most of Fred's hair as well. When she was done she started on his thick beard.

I still want him kissable, she thought, so she didn't cut it too short.

The cabin that night, she thought, smelled like a breath of fresh air.

Fred and George were hunting together now. Fred would take the little Henry rifle and George would take his bow and arrows and the pistol. He had fashioned a shoulder stock for the pistol and had it taped onto the handle. He claimed his hand shook and his aim was bad ever since he had run out of pipe tobacco. He still had the pipe and had been experimenting with different plants in a desperate hope of finding a tobacco substitute. So far every attempt had just resulted in a coughing fit.

George came home all excited one morning. He needed Fred's help. He had come across a cow and calf moose in a little swamp. He had shot the cow and when the calf refused to leave he shot her too. Fred and Ruth went with him and they spent the day gutting and butchering the animals into pieces small enough to carry.

The next few days were very busy, as they had to dig another cold cellar beside the cabin and transfer all the dried fish into that. They reinforced the pole the fish had been hanging from and hung most of the moose meat on it. It was cool enough now that flies probably wouldn't be a problem, but they cautiously built a smudge fire under the hanging meat anyway.

Over the next few days they dined on moose tongue and heart. These were George's favourites. Ruth and Fred were not so fond of heart, but they gamely ate it anyway. Ruth was feeling pretty good about her winter larder. Beside the two moose, they had most of the bear meat and over a hundred dried trout.

She had dried a bunch of the wild mushrooms and vegetables they had found over the summer. Ruth and Fred had harvested berries all summer. They had ten big freezer bags full of dried berry patties and they had another five bags of dried rose hips. They also had collected almost a full bag of juniper berries.

George had suggested putting a few of the berries in stews.

"It gives the bear meat kind of a nice flavour," he said.

There was a bag of cattail roots, some wild onions, and some dried leeks as well. They also had baskets of dried mushrooms.

George had an amazing knowledge of the edible plants available in the local forest. While he hunted for game, he also collected all kinds of edible plants. He routinely found plants like Indian cucumber and wild carrots—although not large, their roots made a tasty addition to the dinner pot. He had a vast knowledge of the many edible mushroom varieties that grew in the neighbouring woods and often provided these to add to the variety of their meals.

He showed Fred a trick for collecting the mushrooms even in the late fall.

"Squirrels gather them all summer," he explained. "They stash them in the spruce trees on the branches above the snow line. I just steal them."

One morning George checked the night-line on the nearby lake and found they'd been rewarded with three good-sized trout. He brought them back to camp when he came to collect Fred for some hunting. It was then that Ruth decided that she would put a plan into place that she'd been hatching now for months.

She'd managed not to use the sushi rice over the course of the summer, and had even gone so far as to tuck it away. *Out of sight, out of mind.* She decided tonight would be the night.

Once the boys were gone, she dug out all the sushi supplies she had been hoarding. She had the Wasabi mustard, the seaweed wraps, the rice, the rice wine and of course, the trout. In the afternoon she started her preparations. She put the pot next to the fire to boil the water for the rice. When the sticky rice was prepared she started making the sushi rolls. Lacking the traditional bamboo mats, she used one of Fred's flying magazines to make the sushi rolls.

First she laid out the seaweed wrap. She spread out a layer of the cooked sushi rice then a spread of wasabi mustard. Finally she laid out a generous portion of the raw trout on top of the rice and some Indian cucumber. Using the magazine, she rolled the whole thing up into a roll. She cut the roll into bite size rolls using a trick of dipping the knife into cold water between each cut. Once the first one was complete, she made two more rolls. She balled the rest of the rice up in small bitesized portions and put a little of the wasabi mustard paste and a slice of the raw trout on top of each one. To top off the meal she heated the saki rice wine in the pot and served it with the meal.

She could hardly have been more pleased with herself.

George ate the meal, but really didn't appreciate the effort Ruth had put into it. Privately he thought eating raw fish was the act of a desperate man, and he didn't really feel that desperate. Fred, however, loved sushi having got a taste for it on the West Coast, and he thanked her profusely.

They were almost out of tea now. Even with rationing, all they had left were ten tea teabags. She decided spruce bough tip tea would be the norm now. The real tea would be saved as a treat for the dead of winter.

George was tanning as many rabbit hides as he could. He had the second bear hide scraped clean of flesh and stretched out on the cabin wall. The deer hide was ready for use and he had several large pieces of moose hide drying.

"What are your plans for those?" Ruth asked.

"Well," he said. "I think that bear hide will be my winter bed. The moose we could use for moccasins and snowshoes. The rabbits can be used for all kinds of warm clothes."

She thought once more, as she did half a dozen times a day, of Mike and his reckless decision to walk out. She hoped that he was still alive though she didn't credit him with much chance of success and she couldn't imagine him surviving the winter with the clothes he packed out. It gave her an ache in her chest to think of him alone and slowly freezing to death.

It's not winter yet, she thought. *But it's coming.*

NINETEEN

The lake seemed to go on forever, of course it didn't help that the shoreline was often impassable and the surrounding terrain rough and irregular. He would have to track away from the lake in order to make any progress south and then push back to find the water again in order to reorient himself. A couple of times he found himself back at the a rocky outcrop he'd left hours before. He had already lost track of the days since leaving the others for these things had seemed easier to keep track of back at camp. Not that it mattered much, he supposed. His calendar was pretty much open so to speak—no one was expecting him anywhere anytime soon.

No one is expecting me at all.

It was an unsettling thought. One day he found three cigarette butts and a pull-tab from either a pop can or a beer can near an old campfire on a rocky beach. Another day he found a red and white fishing bobber washed up on shore.

The nights were getting cold now. Twice in the last week, there was a skiff of snow on the ground when he awoke. While it lasted, he saw lots of tracks in the fresh snow. Moose and deer he could identify. The rest were pretty much a mystery to him. Both snows had been gone by noon, but he knew that eventually there would be snow that would not be so easily dispelled and that his chance of avoiding it by way of rescue was dwindling.

As he walked, he often thought of Cathy and his kids. He wondered how they were coping. Surely Cathy had given up on the thought of him being alive by now, and the thought of it made him almost giddy with unease.

He remembered the way she looked on the night he'd met her in a Vancouver club back in '87. He'd been getting his PhD at UBC, and she'd been a newly minted dental assistant from Victoria in town with a colleague for a night of fun in the big city. He thought of the first time he'd kissed her (it'd been that same night); the first time they'd made love (unexpectedly in a White Rock motel room a few weeks later); and the sweet summer romance that had ensued. He thought about meeting her family. He recalled his offbeat marriage proposal to her just before Christmas and how she'd look the day they'd been married that August.

He desperately needed to see her again, her and the kids, before the life he'd made for them eroded entirely in his absence. That was his biggest fear. Though he hadn't said anything about it, it had upset him to have missed their anniversary—though he'd not actually forgotten it this year—and his son's birthday as well. Time just kept marching forward without him. And though he had told himself that, by walking out of bush, he'd be home for Christmas, he now realized that it likely wasn't going to happen.

It was a late afternoon, and he was making his back down to the lake, hoping to be able to see where the river emptied into it. In his mind he was playing through a dream that had woken him two nights ago. In it he'd walked up to his own front door (somehow still dressed in his stinking tattered housecoat and carrying George's old pack) only to find it unlocked and the house entirely empty—no furniture, no plants, only nails in the walls where pictures once hung...

And without immediately realizing it he stumbled across a path.

Hang on, this is no game trail, he thought—for someone had cleared out the windfall with a saw.

He followed the trail up almost at a run and, to his amazement, there in a tiny clearing overlooking the lake, was a little log cabin.

Mike hallooed the cabin, but there was no answer. He marched right up to the door and pounded. Again there wasn't an answer. He pulled the peg out of the hasp and walked in. It was a tiny little log cabin about twelve feet by twelve feet. It had a half loft with a single foam mattress up there for a bed. Access to the loft was via a steep log ladder. Downstairs there was a tiny airtight wood stove. There was a rough hewn table and two cheap folding camp chairs. There was a homemade set of kitchen cupboards on the wall centred between two small windows.

Mike carefully inventoried the cupboards. He found a few assorted pots and pans, two plates, a big bowl, two forks, a sharp knife and a big spoon. There was some stale coffee, a big container of tea bags, and a box of salt. There was a can of baking powder, but no flour, and an unopened bag of white beans. There were also two boxes of strike anywhere matches, one new and one half full.

A bale of snare wire and a wash pan hung from the wall. By the door was a galvanized water pail. In one cupboard he found a box of .303 shells. This puzzled Mike and made him search further. Under the foam mattress upstairs he discovered an old WWII bolt-action rifle.

Mike was excited over the discovery of the gun. This opened a lot of doors. With this rifle, he thought, he had a solid chance of making it out of here. The problem was he had never fired a gun in his life—but he was determined to figure it out. He spent the next hour teaching himself how it worked. First he figured out how the magazine clip came out of the rifle.

The bullets must go in here, he reasoned, pushing a couple of rounds into the magazine and putting the magazine back into the rifle. He had seen these bolt-action rifles in the movies and, without hesitation, put a bullet into the chamber and pushed on the safety lever.

He went outside and pointed the thing at a tree. He took off the safety and pulled the trigger. He didn't expect the noise. The gunshot was deafening. What he really didn't expect was the kick.

"Wow," he said, rubbing his shoulder as he took the gun back into the cabin and unloaded it.

Beside the cabin was a woodshed. He walked over and poked his head in the door. Hanging on the wall was an axe, a big buck saw, a heavy old splitting maul and a coil of brand new yellow rope still in the plastic package. He picked up the rope and studied the package. There was a computer barcode on it, indicating in his mind that it was probably no more than a few years old.

He carried on with his search in the woodshed. He found a four-litre container of kerosene that made him smile, for there was an old hurricane lantern on the wall outside the cabin. He had given it a shake on his way by, but it was all but empty. Now he thought a least he would have light at night. There were also two old tobacco cans full of rusty looking nails. The woodshed was about half full of dry fire wood already split.

Mike's next stop was the outhouse. He was fully expecting to use a page from his book as wipe when he saw a big coffee can. He opened it and giggled to himself out loud. Inside were two rolls of toilet paper, one new still in its wrapping and one about three quarters full.

From the back of the cabin hung four well oiled traps of some kind. Mike had never even seen one before, so he let them be. But it gave him a clue as to what the owner's occupation might be.

That night Mike boiled some of his dried fish—with a pinch of salt for a change—and had a wonderful cup of coffee. He rolled into his blankets. The cabin was toasty from the evening fire on the airtight stove.

I may be in heaven, he thought.

Shortly after dawn, he awoke sitting bolt upright.
Where am I?

It took a minute for his head to clear. He lay on his bed for twenty minutes at least formulating a plan.

It would be foolhardy to leave now, he thought as he stared at his map spread out on the table. *Even with the rifle, I don't think I would make it. Hell, I don't know if I could even hit an animal with it.*

He decided he would use the cabin as a base for a few days and scout around to see if he could find a road or a trail leading in to this place. Finally he got up and lit the fire in the stove. After breakfast, he got the gun down and re-familiarized himself on how it worked. He put the sling over his shoulder and set off to explore his new surroundings.

It was cold outside.

It must be October by now.

The leaves were dropping fast. Around noon a plane went by in the distance. And though it was little more than a dot, he jumped up and down waving his arms like a mad fool nonetheless. Of course, like the rest of the planes since their crash, it flew on unseeing.

Shit!

TWENTY

George dreamt of Mavis again. Of meeting her at a house party in Kenora in 1965 while he and some buddies were down from the reserve in Red Lake to pick up a car—and of the miles he had put on that buddy's car travelling back and forth the Kenora in the months following that first meeting. George awoke haunted by the fear that he might never his wife, kids, or grandkids again. As he lay in bed wrapped tight in his sleeping bag, he came up with a project to keep him busy and keep him from doing precisely what Mike had done.

"We need to attach the kitchen to the cabin," he blurted out over their morning tea and fish breakfast. "Think about it. We won't have to struggle over here for our meals. And once the snow flies we'll sure be glad of it."

"I think it's a great idea," said Fred. Ruth agreed.

And so for the next few days they worked on dismantling the kitchen shelter and attaching it as a lean-to off the main cabin. Fred's leg was fully healed by now, and he was determined to work hard preparing for the winter. Though he never brought it up, Fred often felt burdened by the knowledge that, were it not for his leg, the four of them would have likely walked out in June or July. He often wondered how George felt about it.

The evening they finished moving the kitchen the two men sat out around an outside campfire, both lost in thoughts of their own.

"How do you think Doc is doing?" Fred asked. It was no coincidence that Ruth was out of earshot.

"He's dead," George said in his usual matter-of-fact tone.

"You don't know that."

"Didn't ask me what I know," he said. "You asked me what I thought."

"Well, don't say anything—"

"I know."

"It's a tough subject for her."

The old guide nodded.

"Be honest, what do you think our chances are, George?"

George shrugged. "Well, we're certainly prepared. If we make it through this winter without getting sick or freezing to death, and there's no guarantee of that, I guess our chances are okay. Cabin won't last though, by next summer, those poplar walls will have shrunk up so bad you'll be able to throw a rabbit through the cracks. Should get us to spring though."

"That's all we need," said Fred. "Come spring, the three of us are walking out of here."

"You don't know that," George said.

———

Mike searched the shore in front of the cabin for all of the next morning. He was sure he would find either a canoe or a rowboat stashed, but he found neither. His heart sunk. This was another sign that whoever used this cabin probably only used it in the winter as a trapline shelter. His hopes of an early rescue were slim now.

Still that meant that, if he stayed put, come winter, someone would arrive.

Unless they give this winter a pass for some reason... then I'll probably die here.

It was a risk. And he changed his mind three or four times a day. Stay or move on.

Indecision aside, he was prepared to stay for the time being at the very least, and so he went to work collecting firewood as part of his daily routine. He didn't want to burn up all the owner's firewood and leave the poor fellow stranded. He felt bad enough using his food and his gun. He still had his wallet with over a hundred dollars in cash, and whenever he was considering moving on, he told himself he would leave a note of explanation, the money, and his contact information on the table.

With the big bucksaw he cut deadfall into stove-sized pieces and hauled them back to the cabin. These he split then piled it into the woodshed. The stove burnt a fair amount of wood, so he worked most afternoons at the chore. He also wanted to fill the woodshed before he left as payment for the use of the cabin.

———

The first skiff of snow in the area fell three days later. George began work on a pair of snowshoes with a bit of urgency. He first cut four spruce saplings and shaved them flat on opposing sides with his knife. Next he cut two sets of notches on each one. One set near one end and the other set near the middle. Using his foot as a break, he slowly bent the tip up until it was at a ninety-degree angle to the rest of the sapling. He then enlisted Ruth's help.

While he held the angle Ruth tied a cord around the notches at the tip then stretched it under George's watchful eye to the centre set of notches and tied it off.

"This forms the toe," George told her. "At least I'm pretty sure that's how it works. I don't really know what I'm doing. I've never made a pair before. I just remember watching an old man on the reserve making them. His were a lot fancier than mine will be."

He spent the next week cutting the crossbars and boring the holes for the webbing with the awl on Ruth's big Swiss army knife. Ruth helped him by cutting thin strips of moose hide to use for the webbing and soaking it in water. As the hide dried, it shrunk making the webbing tight. Every evening before dark,

George would spend an hour or so sitting around the campfire weaving in the moose hide. When the first one was finished they all admired it.

"I wish I had some shellac," he said. "Without it these things will be garbage in a couple of years."

He finished the second shoe that week. He was so happy that his project worked, that he cut the saplings for two more pairs.

At least I'll have something to work on once we get snowed in, he thought.

Ruth was busy with a couple of projects of her own. She had cut out the pieces for some knee high moccasins out of moose hide under advice from George. Again he admitted he had never actually made a pair but had watched his mother and his grandmother making them when he was a kid. Theirs had fur tops and were decorated with coloured beads he had told Ruth.

"Don't hold your breath," was her reply. "These are going to be pretty simple."

She was also cutting evergreen boughs and weaving them into the new kitchen lean-to to act as a bit of a wind block. Fred and George had done a real nice job of this lean-to, considering what they had to work with. They were completely out of rope and bolts now, so the whole thing was tied together with strips of moose and deer hide. The willow bark was too brittle to work with now that the cold weather had set in.

With the first bit of snow came the arrival of the geese and duck migrations. Most of the flocks stayed high overhead honking their presence. One morning, however, they awoke to the sound of geese honking nearby. A flock had landed on the little lake in front of the cabin. George crept down and managed to shoot two of them with the little rifle before the whole flock took off. The carcasses floated off shore just out of reach of the longest pole they could find. Fred boldly volunteered to strip down and swim out to get them.

He didn't get an argument from the other two.

Ruth offered to go back up and build up the fire and have a blanket ready for him to wrap himself in once he got out.

"This might be my last good bath of the year," said Fred and he ran up to the cabin behind Ruth to get a bar of soap.

Once back down at the lake, he stripped down to his long underwear bottoms and quickly waded in. With the cold outside temperature the water actually felt relatively warm. He knew it wasn't really that warm, so he wasted no time in retrieving the geese. He soaped himself down leaving George to deal with cleaning and plucking the geese. Once he was finished his quick bath, he picked up his clothes and stepped gingerly in his bare feet up the path to the cabin. Ruth wrapped a blanket around him as soon as he walked through the door.

"You're such a brave boy," she said kissing him quickly. "Now you get yourself out of that wet underwear and I'll hang it up to dry." She turned her back to give him some privacy, and he complied.

Within the next week, George shot several ducks that landed on the lake for a rest on the migration south. Knowing Fred was not likely to volunteer to swim for a duck, he was very careful to shoot them only when they were close enough to shore that he could drag them in with a pole. The greasy duck and goose meat was a welcome change from the lean moose and fish diet they had been living on.

They emptied the last of their gear from the survival duffle and were collecting all the feathers in it. So far they had amassed quite a collection of grouse, goose and duck feathers. Ruth came up with a plan for their use.

From Mike's suitcases she selected four tee shirts. She took two and put them one inside one another. She sewed the bottoms and the edges of the sleeves together. Next she stuffed the cavity with feathers and down. Once each was filled she sewed up the neck and quilted it to keep the feathers from settling to the bottom. She gave the first one to George who was quite pleased. With the oncoming weather, this new garment would be a lifesaver.

Happy with the results of the first vest, Ruth went to work to create a similar one for Fred. She would have liked one for herself, but there was not enough down and feathers to pull it off. She had plenty of tops and sweaters though, so she settled for the layered effect to keep warm.

TWENTY-ONE

Mike was getting desperate. He needed to fill his larder if he hoped to survive. He managed to catch a few pike and perch over the last couple of days, but had all but consumed them. Every morning he was out with the rifle and the bow hoping to find something he could shoot. He knew there were moose in the area, for he could see their tracks in the fresh snow. Sometimes he would find where they had bedded down packing the grass and snow. At night he could hear them calling. George had told him of experienced hunters who could imitate that call, using a birch bark horn as an amplifier. Mike didn't even try.

Early one morning, his hunting paid off. As he crept along the shore of the lake in the dim dawn light following some fresh tracks in the snow he heard a noise. Up to its knees in water was a huge bull moose standing with its big rump facing him. The moose hadn't heard him. Silently Mike slipped off the safety and dropped to one knee. He decided to wait until the beast was out of the water and he had something better to shoot at than a big hairy ass before he pulled the trigger.It seemed to take forever and he was sure it would hear his heart pounding. Finally the big bull turned and walked out of the water still unaware of Mike's presence. Mike took careful aim and fired. The bull stumbled and Mike fired again. It fell to the ground with a resounding thud and lay there with its sides heaving. Mike ran up and put the gun barrel six inches from its neck and pulled the trigger. The heaving stopped.

Mike had never butchered anything remotely this big before by himself. He had watched George butcher the bear, but this was different. This time he was on his own. This time it was a life or death situation. He had to get this thing cut up and hung today. By nightfall all kinds of creatures would be here to claim a share. There were already two whiskey jacks sitting in a nearby tree eyeing him with their beady black eyes. It was marauding black bears he was most concerned about, so he carried the rifle with him when he went back up to the cabin to retrieve the axe and saw.

When he arrived back at the carcass the birds were already pecking away at it. He chased them off and began gutting the big moose. The smell was revolting, and he actually had to walk away and vomit into the brush. Once he had the moose gutted out, the task didn't seem so bad.

Using the axe and saw he separated the two hindquarters from the animal and dragged them up the trail to the woodshed with the rope. The rest of the moose he cut into manageable sized pieces that he was able to carry or drag up to the shed. On every trip, he had to chase the birds off the carcass again. On his last trip down he considered the heart and the tongue. At this point he felt he shouldn't waste anything edible so he collected the heart, the liver, and the kidneys. Then he sliced out the big guy's tongue.

His audience had now grown to at least ten whiskey jacks and a couple of big jet-black ravens.

"All yours," he said picking up his tools and walking away.

The next task was hanging the meat and constructing a door for the shed so the bears and such couldn't steal his meat. He had to finish the door by lantern light as he just ran out of daylight. The door was simply a series of poplar logs laid out side by side and nailed together with some pole cross bracing. He had nothing for hinges so he simply stood the door against the opening and braced it shut with a couple of stout poles.

Tomorrow I'll think about hinges.

He built a fire in the airtight and boiled the tongue. He was quite pleased with the result. A little salt for flavour and it was not half bad. He made a decision. With the moose, he had enough meat that he could survive for months. It would be impossible to travel carrying it. He decided that, since he hadn't been able to find a trail or a road leading into this place, the owner must come in by air. He would wait for the plane to arrive and then hitch a ride back out.

———

Ruth thought George's moccasins had turned out pretty good, but in comparison Fred's were the best. She had saved his for last, for when she had her skills honed. Her next project was mitts. With Fred's help, they cut out the mitts from moose hide while they were sitting by the fireplace in the evening. George stepped in to help and they all worked at sewing front and back together. She then made an inner mitt of rabbit fur for each one.

"You better get hunting, George," she joked. "I'm running out of sewing materials."

"Yes ma'am."

"You boys are sure hard on your clothes," she said one morning. Both men were wearing threadbare jeans. George still had a pair of work pants in reserve, but the only spare pants Fred had were Mike's, and they were huge on him. He hated wearing them and only put them on when his own jeans were too wet to wear. Today Ruth put her foot down.

"Give me those jeans, Fred," she said. "And you give me yours too, George."

It was a tone neither of them had heard before, so they quickly obeyed.

Over the next two days she carefully mended Fred's jeans. The whole front of each leg was fitted with a deerskin patch. She also reinforced the butt ends with deerskin. Fred was ever so happy to get his jeans back.

"I can wear Doc's pants overtop of these when I'm outside," he said, "to protect them. But they are absolutely huge on me."

George's jeans were beyond repair. He still had his work pants and a pair of Mike's pants, so she wasn't concerned. She put the rag that were his jeans into her scraps pile for future projects. Next she wrestled George's beloved bush jacket from him and patched the elbows with a few small darning mends.

"Thanks, Ruth," he said, admiring the work. "I love this old coat."

Fred and George were cutting firewood every day now. They would need a lot of wood to warm that little shack over the winter. The mornings were quite chilly, so they dressed in as many layers as they could. They reinforced the roof of the lean-to with more poles to carry the snow load. This would now be their woodshed.

Fred was thankful for his old leather flying jacket during these cool fall days, but he knew it would be definitely not suited for the weather that lay ahead. Ruth had taken his old Cessna hat and sewn some rabbit ear protectors on to it—she had cut them from the mitt scraps. His hooded sweatshirt was still in pretty good shape as he hadn't worn it much over summer, but his shirt was almost in tatters. He had long ago cut the arms off at the elbows and now the collar was almost worn through. He still had two pairs of rather threadbare socks that he had salvaged from Mike's suitcases and a pair of Mike's pants for outer protection. With the mitts and the moccasins and his new vest, he felt he could brave all but the subzero weather.

George was in about the same shape as Fred for clothes. His jeans were completely shot, so he had switched over to wearing his work pants. He had just about worn out the plaid shirt and had donated it to the ragbag. Now under his wool jacket, he wore a golf shirt he had pinched from Mike's bag, then a twill work shirt, his new vest and a cardigan sweater.

The wool bush jacket was his pride and joy.

"It's a good one," he told Fred one night as they sat around the fire. "You can't buy these in Kenora. It's got an extra flap in the back. It keeps you warmer and dryer. I had to get my nephew to get it for me in Winnipeg."

He also had an extra pair of Mike's pants that he was going to wear over his own when the weather got colder. He had two pairs of wool socks left. The ones he had been wearing when they crashed were shot. He had kept the tops for darning wool and had kept these last two pairs in pretty good shape. Ruth had made him a headband out of one of her tube tops. It was peacock blue and by the way Fred smirked whenever he put it on probably looked ridiculous. George didn't care it kept his ears from freezing. Ruth promised to make him a fur hat if he could get some fur. He still had his work gloves. He had hoarded them all summer, so they were in fine shape. He preferred them to the mitts this time of year. The mitts were too warm.

Ruth was in the worst shape of them all. Her wardrobe had consisted of mainly shorts and tube tops with a few little sweaters. She had one pair of jeans left and a denim shirt that was still in pretty good shape. She had a hooded sweatshirt and a well worn lined jean jacket. The jacket had been well worn *before* the crash, so she had to mend the elbows with deer hide as well. Her hiking boots were still holding together and, of course, she had her new moccasins and mitts.

She had not brought any long underwear but had brought along a couple of pairs of running tights so was making do with those. She had taken her jaunty little peaked hat and attached a pair of rabbit fur ear protectors. Her pink gardening gloves were shot and the ends of her fingers stuck out of them. She had her mitts so she was okay.

George was determined to have that fur hat Ruth had promised him. He knew where there was a little beaver pond maybe a half a mile inland. He took the little .22 and the axe and headed over there one morning. Once he arrived, he assessed the situation. There was a skim of thin ice over most of the pond, but the water near the dam itself was still open.

He walked out onto the dam and began chopping a hole. An hour later he had done some sizeable damage, and water was pouring out of the breach. Then he went up on the bank and hid behind a big spruce and watched. About a half an hour passed before he saw movement. A big beaver cautiously approached the dam and swam by the hole checking it out. It circled around the open water of the pond looking for danger. George didn't move a muscle. Then a second beaver appeared. He patiently watched as they hauled stick after stick over to repair the breach in the dam. Finally the moment he was waiting for. The big one climbed out of the water onto the dam itself. George waited until it was fully out of the water and had settled into work before he fired two shots in quick succession from the little rifle.

The big beaver dropped dead. The smaller one slapped her broad tail on the water resulting in a loud smack in alarm, but it was too late. George had his beaver. On his way home he managed to bag three snowshoe rabbits as well. They were turning from brown to white this time of year, so were a lot easier to spot.

Fred and Ruth had spent the day in the bush with the saw, cutting firewood. They had to go a little further afield these days to find the dry wood but still managed to collect a sizeable pile ready to be split. They stopped their work when they saw George struggling under his load and ran down the trail to help. They watched with interest as George expertly skinned out the beaver carefully avoiding the scent glands so as not to spoil the meat.

Neither Ruth or Fred had ever tasted beaver before, but they were surprised to find it had a very pleasant taste.

"I generally give it to my dogs when I'm on the trapline," said George. "I much prefer moose."

"I don't know, it's nice to have a change," said Ruth.

They dined on the meat for the next few days to save dipping into their dried meat supply.

George went to work soaking and scraping the hide while Ruth mentally designed his new hat. She thought maybe she could use some of the scraps to make something warmer for Fred as well.

—

As usual Mike proved to be a much better fisherman than he was a hunter. In one day he had managed to use up three of his precious bullets to get one solitary grouse. Even then it was the percussion of the bullet that knocked the bird out of the tree. He grabbed it by the feet as it lay flapping on the ground. Mike unceremoniously whacked its head on the tree trunk to put it out of its misery. He checked it all over before he cleaned it. There was absolutely no sign of a bullet hole.

Fishing, however, was a different story. Mike had found a spot where a fast flowing creek fed into the lake. He experimented with lures and finally got lucky with a yellow feather jig and was rewarded with a nice walleye. Now he was in his element. This is what he had been planning on catching at the lodge.

He quickly cleaned the fish and baited the jig with some of the gut. Normally he would have only kept the fillets but he wanted to use the entire fish. Even the head could be made into a stew. Two hours later he had ten nice fat fish on the ground beside him.

Every morning he was up at dawn and out hunting. Before the week was out, he had shot four rabbits. He was quite proud of himself, as he had managed to only use the required four bullets to do so. During the week, he had also caught another twenty or so fish, mostly pike and walleye. In the afternoon, he manned his smoker and cut firewood nearby.

While he hunted, he collected whatever food he could find. He found a patch of cattails in a little swamp and pulled all he could for their roots. Early one morning, he met a deer face to face on the trail. Four shots later and she was all his. He spent the day skinning her out.

Not a bad job if I do say so myself, he thought after he had finished tacking the hide to the cabin wall. Part of his daily ritual was to scrape the hides with the hatchet to remove the flesh. They were doing nicely. He judged the rabbits and moose hide pieces were ready to work with.

He went to work making himself a pair of crude moose hide mitts with rabbit liners. He straightened out a big fishing hook and filed off the barb on a rock. Fishing line was his thread—this was a trick he learned from Ruth. Truth be known, Ruth had stolen the idea from George. As it was his first attempt at sewing, the mitts were very amateurish but still were quite serviceable. Next he made some rabbit fur socks for his boots. They were nice and comfortable. His feet had been cold almost constantly in the last couple of weeks.

Mike counted his bullets. He only had five left, but his meat larder was not bad considering. He decided he would not waste any more bullets on small game. He was facing a pretty tough winter as it was. He was not the craftsman that George was, but he was inventive. Mike's attempt at making snowshoes was to simply cut some big spruce boughs and tie them together in bunches to his boots with rope.

The big lake was freezing over now, but he could still see open water in the middle. The ice close to shore was thick enough to walk on, but he stuck close to the edge. It was really cold now.

By day he layered up in most of his clothes. He had even taken to wearing the housecoat as an outer layer in the cold mornings before the sun got up. He was contemplating an attempt at making another jacket out of the deer hide, but hadn't quite got there yet. He was still scraping the flesh bits from it. This chore he saved for the night while he sat around the little airtight stove.

PART 4
WINTER

TWENTY-TWO

November hit with a fury.

George opened the door one morning to three feet of fresh snow.

"Wow," he called over his shoulder. "Look at this. Winter is here for sure."

While Ruth made breakfast, Fred and George banked the base of the cabin up with snow. They used the Plexiglas windshield salvaged from the Cessna for the task. One of them held each side of it.

After breakfast, George tried out his new snowshoes. He walked down to the lake to fetch some water and they worked like a charm.

Better get busy on the rest of them, he thought.

He had one of Fred's complete. The other one was ready for webbing.

"So where did you grow up, Fred?" asked George, one day while they were jigging for fish through the ice.

"Kirkland Lake." When he could tell it didn't register with George, he said, "It's a little mining town close to the Quebec border."

"I've never heard of it. I've never been east of Thunder Bay," George said. "So will your folks worry about you?"

"No," said Fred. "Not mine. My parents are both gone. They were killed in a car accident when I was just a teenager. I've got three brothers and two sisters, but I don't see them that often. One of my brothers, Chris, still lives in Kirkland Lake. Once in a while, I see him. My sister lives in southern Ontario. I doubt they know I'm missing. Maybe my landlord will pass on the news if they send me a Christmas card."

Fred fell silent. He was remembering the last time he saw his siblings. It was the first Christmas he had been in Kenora. His brother Chris had organized a Christmas reunion in Kirkland Lake. Fred had planned on flying the Cessna down, but weather wouldn't allow it. He had driven instead, twelve gruelling hours each way. It had been worth it though, for it had been years since they had all been together.

"How about you, George?" asked Fred. "Do you think Mavis thinks you're still alive?"

"Nah," said George, grinning but looking grim nonetheless. "She's probably down in Winnipeg spending my millions."

"Have you ever been to Winnipeg?"

"Oh yeah," said George. "I went down there one time with one of my nephews. My sister lives there. I didn't like it. They took me shopping at one of those malls. It was way too crowded. I went back and sat in the truck for three hours until they were finished shopping. Next day I got my nephew to drive me home. Hell, I don't even like going into Kenora if I don't have to."

———

It was late and Mike was exhausted and so he decided to test the ice on the bay. It seemed really solid now—it had been so cold recently. He jumped up and down on it close to shore without even a crack, and so he decided to take a shortcut across the bay home. At first he walked with the gun held sideways just in case. After a few minutes he confidently slung it under his arm and trudged on.

No problem, he thought.

It was only once he was abreast of the creek that fed his favourite fishing hole that suddenly he broke through without warning. Down he went. He fought his way to the surface only to find ice. In a panic he swam around in a circle until finally he saw the hole. He popped his head through and tread water while he gulped the sweetest air he had ever breathed.

He tried pulling himself up onto firm ice, but it kept crumbling under his weight. He tried a swim up manoeuvre that he had seen on the fishing channel once. He approached the edge of the hole kicking his feet like mad and using both his hands dragged himself up onto the ice shelf. He wiggled forward on the ice until he was well clear of the hole and then cautiously began to crawl. He didn't dare stand until he had crawled a good twenty or thirty feet from the hole.

He stood shaking like a leaf for a few seconds before reality set in. He realized then that, if he didn't get moving and moving *fast*, the cold would take him. He was still unsure of the ice so moved cautiously towards shore. Once on shore he tried to run, but his jeans had quickly frozen into the shape of a couple of stovepipes, so he waddled as fast as he could for the warmth and safety of the cabin.

As he neared the cabin, he was shaking uncontrollably. All he could think about was his two big wool blankets. He started stripping clothing off as he waddled up the trail dropping frozen apparel into the snow as he went. By the time he reached the door, he had only his jeans, long underwear and rubber boots on. Once inside, he stripped completely naked and quickly rolled into his blankets.

Two hours later, he awoke from a fitful shivering sleep. The reality of the situation slowly seeped into his brain. The first thing that came to mind was the fact that he had lost the gun and his bow and arrows. As his faculties came back to him, he had a vague recollection of stripping off his clothes and dropping them on the way up the trail.

There was no way he was going out there to retrieve them until tomorrow though. He got up and put on his big housecoat and got a fire going in the stove. He hung what was left of his clothes to dry. After a meal and a hot cup of tea, he finally quit shivering. The next morning his clothes were still soaking wet when he woke. He dressed in his housecoat, damp rubber boots and wrapped himself up in a blanket. He set off down the trail to retrieve the rest of his stiff clothing. He spent the rest of the day drying clothes over the wood stove, and pondering his plight now that the gun was lost.

Once his clothes were dry, he set out on a quest for materials so that he could get to work on a new bow and some arrows.

Twenty-three

George had established a sizeable snare line over the last couple of months. Using strands of copper wire from the airplane, he made wire nooses. He would seek out the trails that the snow-shoe hares frequented and tie one of his nooses over the trail. Next he would place a barrier of twigs in front of the noose to entice the hare to hop over the barrier and through the hoop. The noose would tighten around the creature and eventually it would either strangle or freeze to death.

Every day he strapped on his snowshoes to check the lines. Most days rewarded with a couple of hares. Although the meat was welcome to conserve their meat supplies, what they really relished were the furs. They had the hides stretched on home-made frames using deer sinew as thread. Ruth was using them as they cured to make what she described as a one-size fits all pull over parka. She doubted that they could possibly snare enough hares to make three of them. It was a garment they would all have to share.

It was the evenings that were the toughest to stay busy. Ruth and George worked on the parka project using George's oil-and-gasoline lantern in a wine bottle for light. Fred watched that lamp like a hawk for a night or two, ready to throw it as far as he could should it flare up. Finally he decided he could trust it. George seemed to have got the right mixture of oil to gasoline, and it was working fine, other than some excess black smoke.

Fred invented a project to keep himself busy as well. He salvaged some large red and white lures from Mike's big tackle box and was busy fashioning handles for them. He thought they would make fine eating spoons.

He was also working on a log bed frame for himself and Ruth, painstakingly notching the logs with the hatchet.

"I should have this ready to use by spring," he joked.

The little fireplace was good for cooking on, but was almost useless for heating the cabin. Most nights after they were finished with their projects, they sat wrapped in blankets before the fire capturing whatever heat they could before they forced themselves to bed. Sitting around the little rock fireplace one night, Fred finally announced his boredom.

"Ruth, I've got to get out of here!"

It took both Ruth and George several hours to convince him to calm down and wait for spring before he tried anything rash.

The trio had settled into a routine now. After the morning tea, Fred would wear the shared parka first and go down to the lake to chop the night's accumulation of ice from the water hole. He would then fill the wine bottles and the scotch bottle with water. He had made himself a funnel and a dipper from aluminium to make this chore a little easier.

Once back at the cabin, he would bring in the day's wood supply before handing the parka over to George so that he could check the nearest of his snares. Ruth would be cooking the morning meal, which was usually leftovers from the night before. She was doing her best to conserve their berry supply, yet serve just enough to keep them all healthy.

Although George was usually a pretty good provider of hares from his snare line, Ruth knew that a diet of lean meat like rabbit was not good for people. They needed some fat. She augmented this diet with the fish, moose, and venison so they could enjoy a bit of variety in their meals. She also rationed the bear meat to ensure they had a bit of extra fat in their diet throughout the winter months.

George was the fire master. Every evening before he went to bed, he banked up the coals with ashes so that, in the morning, he wouldn't have to waste any of their few precious matches. At first light, he would use a tiny bit of his secret formula tinder to coax a flame from the embers.

—

Mike was not as fortunate as the others with his diet. He had moose, deer or fish to choose from. He often vowed to himself that, if he ever got out of there, he would live on fresh garden salads for the rest of his life. He craved cheese and eggs as well. He often woke up a night dreaming of such meals. The lemon tea was all but gone. He had but two bags left. He had about thirty of the regular bags he had found in the cabin. The coffee was a pleasant memory. He augmented the tea bags with spruce bough tea. At least this would provide him with his much-needed vitamin C. All that was left of the rest of his store bought food was a half a box of salt.

He too tried making a snare line for rabbits, but the snow was getting too deep to walk in with only his spruce bough snow-shoes. Every day he packed a trail to the woodshed, the outhouse and down to the lake, stamping along taking baby steps with his funny looking snowshoes. Every few days he had to make a new set, but they did the job.

Part of his daily routine was to chop out his water hole so that the ice wouldn't get too thick. Every morning he would go down to the lake, chop out the ice and fill his pots with water. Then he would bait a hook with some gristle and set a still line. Several times during the day he would stop by and jig for a few minutes. Every couple of days he usually would be rewarded with a slimy little pike. He took them gratefully now. At this time of the year food was food! On warmer days he foraged for firewood and birch bark along the edge of the lake.

Must be December maybe even January by now.

The days were cold, but the nights were far colder. Most nights he guessed the temperature was dropping to at least minus forty. At this rate, his wood supply would not make it. He was forced to move his foam mat down right beside the stove so that he could feed the stove without getting completely out of bed in the middle of the night.

TWENTY-FOUR

George had abandoned all but his closest snares because of the bitter cold. They had been not producing much lately. They were all quite worried. He had been worried lately about his own trapline back in the Lake of the Woods country. As he lay in bed, he wondered if his wife and kids had kept it going or whether they had just walked away from it assuming he was dead. Tomorrow, he decided, he would dress up as warm as possible to try hunting further afield.

He woke up at dawn. While he was having his early morning breakfast, Fred woke up and joined him by the fire. They discussed George's plans for the day in whispers over tea. After breakfast, George put on the shared parka, picked up the little rifle and slipped out. Putting on his snowshoes, he headed for the faint trail leading to the second unnamed lake.

It was overcast and quite a bit warmer today than it had been for a couple of weeks. George walked slowly, pausing every few steps to listen for any sound of small game. Finally after a couple of hours of this slow cat and mouse game, he heard the distinctive peep, peep, peep of a nervous grouse. He paused and crouched trying to spot his prey.

Finally he saw it trying to make itself completely invisible by standing perfectly still. He took careful aim and pulled the trigger. He smiled to himself. This would be a welcome treat back at the cabin tonight. He spent a few minutes cleaning the grouse and stowing the meat in the little backpack he had borrowed from Fred.

By noon it had started to snow. George looked at the sky and made a decision to push on. By the time he made the lake, it was starting to snow a bit heavier. Still George was not concerned. He hiked up to the far end of the lake to chop out a couple of marked fishing holes that they hadn't used in a month. After an hour of chopping, he finally hit water. Using one of his homemade cups he skimmed the floating ice out of the hole. Using the grouse entrails as bait he landed three small trout, all under a pound.

Although he guessed it to be no later than two o'clock in the afternoon, it was growing dark. George took an anxious look upward and quickly realized he had made an error in judgment. He quickly packed up his gear and headed for the trail on the opposite side of the lake.

By the time George made the centre of the lake, it was snowing so hard he couldn't make out the shore in any direction. Then the wind picked up. Soon he was totally confused as to which direction he should go. He resolved to pick one direction and stay the course. This was not that easy. He kept intersecting one of his old trails. Finally at dusk, he found the tree-lined shore. There was no time to build a shelter, so when he stumbled on a big spruce tree with a snow well at the base, he simply crawled down into the shelter and resigned himself to spending the night there.

George thought hard as to how he could build a fire, but could not come up with the tinder to get it going. He picked the least frozen of his fish and ate it raw. He hacked off a few of the low branches with his knife to sit on and put his back to the trunk of the tree. He quickly fell asleep.

Long before dawn, the cold woke George. He waved his arms and kicked his feet trying to stay warm. At first light he was up looking for firewood. The wind had died, and when light came he found some tinder and kindling for a fire. He quickly skewered the two little trout and the grouse on a twig and cooked them over the open fire. After inhaling the fish he decided to keep the bird for the walk back to the cabin. George knew Ruth and Fred would be worried, so he hurried his breakfast and set out.

He was been almost back when he spotted some moose tracks. Intent on following them, he tripped himself up on his snow-shoes. Down he fell head over heels. He grabbed at a little poplar to stop his fall and felt his arm snap.

The little Henry .22 carried on down the slope out of reach. Leaving the rifle behind, he stumbled back in the direction of the cabin with his right arm hanging uselessly at his side. The pain was terrible. At one point he stopped to vomit.

Ruth was in the outdoor kitchen and saw him coming. She ran down the trail to the lake and helped him up the last part of way up the trail and into the cabin.

"Thank God you're back, George! What happened?"

"Broke my arm," he mumbled before he suddenly lost consciousness.

She grabbed him and lowered him to the floor. Quickly she ran to get Fred. He had been chopping firewood and worrying about how long to wait until he should look for George. With George wearing most of the warm clothes, it would be foolhardy to go searching unless it was really necessary.

When George came to an hour later, he found his right arm had been set and expertly splinted by Fred.

"Guess we're even now," said George.

"I was just glad that you had passed out. It was a bit tricky getting you out of that parka. I don't think you would have wanted to be awake for that." said Fred.

"Sure wish we had something to give you for the pain besides a couple of aspirin," said Ruth, patting his forehead.

"I'll tough it out," said George. "Fred, I left that little .22 where I fell."

Fred nodded, picked up the parka, and walked out into the cold to retrieve it. That gun was critical to their survival. Fred was worried. As he followed Georges track's back to retrieve the rifle, he thought over the situation. At last count, they only had sixty shells left for the .22 and twelve for the pistol.

With George laid up, the hunting duties would fall to him. He knew he was nowhere near the hunter that George was. The pistol was pretty foreign to him and he would have to get some coaching from George. As for the bow and arrows, he wouldn't even bother to try. The learning curve would be far too steep.

George felt absolutely useless.

"Why couldn't it have been my *left* arm," he said repeatedly that first day.

Even the smallest task like dressing himself was awkward. Ruth had made him a sling out of one of her tube tops that helped immobilize it. He was in constant pain, but tried not to take any of their meagre supply of painkillers.

The next morning, the weather improved, and the day looked to be much warmer. Fred decided to take advantage of the weather and start his hunting duties right away. After some lessons from George on the use of the pistol, Fred set out, determined to bring back some fresh game. Kissing Ruth goodbye, he tucked the pistol firmly into his waist, picked up the little survival .22, put on his snowshoes and headed for the lake. Once there he began a slow circle around the lake looking for fresh tracks.

About a third of the way around the shore, he intersected a single set of deer tracks. He reasoned they had to be quite fresh as it had snowed in the night and these tracks didn't have any fresh snow in them. He followed the tracks as quietly as he could, trying not to bump the snowshoes together. By noon he was still on the trail. Studying the tracks he was sure the deer was unaware it was being followed. The tracks meandered from bush to bush, indicating it was browsing on whatever dead leaf it could find.

Fred came upon the deer in a little clearing. It had its head down, browsing, and did not see or hear him. Slowly and silently he pushed the butt of the rifle into the snow far enough to hold it. He pulled the pistol out of his belt and slipped off the safety. George had shown him the two-hand pistol grip just this morning.

He took careful aim at where he judged the big buck's heart was and squeezed the trigger. The deer stumbled and then started to run. Fred panicked and blindly fired two more shots after it as it vanished into the brush. He went quickly over to where he had last seen it. There was fresh blood on the snow. He followed its trail all afternoon. The deer was bleeding badly. He found places where it had laid down to rest a couple of times but then must have heard him coming and forced itself up and onward.

Late in the afternoon he came upon it. It was lying in the middle of a clearing. Seeing him approach it struggled trying to get up but couldn't manage. It was spent. Fred put the pistol close to its head and fired. The struggle was over. Only then did he remember that he left the little Henry behind standing in the snow.

I'll get it on the way home, he thought. *Who's going to steal it anyway?*

Pulling out his knife, he went about the task of gutting out the deer.

"Sorry I'm such a shitty shot, old guy," he said to the deer as he realized he had missed the heart completely but had hit a lung.

One of his other shots had hit it in the rump. As he worked he watched the light failing.

I'll have to spend the night, he thought. *Ruth is going to be really worried now. First George and now me.*

Leaving the carcass he began a hunt for firewood. Soon he had a good supply of small dead poplar and birch branches that he was able to just snap off the trees. Using his snowshoe, he dug a pit in the snow down to the frozen ground. Within a few minutes he had a nice fire going.

Dinner was deer heart. This was not usually his first choice, but it was getting too dark to start butchering the animal. He roasted the heart in pieces over the fire.

Not bad, he thought. *If only I had a bit of salt.*

He dragged the deer carcass closer to the fire as a deterrent to night critters. This was a big buck. He decided he would have to enlist Ruth's help tomorrow to get this thing out of the bush. All and all he was quite comfortable. He was wearing the shared parka and was quite happy to have it. He sat on one snowshoe and used the other as a backrest leaned up against a big poplar tree. He put a few larger sticks on the fire, and with his belly full, he soon drifted off to a dreamless sleep.

Something woke him in the night. He sat bolt upright and listened hard. Then he heard it again—the eerie cry of a wolf. He automatically reached for some firewood and stirred the coals alive. A few puffs on the coals and the fire was blazing again. He was nodding off when he heard the wolf call again. Then another answered.

Then another.

They were getting closer. They were on the bloody trail of the deer! Quickly he pulled out the pistol and dropped out the clip. He pulled the remaining shells out of his pocket and fully loaded gun, his hand shaking.

Within a few minutes the cries stopped and glowing eyes started appearing from the edge of the clearing. First one pair, and then another appeared. At one point he counted seven pairs of eyes. He heard a twig snap and whirled to see a pair of eyes not thirty feet behind him.

"GET OUT OF HERE YOU BASTARDS," he yelled at the top of his lungs.

And all the eyes disappeared.

That's better.

———

Meanwhile back at the cabin, Ruth was frantic.

"Fred should have been back by now," she said to George as he woke from a troubled sleep.

"He's not back?"

George was really worried but tried not to show it to Ruth.

"I'll go looking for him at first light, Ruth. He probably decided to do the smart thing and settled in when he realized he wouldn't get back before dark. It comes so quickly this time of year."

"Yes, I guess you're right. But you're not going anywhere with that arm. I'll go for him if he's not back by midmorning."

As soon as there was enough light to see, she was up and dressed. George got up and built up the fire. He put a pot of water on to boil.

"You're not going anywhere until you have some breakfast. I'll make you a quick cup of tea too," he said.

While she was eating he got some sliced rabbit and put it into a plastic bag. The whole operation was quite difficult using his left hand.

"Here," he said. "Put this in a pocket. It's not much, but you will want it later."

She gulped her tea and grabbed another slice of rabbit while she was getting her moccasins on.

"Take the axe," said George, "And that piece of rope. Fred might have got a moose or something."

She put on George's snowshoes and headed down to the lake. She soon found Fred's tracks in the snow and began to follow them. It was cold. She had layered up as much as possible with her hooded sweatshirt and finally her old jean jacket. She had on one of her homemade rabbit fur hats tied snugly under her chin and her big oversized mitts clutching the axe.

Before long she came upon where Fred had left the lake and headed inland. She immediately saw the deer tracks and realized what he had been doing. All morning she followed the tracks. A couple of hours later the trail led her into a clearing. As she came into a little clearing, she saw a strange sight. There, standing butt first in the snow was the little Henry survival rifle.

She picked it up and slowly looked around. At her feet lay a spent pistol cartridge. A few feet further lay two more. She moved through the clearing studying the tracks. There was blood in the deer tracks.

So he hit it, she thought and set to following the tracks.

A few minutes later more tracks joined the trail. A wolf she decided. One wolf was not a huge worry but within the next few hundred yards more tracks joined. How many she couldn't tell. Panic began to set in. She tried to hurry, but with both the rifle and the axe to carry, the going was slow. She thought about stashing the rifle, as she had no clue how to use it. Reasoning that Fred might need it, she soldiered on.

———

As dawn approached, the fire was almost out. Fred had a bed of coals and only a few small sticks within reach to burn. The eyes had returned. His shouting had no effect on them now. They desperately wanted that deer. In the grey light, he could just barely make them out. He counted five, but he knew there were probably more. These were just the bold ones.

The wolves slowly edged forward. Now he could clearly make out a large one not thirty feet from him. He slipped off the safety on the pistol and took careful aim with a two-handed grip. His elbows were rested firmly on his knees. He took a breath, held it, and squeezed the trigger. The boom of the pistol shattered the dawn silence. The big wolf dropped dead in its tracks, the rest scattered. Quickly Fred rose and fastened his snowshoes. He slowly backed away from the clearing. As soon as he was at the edge of the brush, the rest of the pack tore into the clearing and fell upon the body of the dead wolf, tearing it to shreds. They paid no notice to Fred as he slunk back onto the trail. He looked back once and saw two of them were advancing on the deer carcass. He sighed, they really needed that deer themselves, but at least he was alive.

Two hours later he came upon Ruth trudging along near exhaustion, the big axe in one hand and the little Henry .22 rifle in the other. She waddled up on her snowshoes and threw her arms around him. He threw his around her as well.

"Oh my God, Fred! I was so worried. I saw wolf tracks."

"I don't doubt it, I saw the wolves that made them," he said with a smile. "Let's get going. I still don't trust them."

They were almost at the lake when Fred spotted a little snowshoe rabbit doing its utmost to appear invisible. Silently Ruth handed him the rifle, and with one shot he had it.

"At least we have fresh meat for tonight," he said.

"And another skin," she said. "Don't forget that."

TWENTY-FIVE

That same morning, miles away, Mike brought one of the traps in from the woodshed. The previous evening he had seen tracks in the snow he thought were from a big cat, probably a lynx. The trap was the largest of the four he had found hanging in the wood-shed. He'd had never seen a trap before nor had he ever seen how an animal was fooled into such a thing. But he was clever and analytical, and so he sat down at the kitchen table to study it.

It seemed to him that once it was set, the animal would have to stick its head right into the trap for it to work.

Bait must have to hang right behind the trap to entice it into sticking its head in, he thought.

In his mind he designed a three-sided stick enclosure to prevent it from just walking around behind the trap and taking the bait.

He spent a couple of hours cutting sticks to fashion a stick tepee with one open side. Then he took off back to where he had seen the tracks. Picking what he hoped was the right spot, he started to set the trap. In the back of the enclosure, behind the trap, he placed some fresh rabbit entrails on a stick. He hung the trap from wire and secured both sides, then he carefully set it. Finally he stuck twigs on end under the trap to block off the bottom to ensure that the only way the cat had of getting the meat was to stick its head through the trap which would of course trigger it.

He checked the trap daily on his way down to the lake. On the third morning, a snow-covered animal lay in the trap. He approached it carefully, axe held high, making sure it was dead before he touched it. Carefully he released it from the trap and carried it back up to the cabin. He had been right—it was a nice sized lynx.

He gutted it and carefully skinned the cat out. He was unsure if the meat was edible but decided to give it the old college try. He boiled up some and tasted it. It was definitely edible. He hung the meat in the woodshed so that he could augment his diet with it. After all these were desperate times. He spent the next couple of evenings cleaning the hide. Once he scraped all the flesh off the hide, he tacked it to the cabin wall to let it dry and cure.

It was a few days later, as Mike was busy boiling part of a little pike for a late lunch, when the door of the cabin opened and in walked a huge native followed by the biggest Malamute husky Mike had ever seen. The dog approached him slowly, growling the whole time. Mike didn't move, more shocked at the sight of another human being than scared of the dog. He let the dog come near so that it could sniff him.

"I'm Joe," said the man with a smile. "That's Yukon."

By now the big dog had jammed his nose into Mike's crotch and had apparently decided that Mike was okay based on that—Yukon was now wagging his tail like crazy.

"I'm Mike," stammered Mike with a stunned look on his face.

"I knew *someone* was here," said Joe. "I saw your trail coming up from the lake."

"Is this your place?"

"Yup, it's one of my trapline cabins."

"Sorry for trespassing," said Mike. "I'm lost and I just happened upon it. I've been here since the fall."

"That's no problem." Joe stepped around Mike to inspect the boiling pot. "Is that what you were going to have for dinner?" he asked laughing.

"That's it," replied Mike.

"Well Mike, give me a hand to unload my sled, and I'll fix us something *good* to eat. The dog can eat the fish."

Outside he had a big toboggan with a box built onto it. The box held a couple of old school canvas packs and a big arctic sleeping bag. There was a gun scabbard tied to the outside of the box. Joe unzipped the scabbard and handed Mike an old Cooey single shot .22 and one of the packs to carry into the cabin. He grabbed the other pack and the sleeping bag, and they went back inside.

The sight of the little rifle reminded Mike of the loss of the gun through the ice.

"I've got a bit of bad news for you, Joe," said Mike, after they were inside and had put down their loads.

"What's that?"

"Well, I fell through the ice on the lake last fall and lost your big rifle in the process. I'll gladly pay you for it when we get back to civilization."

Joe just chuckled. "I always hated that gun," he said. "It was just too damned heavy. I bought a new one a few years ago. I just left that one up here in case I ever ran low on grub and had to shoot a moose or something."

"So did you walk all the way in from the highway?" asked Mike.

Joe looked at him for a moment.

"Man you *are* lost. No, the highway is a long way from here, Mike. I actually came in by plane. A pilot from Kenora dropped me off at my big cabin over on Susan Lake. I have another little cabin in between the one at Susan Lake and this one."

"How do you get back out." Mike was almost giddy with excitement. "Do you have a radio or something?"

"Nope," said Joe. "Afraid not. That same pilot will pick me up from my cabin around the middle of April before break up. Usually I expect him the first nice day after the fifteenth. Sometimes it takes a week if the weather is bad before he shows up, but he always shows up."

"Well what's the date now?" asked Mike, hardly breathing.

Joe smiled. "March third, my birthday, in fact."

"Well, happy birthday. I gotta say it feels more like *my* birthday. You finding me is the best news I've had in months."

"You found *me* really," Joe said. "This is my cabin, remember. You just got here first."

Six more weeks! I can make it! Just six more weeks and I'll be home. He turned away from Joe so that his tears wouldn't show.

Joe rooted through his supplies and produced a package of onion soup mix, a can of corned beef and a can of green beans from his pack.

"How 'bout I make us something better than boiled pike?"

Mike was drooling in anticipation of the meal to come.

Over dinner Mike told Joe the story of the plane crash and his attempt to walk out to safety. He had been so long alone without anyone to speak to that, once he started he couldn't stop talking. He even tried to apologize at one point, but Joe waved him off.

"Don't worry about it. We trappers are used to cabin fever."

After they were done eating and the dishes were cleared away, Mike got out his map and spread it out on the table. He pointed to an area on the map to Joe.

"That's where the others are if they are still alive."

Once he mentioned George White, Joe sat back and smiled.

"Oh I know George quite well," he said. "He knows his way around the bush. I wouldn't worry. I suspect they are doing just fine."

Joe spotted Mike's harmonica on the counter. "Do you know how to play that thing, Mike?"

Mike smiled, picked it up, and proceeded to play a few songs while Joe sat by the fire with a big grin on his face.

"That was nice," he said once Mike put it away. "Y'know I have one of those at the big cabin, but I don't know how to play it."

Before bed, Joe put some white beans in a pot with some water to soak.

"This is dinner tomorrow night. Maybe I'll get lucky tomorrow and shoot a rabbit to go with it," he said with a big wide grin.

The next morning Joe made them breakfast. He cut off a few slices of bacon from a big slab wrapped in brown paper and cooked them in the frying pan. Once the bacon was done, he cooked pancakes in the fat. They sprinkled a little sugar on them and washed it down with mugs of steaming black coffee.

"Oh God, that's wonderful," murmured Mike.

"Well I had better get at it," said Joe. "I've got a lot of traps to set today."

He picked up the little rifle and without Joe saying a word the big dog got suddenly up from where he had been sleeping and trotted to the door whining.

"He doesn't much like being in the cabin," said Joe. "But if I let him out at night the wolves will probably get him."

"I could help you," said Mike.

"No," said Joe. "Without proper snowshoes you would just slow me down. Thanks anyway, I'll see you tonight."

Outside, Joe harnessed Yukon to the sled, stowed the gun, and donned his snowshoes.

"Come on, Yukon," he said softly, and the dog fell into place behind him dragging the toboggan along.

Mike spent his day doing his usual chores, chopping out the ice hole, collecting the day's water and bringing in the night's firewood. He then spent an hour or so jigging for fish through the ice. He caught a couple of small pike. One he put in the woodshed to freeze, and one he kept for the dog's dinner.

At dusk the door opened and in bounded Yukon with Joe right behind. The big dog walked right up to Mike and put his head in Mike's lap to have his ears scratched.

"I think he likes you," said Joe. "He's usually not that friendly."

Joe handed Mike two snowshoe hares. He had already cleaned them. "If you want to skin these guys, Mike, I'll start dinner."

Mike got out his filleting knife and happily went about the chore. He hadn't had rabbit for a couple of weeks.

While Mike was skinning the rabbits, Joe dug out a plastic jar of molasses out of his pack and started doctoring up the beans. Besides the molasses, he added a package of onion soup mix and some salt and pepper. Next he fried up a couple of thick slices of bacon and added them to the beans. From his pack he produced a little bag of flour and got the baking powder from the cupboard. In a bowl, he mixed some flour, a couple of teaspoons of baking powder, a pinch of salt and some water together to form little cakes which he then fried in the bacon fat.

"Bush bread," he said smiling when he saw Mike watching him.

Once the bread was finished they fried up some of the rabbit meat to add to the meal.

After dinner, they sat around the stove enjoying yet another cup of sweet black coffee. Joe said the coffee was what Calgary folk called cowboy coffee. It was made in a beat up old percolator so the result was a good helping of grounds in the bottom of every cup.

Joe begged Mike to play some more on the harmonica. He really seemed to enjoy the music, and Mike by now was pretty good at playing it. Over the early winter, he had found that the instruction book was more valuable to him as toilet paper, so he had spent a fair amount of time memorizing the songs before he used up that particular page. The book was now long gone. He also had been experimenting playing songs he knew by ear and had taught himself quite a few more to add to those he had learned from the song book.

The next morning after breakfast, Joe dumped the contents of his grub pack on the table. He was heading out to his other line cabin to check his traps. He quickly started dividing things up.

"Here Mike," he said. "You can have the bacon and the flour. I have more back at the big cabin. Take the coffee too. I have some tea bags at the line shack."

He rummaged around in the other pack and pulled out a pair of old grey wool socks.

"Here," he said looking down at Mike's rubber boots. "Take these, your feet must be freezing."

Mike didn't argue. In fact it was all he could do to keep from weeping. He sat down and pulled off his rubber boots. His rabbit skin socks were completely worn out. He pulled on the socks and sighed with pleasure.

"Thanks Joe," he said quietly.

Outside Joe put on his snowshoes and hitched Yukon up to the toboggan. With Joe out front breaking trail, the big dog obediently followed along behind.

"See you in a couple of weeks!" yelled Joe, as he and Yukon hit the trail to the lake.

"See you," Mike called after him and turned back into the warmth of the little cabin.

TWENTY-SIX

Joe and Yukon plodded along all day, checking and resetting traps as they went. Progress was slow, and Joe realized late in the afternoon that he wasn't going to make the line cabin that night, so he stopped in a little clearing where he quickly began building a lean-to and collecting a stack of deadfall for firewood. Once the fire was roaring, he boiled water in a little pot and threw in some oatmeal for a hot dinner. After dinner, he built up the fire with some bigger logs and curled up in his big sleeping bag. He fell almost immediately asleep. Yukon curled up in the snow nearby and also drifted off to sleep.

Joe was up at dawn. He built a fire and made another little pot of oatmeal that he shared with the dog.

"I'll fix you a proper meal when we get to the cabin."

By noon they arrived at the cabin on Long Lake. It was pretty much the same design as one on Big Buck Lake.

Joe got the fire going and fried up two big moose steaks—one for him and, as promised, one for Yukon. After lunch he donned his snowshoes and, with the little .22 under his arm, set out to check his snares and a couple of nearby marten traps. He was rewarded with a marten in one trap and two snowshoe hares caught up in the snares.

That evening he spent a couple of hours skinning all the animals he had harvested since leaving the Big Buck Lake cabin. He had three beavers, two otters, three martens and the two rabbits to skin. The rabbits skins weren't worth anything really, but he knew he could swap them for a few home cooked meals to a woman he knew in Kenora. She made crafts with them to sell to the tourists.

Early the next morning, he packed the sled and harnessed the dog. They meandered down the trail, checking traps as they went. By late afternoon, they had arrived at the Susan Lake cabin. The main trapline was situated around this cabin. It usually took ten full days to visit every one of his traps. He used to have a little snowmobile to check his trapline until a few years ago. It was still laying up by the cabin with a hole in the piston and a worn out track. The last couple of years that he had used that confounded machine, it was broke down more it than it ran. He had gotten pretty sick of making emergency camps at the side of the trail while he rigged up some repair. Sometimes he had to hike all the way back to the cabin for parts or specialty tools.

A couple of years ago, he had an offer he couldn't refuse. One of his friends had a female Malamute bitch with a litter of puppies. She offered Joe the pick of the litter. He picked the biggest one who also turned out to be the most stubborn of the bunch. Even with this stubborn streak, he thought the dog was a lot more reliable than those damned snowmobiles.

Once all the traps had been visited and the animals were skinned, he began packing up for the trip back to Big Buck Lake where he had left Mike. He looked around the Susan Lake cabin for anything Mike might be able to use to make the trip back easier. He was working on a pair of snowshoes for him and had one almost complete.

———

Back at the Big Buck Lake cabin, Mike spent his time ice fishing and collecting firewood. He waited with anticipation for the arrival of his new friend. He even missed the big husky. Knowing he was only weeks away from getting home led him to do some serious reflections on his life.

Before he had met Joe a couple of weeks ago, he saw his situation as almost hopeless. Now that rescue was close, he was forced to think about what he might have to face when he did get back. Had Cathy waited for him, or had she moved on to someone else? What could he do if she had done so? Obviously they all thought he was dead. Cathy was still a good-looking woman. There would be any number of men interested in a catch like her.

He spent his evenings working on a new pair of rabbit boot liners. He also made himself a new pair of crude moose hide mitts with rabbit fur liners. True to form, Joe arrived back in a couple of weeks. Sixteen days to be precise according to Mike's notched stick. This time, when Yukon saw him, he almost knocked him over with affection.

"I brought you a few things," said Joe as Mike helped him unload the sled.

Once inside Joe unpacked his things, handing Mike gifts as he came across them.

"I found another blanket for you," he said, "and my old boots."

Mike gratefully accepted the items. The boots were old but they had felt liners, which were a huge improvement over his unlined rubber boots. The blanket was a heavy wool Hudson Bay style. It had a heavy musty smell, but Mike didn't care. He would be that much warmer tonight. The last gift was one homemade snowshoe. Joe had all the moose hide strips cut to make the second one and had cut the frames.

"Maybe you could finish that one while I'm gone checking my traps," Joe said. "When I get finished, we'll be heading out to the Susan Lake cabin to catch our plane ride home."

Mike was speechless. He couldn't quite believe that he was going to make it after all.

Joe took a few more things out of his grub pack and handed them to Mike.

"I hope this gets you by until I get back."

There was a bag of loose tea leaves, four packs of onion soup mix, a bag of white beans and a little jar of sugar. Joe also gave Mike a candle and a little bar of soap. Mike was really grateful for the gifts. It felt like Christmas morning when he was a kid to him. He thanked Joe profusely.

"Don't mention it," said Joe and changed the subject. "Say I was thinking about that gun of mine that you lost." He pointed at the lynx hide still hanging on the cabin wall. "If you give me that lynx, I'll call it even."

"Done deal," said Mike.

He had been feeling extremely guilty about losing that rifle since the day it happened. He was more than happy to have the debt repaid. After dinner Joe produced his own harmonica from his jacket pocket and showed it to Mike. Mike was pleased to see that it too was tuned to the key of C. Joe began his lessons that evening in earnest. By the end of the night he had almost mastered "Amazing Grace". They worked on a different song every night after that.

Joe spent the next two days checking his local traps. As he tramped along the trail, he practiced his harmonica. At night he and Mike would play together. On the third morning he arose at dawn and after a quick cup of tea and a bit of rabbit meat, he and Yukon hit the trail.

"I want to make the other line cabin on Long Lake before dark," he said. "I'm getting too old for this camping on the trail stuff. Keep working on that snowshoe, Mike! I'll see you in a couple of weeks." And with that, he disappeared down the trail.

"You keep practising that harmonica," called Mike.

"You bet I will."

Mike could hear Joe blowing away on his harmonica for the next few minutes.

Joe pushed hard all day and arrived at the line shack before nightfall. Along the way he had collected a few more furs to add to the growing pile.

Two weeks to the day, Joe was back at Big Buck Lake. Mike was on the lake jigging for fish through the ice, when they appeared, two dots at the far end of the lake. Mike walked out to meet Joe and the big dog. Mike was wearing his newly finished snowshoes. Joe inspected Mike's handy work.

"Nice job, Mike," said Joe. "I can't tell the difference between the two."

Mike knew he was lying, but he blushed with pride anyway. Mike helped Joe and Yukon pull the sled up the hill to the little cabin and together they unloaded it and moved the gear indoors.

The next day, Mike went out on the trapline with Joe. He wanted a little more practice on the big clumsy snowshoes before they left on the trip to the big cabin. Yukon trotted along behind them pulling the almost empty sled. Their first stop was a little beaver dam about a mile inland from the lake.

Joe tramped over to the middle of the frozen pond near the beaver house. A couple of sticks stuck out of the ice. He took a long handled ice chisel out of the sled and expertly began chopping out the ice around these sticks. Once they were free he grabbed them both and hauled them up onto the ice. Their reward was a big fat beaver caught firmly in the trap.

Mike was fascinated.

"How did you know where to put the trap?" he asked.

"Bubbles. When I came here for the first time this year, I cleaned the snow off the ice and looked for bubbles trapped in the ice. The bubbles are from their exhaled breath when they are swimming from the lodge. Once you find the bubbles you know which way their runway to and from the exits are. Sometimes they have two exits, so you have to look carefully."

"So what do you do once you find the bubbles?"

"Well, you go and find yourself a couple of dead sticks, they have to be dead not green, and you take an old piece of one by six lumber and nail it across for a platform for your trap. Now you take a couple more pieces of dead wood and brace it. Now put a piece of green poplar in the trap as a bait stick. The other thing is to make sure your platform is no more than a foot below the ice. If it's any lower, the beaver can swim right over your trap and set it off, and you'll miss him."

Joe removed the beaver from the trap and undid the anchor chain. He threw both into the sled and walked over to the other trap and started chopping out the stakes. The trap was empty, so Joe simply unwired it and threw it in the sled. He dragged the stakes and platform over to the sled, and with Mike's help, they balanced both trap sets onto the sled.

"We'll leave the wood up on shore," he said. "If they are still there next year, I can use them again. It saves me time."

On shore Mike was amazed when Joe pointed out a huge poplar that the beavers had chewed down.

"They're after the more tender branches that they can't reach so they just chew the whole damn tree down," Joe said. "It doesn't matter much up here where there are no people and nothing but trees, but down south the landowners get pretty pissed over it"

Their next stop was back down by the lake to the mouth of the creek where Mike had liked to fish in the fall. A stout pole lay across the ice. Joe chopped a hole in the ice, and they each grabbed an end of the pole and lifted the trap out of the ice. It contained a muskrat.

Mike had never seen a muskrat and inspected it with interest before he tossed it and the trap into the sled. They checked and pulled another empty muskrat set and three empty otter traps before they started home. Mike was secretly happy to see the otter traps empty. He had watched the creatures playing on several occasions over the past year and quite liked the playful little guys.

"We had better get a move on," said Joe pointing at the darkening sky. "Looks like we're going to get some snow."

Sure enough, within fifteen minutes they were in the heart of a blizzard.

"Let's get in close to shore, so we don't miss the trail."

Visibility was now no more than a few feet. A bitter cold wind had picked up and the blowing snow stung their eyes. Suddenly Yukon stopped and whined.

"What's up with you?" Joe growled.

The dog whined again and then turned towards shore.

"We almost walked right by the trail," laughed Mike and turned to follow the dog.

Once in the trees and out of the wind, the storm was not nearly as bad. They tied a couple of towropes on the front of the sled and helped the big dog pull the sled up the trail to the cabin.

It snowed hard all night. By morning, two feet of fresh snow had fallen and it was still snowing hard.

"We had better stay put today," said Joe. With nothing much to do, they ate a leisurely breakfast and sat chatting over mugs of hot tea.

"Too bad we're not at the big cabin," said Joe. "I've got a deck of cards there."

"I had a deck of cards and a homemade crib board myself, but I left it behind for the others when I left." said Mike. "I really liked that crib board."

Joe started skinning out the beaver and the muskrat. Mike pulled up a chair to watch Joe work. He started with the beaver.

"Can you eat these things?" asked Mike.

"Oh sure, I quite often eat them toward the end of the year when I run out of moose meat. Usually I cook it for the dog."

"What part do you eat?" asked Mike.

"Pretty much all of it. My dad used to even cook the tail."

Mike wanted to taste it, so they cut off some of the meat for dinner. Joe produced a bag of wild rice to augment it. It was a delicious meal.

It would be hard to describe, thought Mike.

It had a wild gamy taste to it but was quite edible. He thought he might even give the tail a go if he got the chance someday. After dinner, they packed up the cabin to get ready for an early start and went to bed early.

Joe was up long before dawn, building up the fire and making the morning meal. With the sled packed, they set off down the trail with the first grey light of dawn barely visible in the eastern sky. Joe broke trail followed by Mike, pulling a long trace line to help the dog with the heavy load. Along the way they stopped to check the traps and to pull them for the season.

All the sets now were for marten. Mike had never even seen a marten before so was quite intrigued with the process of trapping them. The first trap was empty, so they just threw it onto the already laden sled. Joe showed Mike how the trap worked.

He had spiked a pole onto a tree trunk at about a forty-five degree angle. At the top end of the pole a piece of meat was wired. The trap itself was set about two thirds of the way up the pole.

"The marten smells the meat, runs up the pole to get it, and *whack!*" Joe said with an impish grin.

The next trap contained a marten. Mike picked it up and stroked its luxurious fur. It was a beautiful creature. It was almost a shame to kill these things, but he realized that was how Joe had to make a living.

Late in the afternoon, they at the frozen shore Long Lake. They trudged down the lake for a half an hour before they came to a trail heading inland. At dusk they arrived at the line cabin. Looking down through the trees, Mike could make out the white vast plain of the frozen lake.

"Who built these cabins?"

He was admiring the workmanship. The logs fit together at the corners almost perfectly.

"My dad did. My older brother helped him. I built the porch."

Mike glanced over at the porch. There was no comparison to the craftsmanship of the original structure.

"Very nice work," he lied.

Joe got Yukon out of his harness while Mike began unpacking the sled.

"My dad had this trapline the whole time I was growing up," said Joe. "As kids we lived out here year round until my oldest brother was old enough for school. He was already eight when my mother finally insisted we move to town. We rented a place in Kenora for the school year and then the whole family spent the summers out here with Dad."

"So did you go to high school?" asked Mike.

"No, I quit after grade eight and came out here to help my dad. He was getting pretty old. My brother was helping him for a couple of years, but then he bought his own trapline. My sister went to high school and even to college down in Winnipeg. She works for a bank in Calgary now."

"So you have been doing this ever since?"

"Yeah, I bought the trapline from Dad fifteen years ago."

"So did you ever marry?"

"Nah," said Joe. "I had a serious girlfriend a few years ago, but she got too lonely in Kenora while I was up here. She left me for some white guy and moved down to Winnipeg. I have a couple of girls that I hang out with in town once in a while, but I have never got too serious with them. It's just not worth it. This is my life. It's hard to find a woman these days who's willing to give up the comforts of town to live out here with an old codger like me."

That night they feasted on a prime rib roast of moose. The last decent cut of meat left from Mike's moose. Joe produced a package of instant mashed potatoes to go with it. After dinner they sat by the fire for a couple of hours playing their harmonicas and chatting before Joe decided it was time for his bed and climbed up into the loft.

Mike lay in his blankets by the fire in absolute wonderment. A couple of years ago he probably would have crossed the street if he saw Joe coming. He now considered Joe one of the nicest people he had ever met. It was a marvel to Mike that here was a guy who had accumulated as many down to earth skills as could be imagined. His own PhD in chemistry seemed pretty poor by comparison. He was in absolute awe of this bushmaster. Joe didn't ever ask Mike what he did for a living. Mike would have been embarrassed to tell him.

The next morning they were up at first light.

"You pack the cabin up, Mike," said Joe. "I've got a couple of beaver sets to pick up. I should be back before noon. I'll leave the dog with you. Let him rest, he has a couple of tough days ahead of him."

They had talked about this the night before. With the load on the sled it was doubtful they would make the big cabin in one go. Joe had a lean-to shed about four hours walk from the cabin that they could hole up for the night in.

"It's not much. I use it from time to time if the weather is bad."

He emptied out one of his packs to put the collected traps in, threw in a coil of rope to drag the beavers back with, and started off to the lake.

———

Joe followed the shore for about a kilometre or so before he headed inland following a creek bed. The creek fed into a frozen marsh and finally to a dam and an iced-over pond with the snow covered mound of the beaver lodge.

He walked a couple of dozen feet past the dam before he ventured out onto the ice. Experience had taught him that the ice was always thinnest closest to the dam. As he walked, he looked for signs of his wooden stakes but they were buried in snow. As he neared the spot where he thought the first one was he stopped and took off his snowshoes. Using one of them for a shovel he soon uncovered the first hole. Taking the axe he chopped it out. The ice on the hole was not very thick. Joe's father had taught him a little time saver years ago. He had showed him how to fill the hole with snow after the trap was set so the ice wouldn't freeze as thick. He pulled up the trap and was rewarded with a fat beaver. Smiling he released it from the trap and put the beaver and the trap in a pile on the snow. Picking up his snowshoe, he walked around to the back of the beaver house to look for the other hole. Suddenly he was up to his armpits in ice-cold water he had fallen into the hole he had been looking for. His dad's trick had bit him back hard!

He struggled and tried to pull himself out but he was stuck. He started to panic. With an adrenalin fuelled last-ditch effort he hauled himself up with his arms and hurled himself forward kicking and clawing at the ice as he went. Exhausted he lay panting on the snow. He quickly sat up and took off his boots to dump the water out. He slipped them back on and began struggling for shore. The snowshoes were left where they lay. He focused on a big birch tree and made for it.

By the time he reached shore, his boots were full of water again, run off from his clothing had filled them. He slogged up to the birch and began stripping bark off the tree. All the while he was shaking uncontrollably.

He snapped off a few dead sticks and laid them on the birch bark pile on the shore. From his pocket he pulled a little waterproof container full of strike anywhere matches. He tried to aim the match at the striker and light it. The match snapped in half. He dropped that match and quickly tried another. His hands were shaking so bad he couldn't hold the match.

TWENTY-EIGHT

Once Joe was gone, Mike started packing up the cabin, whistling as he worked. He daydreamed about the big cabin at Susan Lake. Joe told him it had a big cook stove with an oven that you could bake bread in. Joe had promised to bake a big loaf with yeast as soon as they got the stove warmed up. He had promised a wonderful meal of canned beans and bacon to go with the hot bread. Mike's mouth watered at the thought. He packed the sled with all the supplies leaving out only the remainder of the moose roast and a tea bag for a quick lunch before they hit the trail. At noon, he put a pot of water on the stove to boil expecting Joe any second.

By three o'clock, he was really worried. He untarped the sled and retrieved the little Henry. Quickly he slipped one shell into the breach and the rest of the box into his pocket. Picking up his snowshoes, Mike walked down to the lake with the big dog following in his footsteps. The whole way down Mike expected to meet Joe on the trail. When they arrived at the lake, Mike scanned the ice. Not a sign of Joe.

"Come on Yukon," he ordered and fell in following Joe's snowshoe prints down to the lake. Mike turned and followed Joe's tracks up the lake. When he reached the spot where the tracks turned inland he stopped and looked at the sky. The sun was setting, and it would soon be dark. He only hesitated a moment before heading inland.

He sure as hell wouldn't leave me out here, he thought.

"Okay Yukon, let's go."

The big dog immediately fell into step behind him. As they approached the marsh, Yukon suddenly whined and bolted around him. A dark figure lay on the trail ahead. Hurrying as fast as he could on his clumsy snowshoes Mike approached. As he got near, he realized it was Joe. Quickly he bent and rolled the body over and found himself staring into Joe's wide-open but very dead eyes. He felt numb. Automatically he checked Joe's pulse to be sure. A quick look at his buddy's clothing told the tale. Joe had fallen through the ice. He noticed something strange as he rose. Joe wasn't wearing his boots.

Mike had to make a decision. It was almost dark. Without shelter he would be in trouble himself.

Can't just leave him here, but I can't move him without the toboggan.

He decided to make a dash for the cabin and return to deal with Joe's body in the morning. He refused to think about anything but the practicalities of the situation. He stood up and called the dog. Yukon wouldn't move. Mike pulled on his collar. Yukon growled and even snapped at him.

"Stay then," he said and headed home down the trail. He had to concentrate on his back trail in the gathering darkness and even so almost missed the turn off to the cabin. Once back at the cabin and the fire lit, Mike began to sob, first quietly and then uncontrollably.

Emotionally exhausted, Mike was up and dressed at first light. Skipping breakfast, he unloaded the toboggan and began hauling all the goods they had packed for their trip to the big cabin inside and dumped them on the floor. He unlashed the cargo box from the sled and tied on the Hudson Bay blanket, some rope, the rifle and the harness and traces for the big dog. He stepped out into the bitter cold, put on his snowshoes, picked up the towrope and headed down the trail to the lake.

An hour later he arrived at Joe's body. The big dog was still lying faithfully guarding his master. Yukon rose and walked over to greet Mike. In a soft voice Mike praised him for his loyalty and bravery all the while stroking the big guy's ears. After a few minutes he felt he had the dog's confidence and rose to deal with the body.

He spread the blanket on the snow and rolled Joe's body onto it. Holding one edge of the blanket, he rolled it and Joe into a cocoon. Finally he tied the whole parcel with rope. He brought the toboggan along side, then rolled his cargo onto the sled and tied it down. He couldn't leave until he had solved the mystery of the boots. Leaving Yukon to guard his master Mike followed his buddy's tracks.

He found the boots at the shoreline where Joe had taken them off in some strange hypothermia induced thought process. A pile of matches lay on some birch bark kindling, most unburned. Joe's mitts lay beside the attempted fire. Mike picked up his buddies scattered belongings including the snowshoes and walked back to the waiting dog. Yukon stood, still guarding his master's dead body. It was a slow trip down the lake pulling Joe's corpse along behind them on the toboggan. Yukon strained in the harness, and Mike did his level best to pull his share of the load.

Once back at the cabin, Mike had to decide what to do with Joe's body. He yelled to the sky in anger and frustration. He couldn't bury, it as the ground was frozen. He finally decided on the woodshed. He spent a couple of hours hauling the remainder of the firewood into the cabin then dragged Joe's frozen body into the shed and nailed up the door to prevent animals from getting to the corpse. Tomorrow, he decided, he would load up the toboggan with supplies and attempt to find his way to the big cabin at Susan Lake.

For the second night in a row, Mike hardly slept. At first light he began to pack. He had no real idea how to get to the big cabin. He found it on the map but still had to find the trail. He loaded the sled with as much food and equipment that he dared and with both he and Yukon pulling they hit the trail to the lake. This time Yukon came willingly. Mike had shown the dog where Joe's body was and explained to him the situation. It was strange but he seemed to understand.

Near the end of the lake, Mike found what he was looking for—a trail blaze and the faint imprint of Joe's last snowshoe tracks. It was snowing now, so he had to be careful watching the trail. It was not well marked, only a sporadic axe blaze scattered along the way. Mike added a few for good measure whenever a tree was within easy striking distance. Mid-afternoon they came upon a clearing with the little midway hut Joe had described. He took off his snowshoes and went over to investigate.

Inside was pretty barren. There was a log bench for a bed and a little tin airtight stove. There was only one tiny little window and a shelf with a part box of wooden matches and a candle butt. He spent the rest of the daylight hours cutting firewood and keeping a fire going in the little stove to thaw the place out. By dark it was warm enough that he could shed a layer of clothing and prepare an evening meal. He had brought along as much food as he could but still felt he should ration it until he was actually at the big cabin. Not wanting to waste the candle he turned in early. Exhausted and emotionally drained, he had the best sleep he had had in months.

It snowed hard all night. It was over Mike's knees when he rolled out in the morning to relieve himself. The toboggan was out of the question now. He would have to pack whatever he needed . He laid out the gear and tried to decide what to leave and what to take.

Yukon, he decided, would have to help so he strapped Joe's big sleeping bag on the dog's back. He had brought Joe's boots with him as they were in a lot better shape than his. They had never been thawed so were still caked in ice. He decided to leave them behind along with a blanket and the axe. He had the hatchet after all. He wanted to keep the load as light as possible. The little rifle and the snare wire were a must take.

The dog did not like the idea of the pack and even growled at Mike when he slipped the rope under his belly. Mike donned his snowshoes, shouldered his pack and with a word of encouragement to the dog set off to find the Susan Lake trail. All day he circled trying to find the trailhead. Finally at dusk he found himself back at the little hut exhausted. He had a decision to make. In this snow he couldn't find the trail. The choice was to wait out spring in the hut or return to the line cabin. The other cabin was better equipped and because of the lake there was more game and of course fish.

It snowed hard all night again. The next morning he awoke to near blizzard conditions. Snow had drifted under the door and through every crack in the little shack. He spent a lazy day dozing only stirring outside to collect firewood for the night. In the morning Mike arose to a bright blue sky. He dressed and spent an hour or so trudging around the cabin looking for any signs of the trail he might have missed before. Finally he gave up and went back to the hut for a quick meal before the trip back to the line cabin.

He broke trail while Yukon followed in his tracks, begrudgingly carrying his sleeping bag pack. Every so often the dog would step on the tails of Mike's snowshoes and trip him up so that he would pitch headlong into the deep snow. After a few sharp words he finally got the dog to follow at a proper distance.

By mid-afternoon they reached the lake. They rested for a few minutes on the shore then set out down the lake ice on the final leg home. Once back at the cabin, he lit a fire and finished off the last bit of rabbit meat. The dog had to be content with the bones.

Yukon had gotten painfully thin over the winter, as had he. Tomorrow he would get busy fishing and trapping to fill his larder. The next couple of weeks were busy as he hunted grouse and rabbits and ice fished. Spring was coming rapidly and he relished the warm afternoons. He was cautious going out on the ice now remembering Joe's demise as well as his own near death experience last fall.

Something woke Mike up from a deep sleep in the middle of the night, and he listened intently. It was Yukon whining at the base of the ladder. He rose quickly and was instantly coughing on thick smoke. Fire! He grabbed his sleeping bag and hurled it down the ladder in front of him. He wrapped his bathrobe around his mouth and nose and climbed down to the main floor. The whole back wall behind the stove was on fire. He grabbed the end of his sleeping bag and ran for the door, opened it and rolled out into the snow gulping the cold night air. The dog was right behind him. Now that the door was open, the fire had plenty of oxygen and the whole cabin erupted into flames. The heat was incredible, forcing them to retreat almost to the edge of the clearing.

He braved the heat one more time to run back and grab his snowshoes that were stuck in the snow by the door to the porch. Once safely back at the edge of the clearing, Mike took stock of what he was wearing. He had on his long underwear bottoms and a tee shirt. He had no socks or boots. He had his housecoat and the sleeping bag. He would be fine for tonight but tomorrow would be a real problem. He sat on his snowshoes wrapped in the sleeping bag with his back propped up against a tree watching the fire burn. First it was just the cabin, but then the woodshed caught. The two buildings burned with such intensity he was afraid the whole forest would go up. If it had been summer that's exactly what would have happened.

As he sat there watching the fire burn, he started thinking about the stories George had told him of the Indian life before the arrival of the white man. The natives had nothing except what they could collect from the land. Mike reflected that, in comparison, he was quite well off. He had this nice sleeping bag. With that thought in mind he curled up into his bed and drifted off to sleep.

By early morning, when he awoke, both buildings were reduced to piles of smoldering ashes. The only building saved was the little outhouse. The problem of how to deal with Joe's body was now solved. Mike said a little prayer and wished Joe well.

Mike dozed until the sun came out. When he awoke the second time, he lay in the sleeping bag for a few minutes trying to formulate a plan. He decided he needed to make it back to the little shack between the lakes. It was shelter and he had left Joes' boots there. He had also left behind a blanket, the axe and some matches as well. All would be very handy right now. Without clothing, especially boots, he would not make it to the Susan Lake cabin in time for rescue.

He rose and hobbled in his bare feet through the slushy snow to the outhouse to see if there was anything useful in there. There was an empty coffee can with a plastic lid that had contained the long gone toilet paper. He used it to collect some hot coals from the cabin fire. He collected a bit of wood from the nearby bush and built a fire. He had to act quickly to keep his feet from freezing.

Once the fire was going he used the coffee can as a pot to melt snow. He added some spruce bough tips to the water for tea. Once he was nourished and with the sun up his body began to warm. Mike started to feel a little better about the situation. He saw it as a yet another survival challenge. He realized that his first problem was his lack of footwear. He knew he had to sacrifice something for temporary boots. He decided that the bottom half of the bathrobe could be cut up to fashion some crude socks. The top half he could still wear as a jacket.

He had seen the hatchet head in the ashes and fished it out with a long stick. It was still too hot to handle so he cooled it in snow. He used it to cut the terry cloth housecoat off just below the pockets. Then he cut the bottom piece into strips. Binding his feet he now had footwear. These terry cloth boots would not last very long. They would soon be soaking wet. He took the hatchet head and went searching for a birch tree. He worked away at peeling off a good size bit of bark and took it back to the fire to work on. He cut the birch bark into strips and began the process of weaving the strips into a pair of really crude boots. It took him until early afternoon before they were finished to his satisfaction.

The sun was quite warm now, so he felt he could get a few things done before the cool of evening. The first thing was to bank up the fire with more coals so that he could have an evening fire. Strapping on his snowshoes he went to check his close in snares. Out of five snares he had caught two hares. Their fur was already turning from white to brown. He collected up the snare wire as he went. He might need it later and he had no intention of staying here without shelter.

Next he went down to the shore to check his night fishing line. The water was open along the edge now. He had caught a little perch. He gave it to the dog. Yukon devoured it in about three wolf like gulps, hardly tasting it. He swallowed it guts and all. Mike wound up the line and brought it back to the camp with him. He was so hungry he could hardly wait for dinner. His feet were cold in his new boots. Quickly he built up the fire and unwrapped his feet from the wet socks. He fashioned another set of socks from the bottom of house coat and hung the first set up by the fire to dry. He rewrapped his feet and put his birch bark boots back on.

He set to work on a shelter. He decided that he would chance the weather and just cut enough boughs to keep the sleeping bag off the ground as he only had the hatchet head to work with. He tried to skin the rabbits so he could use the fur in his boots. The hatchet was just too dull. He went over to where the cabin was and poked through the ashes with a stick until he found what he was looking for, the butcher knife.

The wooden handle had burned off, but it was a knife. He found a rock near where the cabin had stood and spent a few minutes sitting by the fire putting an edge on the blade before he skinned out the rabbits. While the rabbits roasted over the fire, he fashioned the hides into crude boot liners using the ter-rycloth strips to tie them onto his feet. With the fur on the inside the new boots were very comfortable, but he knew they wouldn't last long.

Mike made another pot of spruce tea while he dined on one of the rabbits, He felt compelled to share some with the dog who stared longingly at him from across the fire. He decided he would save the other rabbit for tomorrow's journey. He would wait until the sun was well up before he made his start. He would have to walk along the shore of the lake instead of taking the ice shortcut so he doubted it was possible to make it in one day. The snowshoes were probably not necessary because of the crust but they would perhaps make his footwear last the journey.

Mike slept soundly through the night and awoke at first light. Once he had his homemade boots on, he went over to last night's campfire and stirred up the coals to get a fire going. He added some tinder and soon had a nice warm blaze going. He filled the coffee can with snow and set it at the edge of the fire. While he waited for the snow to melt, he walked over to the still smolder-ing pile of ashes where the cabin had stood. He poked around in the ashes trying to find anything useful. The only thing he came up with was a couple of six-inch spikes. He added these to his gear for future consideration.

He left mid-morning. Walking along the bush at the shoreline was a pain with the snowshoes. Several times he had to take them off to get over fallen logs or to go through thick brush. In the morning chill, he used the sleeping bag as a cape but by noon he was sweating profusely and had to remove it. He had brought along the coffee can. He punched a couple of holes in it and added a handle made of snare wire. He used the belt from his bathrobe to hang the can and the hatchet head from. The knife was securely wired to the top of one of his snowshoes.

In the afternoon, Yukon scared up a spruce grouse and with a mighty leap snatched it out of flight. He skulked off to eat it alone in the brush. Mike rested a few minutes and waited for him to come back. While he rested, he had a small snack of rabbit meat he had stashed in his coffee can. At dusk they arrived at the trailhead leading inland. Mike decided to stop for the night. He made a crude lean-to out of evergreen branches. When darkness fell, he crawled into his sleeping bag for the night. Without a fire, he simply ate the rest of the rabbit meat and went to sleep.

Mike woke to a wet snowstorm. He arose and immediately continued his journey. The snowshoes were absolutely useless in this stuff, wet snow collecting on the tips doubled the weight. Within a few feet he gave up. He thought about carrying them but couldn't see a use. He stuck them in the snow and started off down the trail. Suddenly he changed his mind. He had so few things he owned now it seemed senseless to just abandon a tool like that. He turned and walked back to get them. He slung them over his shoulder with the rest of the load and trudged onward.

They arrived at Joe's little halfway hut in early afternoon. Mike's feet were soaked as was the sleeping bag. The snow had turned to rain by mid-morning and had made the trip a living hell. As soon as Mike opened the door, Yukon rushed in and killed a mouse and gobbled it down in one bite. Mike looked at him with envy. He hadn't eaten himself all day and the prospect of a meal wasn't good. He went out and collected some firewood.

He cut some spruce boughs for his bed, saving some of the tender tips for tea. Once the hut warmed up, Mike stripped down and wrapped himself up in the blanket. He hung his clothes and the sleeping bag up to dry. He found Joe's boots and pulled the liners out and placed them near the warmth of the stove to dry them out. His own birch bark and rabbit boots had just barely made the trip.

Of all the possessions he had lost in the cabin fire, the thing he missed the most was his harmonica. That and the map—the map that showed the approximate crash site.

I can find it on a map when I get out, God knows I studied the other one enough times. Besides by the time I get out, they may be walking out themselves.

Still, he felt bad knowing that, if the others did resort to walking out in the spring, they wouldn't have a map, and suspecting that George and Fred would have made better use if it than he ultimately had.

Joe's little lean-to hut was quite cozy as long as the fire was burning. As soon as the fire would burn down in the stove the shack chilled off quickly. He kept the fire going all night, waking up every couple of hours to throw a few more sticks on.

By morning his new boots were dry. He made a poncho for himself by cutting a hole in the blanket for his head and tying his terrycloth belt around his waist to keep it from flapping around. He spent all morning collecting firewood and foraging for food. He had to stop several times to come into the cabin and warm up his bare hands. By noon the sun had warmed everything up to a tolerable temperature. Spring was definitely here. Water ran off the roof of the hut in torrents from the melting snow.

Yukon vanished into the woods as soon as Mike let him out in the morning. Mike tried calling him several times during the day, but there was no sign of him. Mike figured he was off hunting somewhere. He didn't really blame the big dog, as he was not getting much to eat around the cabin.

While he had been collecting firewood that morning, Mike had seen a couple of red squirrels chasing each other around in a big spruce tree. He went back to the cabin and got the axe and some snare wire. He cut a small poplar tree and leaned it against the spruce tree at about a forty-degree angle. He wired a couple of snares onto the poplar hoping the squirrels would use the poplar for a shortcut to the ground. Mike also set a couple of rabbit snares on some runs he had found in the snow not too far from the cabin. In the late afternoon he went out to check the traps. The rabbit snares were empty but the squirrels had fallen for his trick. He had got them both. He went back to the cabin and began the delicate job of cleaning and skinning them. He wrapped the entrails into the remains of one of his old foot wraps and tied it with wire. If the weather was nice tomorrow, he planned on hiking back down to the lake to try ice fishing. This would be his bait.

He cooked the squirrels outside. He skewered them onto a green stick and roasted them over a fire. He was secretly happy Yukon wasn't here so he didn't have to share. It was all he could do to refrain from eating every last morsel. He saved a few bites for a morning meal. After dinner, he melted some snow in his coffee can on the stove and made some spruce bough tea. He sat by the fire working on his latest project. He was making a spear. He had found a nice straight birch pole and had split the end with the axe. He then inserted one of the spikes he had salvaged from the cabin. Using a piece of snare wire, he wrapped the end of the spear to secure the spike. Now at least he had a weapon. When darkness came, he banked up the coals and crawled into his big warm sleeping bag for the night.

PART 5

SPRING

TWENTY-NINE

Frozen lake after frozen lake drifted lazily beneath the little Cessna's wings while Danny Gallagher followed his course on the chart he had strapped to his leg. It was pretty hard to miss Susan Lake as it had a very distinctive outline. As he neared, he circled the lake. Danny pulled back on the throttle and set the trim for a slow descent to the south shore where the cabin was located. At about five hundred feet above ground, he levelled off and headed straight for the cabin to buzz it.

There wasn't any visible smoke coming from the chimney, and there was no sign of life to be seen on the first pass, so he flew out onto the lake and turned for a second look. Still there didn't seem to be any sign of life. He flew back over the lake, turned up wind and set up for a landing.

This time of year, landings on unfamiliar lakes could be risky. Danny watched carefully to make sure there were no signs of open water or yellow ice in his glide path before he made his final decision to touch down. Once firmly down on the lake, he kept the power on with a slight back- pressure on the yoke to keep the ski tips up above the snow. He taxied up within fifty feet of shore and turned the plane facing back down the lake before he shut the engine down.

The ever-nervous Danny reached back and grabbed his snow-shoes. He gently climbed down from the cockpit and with both hands wrapped around the strut, gingerly tested the ice. Still not satisfied it was safe, he pushed his toes into the bindings of the snowshoes and shuffled towards shore refusing to do up the heel buckle in case he broke through the ice. Once on shore he shed the awkward snowshoes and hiked the rest of the way up to the cabin in his boots.

There was no sign of life at the cabin. Danny knocked at the door and, when there wasn't any answer, cautiously pushed open the door, half expecting to find Joe's dead body inside. A quick scan revealed nobody on the first floor so he crept up the steep staircase to the loft to have a look. One of the little bedrooms was completely empty. The other had a bunk with a foam mattresses and a little dresser. There was no sign of Joe.

Back downstairs Danny looked around the cabin. There was a big bale of furs in the corner. He sat down in the chair at the little table with his head in his hands and studied the situation. Obviously Joe had been back here over the winter—otherwise how did the furs get here? Again it was obvious he was still out on the trapline because his sleeping bag was missing.

And the dog's missing, he thought, *sled too.*

He found a pencil and paper and wrote a note to Joe, telling him he would be back within the week to check on him. Danny hiked down to the shore, put his toes into the snowshoes and shuffled his way back out to the plane and firm ice. Once back in the air, he did a low pass of the far end on the lake. The ice was breaking up in the northern most bays. In fact close to shore, where a creek ran out of the lake it was wide open. Other than a couple of sets of what looked to be wolf tracks on the frozen part of the lake, he saw no other sign of life. He climbed back up to his cruising altitude and headed back home to Kenora.

—

Ruth was quite content these days. The days were getting longer, and the weather was quite bearable. Most days they had highs of five to ten degrees. They thought it was early April although they didn't know for sure. They had not thought to notch a stick in the early months. George and Fred were both wearing watches when they crashed, but the batteries had died some time ago. They were using the sun now as their only clock. Time really didn't matter much now.

George had resumed setting his snare line again now that the weather had warmed. He had ten hides drying and almost ready for use. The rabbit meat was a welcome change to the almost constant moose diet. Fred had stamped a big SOS on the lake with snowshoes and was busy cutting boughs to trace out the letters to make them stand out. He wasn't too hopeful as they hadn't seen or heard a plane in weeks now. Still, it gave him a project to work on.

Their food supply was a bit worrisome. For meat, they still had almost a full side of the calf moose left and a few frozen fish and a half bag of sushi rice left. The berry patties were long gone as were the rose hips. Ruth made sure they had their spruce bough tea with every meal. This was the best source of vitamin C that they had now.

The broken bone in George's arm had set nicely over the last couple of months. He started using it very carefully at first but was now giving it more and more exercise every day. He was back hunting again, venturing out a little further all the time. He carried only the little .22 rifle with him now. They were almost out of ammunition for the pistol. Fred had shot a bull moose shortly after the wolf incident and, in the process, had used up all but one of the pistol shells. George tried to add a bit of variety to their diet by shooting a grouse now and then. His snares paid off only occasionally now. They had severely thinned out the rabbit population in the area over the winter months.

Spring was definitely here now. The snow had melted off the ground everywhere but in the thickest bush where the warm sun couldn't find it. The lake was still frozen. They had a few holes chopped in for ice fishing, but like the rabbits, the fish were getting scarce.

George had found a few tender fiddlehead fern shoots in some bare ground where the sun had warmed the earth. He picked all he could for dinner. He checked his close in snares and found nothing. He checked the fishing lines on the lake. They were empty as well. He decided he would hike over to the other little lake and check his fishing lines and snares there. It was mid-morning so he felt he had plenty of time to get there and back before dark. In the whole afternoon, the only game he saw was a red squirrel, which he expertly shot.

That night after dinner they sat drinking their spruce tea around the fire.

"It's time for us to leave," George said. "Spring is here, and the game is getting really scarce around here."

Fred nodded. "It *must* be April by now. Even the nights are getting warmer."

"Well," said Ruth. "it will take us a week or two to get ready. We have to get as much of the meat smoked as possible."

They went to work the next day. The men cut wood for the smoke fire while Ruth got to work creating back packs for the three of them. She sewed straps on both of the duffle bags for the boys to carry. For herself she would use Fred's little daypack.

———

Mike decided that he would hike back from his little hut down to Long Lake to try ice fishing. He arose in the morning at first light. It was fairly warm in the morning relatively speaking. At least it was above zero and the sky was clear. It looked like it would be a nice day. The trail was quite dry. The only sign of snow was in the deeper bush at the side of the path where the sun couldn't find it.

When he got to the lake he walked out twenty feet or so from shore and dropped his gear. He took his axe and started chopping a hole in the ice. There was still two feet of solid ice to cut through before he hit water. It was hard work but it kept him warm. Once he was through he baited his hook and lowered it through the hole in the ice. He tied the other end to a good strong branch and suspended the branch over the hole.

Now he went back to shore and cut a pile of spruce boughs and carried them back out onto the ice for a seat. He didn't want to get his meagre clothing wet. Within a few minutes, he had his first fish. He gutted it and baited the hook again with some of the entrails and continued jigging.

Suddenly he caught a movement out of the corner of his eye.

He turned to see Yukon bound out onto the ice and rush over to greet him. The dog must have come back from his travels only to find his new master missing. He had tracked him here. Yukon's ruff was covered in blood and his belly bulged. It was quite obvious he had found a good meal somewhere. Mike offered him some of the fish guts. He sniffed at them and finally ate them but with nowhere near the gusto that he would have a couple of days ago.

By mid-afternoon Mike had added four more pike to the pile all weighing three to five pounds. He was about to call it a day and pull in his line when suddenly the line went taut. Mike pulled the fish in as fast as he could. He did not want to give it a chance to get off the hook. With a mighty heave he pulled it through the hole. The fish flopped around on the ice desperately trying to breathe. Mike knocked the big pike on the head with the back of the axe and it lay motionless.

He stood back and admired his catch. It was musky, at least twenty pounds, a huge fish. Mike was ecstatic. He did a victory dance on the ice while the big dog looked on with his head cocked to one side in curiosity. He gutted the fish and threw Yukon the guts. Mike had brought along a piece of snare wire. He tied a stick on one end. Next he threaded the wire in one gill and out the mouth then in the gill of the next fish and out its mouth. He carried on until he had all the fish wired together then wired a handle onto the other end. He hoisted the whole works up onto his back, picked up the axe and headed back to the hut. Yukon fell in behind him. He wasn't going to let this meal out of his sight.

THIRTY

It had been a week, and Danny noticed that the area of open water at the north end of Susan Lake was larger. Now the entire end of the bay was open.

Danny pulled back the throttle and bled off some elevation. Once he was down to a couple of hundred feet above the treetops, he circled and buzzed the cabin. There was no sign of life. He circled the lake once more watching the cabin as he did so. Still nothing.

When he'd returned last week and reported not finding Joe, Bud had put him in touch with Joe's older brother, Jimmy, who told Joe of the cabins on Long Lake and Big Buck Lake. Jimmy wasn't overly concerned but had said that if he didn't find Joe again that he sure would appreciate if Danny would look in on the other cabins.

Danny had said he would.

He decided against landing on Susan Lake, opting instead to give the other two cabins fly-overs to see what he could see. If he didn't find Joe at one of the other two cabins, he would come back here and land.

He pulled up and climbed to a comfortable cruising altitude. He found Long Lake without any problem and dropped down, looking for the cabin. When he couldn't locate the cabin on the first pass, he climbed up in elevation a couple of hundred feet and tried again. Still he had no luck finding the cabin. Was it possible that Joe's brother got the name of the lake wrong?

He decided to fly over to Big Buck Lake. Big Buck Lake was easy to find. He identified it by a couple of distinctive islands. He dropped down and easily spotted the cabin. The ice looked good so he landed and taxied over close to the shore, but not too close. Again he used the trick of shuffling over the ice without doing up the back strap of his snowshoes.

Once on shore he took off the snowshoes and hiked up the path to the cabin. He checked the cabin for signs of life. He opened the door and called. There was no one about. He checked the cupboards and the loft. It had been a while since anyone had been here he decided, judging from the mouse poop on the kitchen table. Danny walked back down to the shore and shuffled his way back across the ice to the plane.

Once he got into the plane, Danny got out his thermos and poured himself a hot cup of coffee. He studied the map for a few minutes while he drank the brew. Long Lake was the only lake in the area that made any sense. It was located directly between Big Buck and Susan Lake. He decided fly back over to try to find the cabin one more time.

On his third pass over the lake, he saw the clearing and the outhouse.

He landed the plane and hiked up to the clearing. Once he arrived at the clearing, the tale began to unfold. There were the burnt remains of the two buildings. He poked around in the ashes and found the rusted remains of a bolt action .22 as well as a few other utensils and animal traps that the fire hadn't consumed. This was more than likely one of Joe's cabins.

He walked over to the other burnt building and poked around the ashes for a bit. There was not much of interest, and he was about to leave when something caught his eye. It was a partially burnt jawbone. He picked it up trying to figure out what kind of animal it had came from. When he saw the fillings in the back teeth he threw it down in horror.

Danny walked down to the plane, his mind in a whirl. The jawbone he had found likely belonged to Joe. But why wasn't it in the burnt out cabin? He was going to fly back to Kenora to report his findings but decided to make a quick stop at the Susan Lake cabin to make sure no one had been there since last week. He landed close to the dock and shuffled across the ice on his snowshoes.

Once up at the cabin he unlatched the door and walked in. Nothing had changed since he had been here last. The note lay on the table with the pencil on top exactly how he had left it. The bale of furs still sat in the corner. He decided to take the furs back to town with him. At least the family would have something to remember Joe by.

Danny hoisted up the bale of furs onto his back and carried it down to the shore. He dropped it there while he made a quick trip to the plane on snowshoes to get a length of yellow rope so that he could drag the bale of furs behind him over the ice. He guessed it weighed close to a hundred pounds and didn't want to chance carrying it on his back in case the extra weight caused him to break through. He was a very cautious man!

—

Mike carefully honed the edge of the butcher knife with a rock when he got back to the hut from his ice fishing trip. Once he had the blade almost razor sharp, he skilfully filleted all of the fish and hung them on the rack over the smoke fire The rest of the fish parts, back, head and tail were roasted closer to the flames for the evening meal.

He shared the fish with the dog, saving only the head and tail of the biggest fish for breakfast. That night he hung the partially dried fillets from wires inside the hut, far up and out of Yukon's reach.

The next morning, he built up his smoke fires and hung the fillets back up on the drying rack. He filled a pot with water to stew the head of the big fish in. While his stew was cooking he went over to the edge of the clearing and cut some thin willow branches. He kept close watch on the fire and the dog while he worked. He didn't trust that dog around food, and he certainly didn't trust the two Canada Jays that had landed in a nearby tree.

Once back at the fire, he began work on a willow basket. He had absolutely no idea what he was doing. He worked away at the project for an hour or so and finally threw the thing down in disgust. After his lunch he went over to the hut and retrieved one of his snowshoes. He cut the end knot and began unravelling the rawhide from the frame. Next he cut willow sticks together and tied them such that they formed the frame of a box. Once he had the box shape, he began weaving the rawhide back and forth to fill in the bottom and sides.

He worked on the basket all day, pausing only long enough to turn the fish fillets on the drying rack from time to time. The basket complete, he went to work weaving a lid for it. He fashioned a couple of rawhide hinges for it and a couple of loops so that he could wear it around his waist with his dressing gown belt.

Mike went to bed early and was up at first light. He went out to check his snares. They were empty so he just collected up the wire and came back to the hut. After he ate he began the process of packing. He rolled his sleeping bag as tight as he could and tied it with snare wire. He packed the knife, his coffee can and the fish into the basket and tied it onto his belt The basket reminded him of an old-fashioned fishing creels like the one his grandfather used to wear when he was fly fishing.

He picked up the axe and his sleeping bag and set off. The dog followed without Mike saying a word. Without a map, Mike wasn't sure which way Susan Lake was, but he figured it had to be opposite to the way to Long Lake. He headed into the bush looking for any sign of a trail. After an hour or so of tramping through the dense brush he sat down exhausted. The long winter had taken a toll on his muscles Mike realized as he struggled through the thick brush.

He thought he heard a small plane engine and his heart leapt—then sank. He was deep in the bush. If he tried to run for a clearing, even if he didn't twist an ankle or break a leg, it would be long gone.

Someone looking for Joe. Okay well Susan Lake is still the place to be. Can't afford to do anything stupid now.

Yukon whined at him like he was trying to tell him something. It suddenly occurred to Mike, that the dog knew where the trail was.

"Let's go, Yukon," he said pointing ahead.

The dog pushed through the underbrush for no more than a hundred yards before emerging on a fairly well defined trail that they had probably been on a parallel track with since they left the hut.

"Good boy, Yukon. What a good dog."

There was the sound of a second plane overhead moving in the opposite direction. It diminished until it was displaced by the call of jays and ravens. Mike wanted to scream, but he didn't want to spook the Malamute.

Jesus Christ!

Late in the afternoon they came to a spot where he could get a glimpse of the lake through the trees ahead.

He hurried forward and soon came to the shore. Most of the lake was still frozen except for the little bay they had arrived at. Yukon drank thirstily from the lake water. Mike was thirsty as well but decided he would boil his water first. He cast his eyes around the lake trying to spot the cabin but had no luck.

Mike looked at the sky and could see dark clouds forming out over the lake. He put down his gear and took the axe into the bush to cut materials for a shelter. He found a likely spot and went to work building a lean-to. He wasn't sure whether those clouds meant rain or snow, but he spent extra time and materials building the roof. He saved some of the softer boughs for his bed. Once the shelter was completed to his satisfaction, he laid out his sleeping bag and went to work collecting firewood. As a precaution, he collected some extra wood and birch bark and stashed it in the lean-to so that, if it did rain, he would still be able to get a fire going tomorrow.

It started snowing just before dark, so he decided it to make it another early night and crawled into his sleeping bag. It snowed all night. It was a wet heavy snow, but the shelter was amazingly dry. Mike woke in the morning surprised to find Yukon curled up beside him. This was something the dog would normally never do. Mike rolled over and scratched the dog's ears.

"Look at you," he said.

Yukon rolled lazily over on his back so that Mike could scratch his belly. Mike propped himself up on one elbow and looked outside. It had stopped snowing but was still quite overcast.

Mike rolled out of the bag. He put on what was left of his dressing gown, then his poncho and his boots. He relieved himself behind the shelter then got the coffee can and headed down towards the lake. Yukon followed along.

Mike filled the can with lake water and was about to leave to go back up to the fire when he noticed the dog staring at something in the water. He took a couple of steps closer and he saw what the dog was interested in. It was a frog, the first one he had seen this year.

He shooed the dog away but the movement startled the frog and it ducked down below the surface. Mike waited for it to resurface. Finally it came up for air a few feet away. He got down on his knees and crept towards it. When he was within striking distance he slowly moved his hand behind it.

The frog ducked under the surface of the water again, but Mike could see its legs sticking out from under the bank. He pushed up his sleeve further then plunged his hand under the water and grabbed onto one of the legs. The frog desperately tried to free himself, but Mike gamely held on. He pulled it from the water and walked over to a tree and smacked its head on it. He picked up his can of water and went back up to the lean-to.

He got the knife and cut off both the legs. He knew they were edible but was not sure about the rest. He offered it to the dog. Yukon took it and gobbled it down in one bite.

"God, you're a pig," said Mike. "We make a good team, you and I. No waste."

He started a fire to cook the frog's legs and spread his clothes around to dry. His underwear was dry about the same time the soup was ready. It was looking like rain or snow, so he went back to the shelter to eat his meal. It was delicious. The frog's legs tasted like boiled chicken. He drank the thin broth down greedily.

Yukon watched him with the most mournful eyes. His only reward was the frog leg bones—after Mike was done carefully sucking them clean of meat. Two snaps of the big dog's jaw and they were history.

After he had eaten, it started to rain. He crawled back into his sleeping bag. The rain was quite steady now, so he saw no need to go outside and get soaked. He fell asleep and slept until mid-afternoon.

What woke him was a steady drip on his face. He scrambled out of bed and looked out. The rain had stopped and the sun was peeking out from behind the clouds. The drips must have been from rain that had worked its way through the boughs over the course of the afternoon.

Mike pulled the sleeping bag out from the shelter. Luckily it was only wet in a few spots so he laid it out over a couple of bushes to dry. He collected some more dry boughs from the underside of big spruce trees. The legs of his long underwear were soon soaked through from the wet brush. Mike's plan was to carry on his journey, but he now realized how unpleasant this would be. He went back over to the fire and built it up with some more wood. As he stood close drying his clothing, an idea came to him.

He got his knife and went to find a birch tree. He found a fairly large one close by and went to work. With the knife he cut a long slit lengthways on the bark. Once this was done he started prying the edge of the slit with the knife. Finally he got enough peeled back that he was able to grab the bark with his hands and pulled it off in one piece. The piece of bark was about six feet long.

He went back to the fire to finish his project. He measured carefully then cut the bark into four pieces. One piece fit from just below his knee to just below the top of his boot. Another fit just above the knee to just about the top of his thigh. He made a set for each leg. He hoped these homemade rain pants would keep his underwear from getting soaked in the wet brush tomorrow. To tie them on he cut strips of bark from willow saplings and braided them together to make a cord. Now he felt he was ready to continue his journey. He ate a leisurely dinner of roast fish and bush tea, saving half the fish for his breakfast. He lazed around the fire for a few hours before he finally felt ready for sleep.

Mike woke at first light and got up to pee. He studied the sky. The day looked promising. There were no visible clouds in the sky. He started to collect some dry branches to build a fire so he could make breakfast but then changed his mind.

"If we leave now, Yukon," he said, "we would just get soaked in the brush. Let's wait until the sun has a chance to dry things a bit."

He went back to bed for an hour or so then got up to make breakfast. After breakfast, Mike packed up his meagre kit and set off. The bush was still a bit wet, but his birch bark rain pants worked remarkably well He walked the shore until he was past the open water. The ice on rest of the lake looked good and solid but he was still gun shy—not only because of his own past experiences, but also because this was how Joe had died. He made a decision to stick to solid ground even though it meant taking the long way around, following the contours of the lake.

For the most part, he was following a pretty good game trail. Mostly moose, thought Mike, as he studied the tracks. There were a few rabbit tracks here and there in the sparse snow patches mixed in with the moose tracks, and a few tracks that he couldn't figure out.

When late afternoon arrived, Mike decided to hole up for the night. He found a nice sheltered spot overlooking the lake. It had a little stream that was partially open. The sky was clear, so he simply found a big spruce tree with overhanging branches under which to camp. He cut some boughs for bedding and laid out his sleeping bag.

After a meal of dried fish, he built a fire and turned in. The mosquitoes were unbearable. Mike found he had to wrap his head in his housecoat while he slept. Even then a few found exposed skin to dine on.

He awoke at dawn. He rolled up his sleeping bag and packed up the rest of his gear. They tramped until mid-afternoon. Mike was almost ready to make camp for the night when they broke out into a little clearing with a cabin at the far end. Yukon stopped and actually howled at the sight of the cabin. He was so happy. He bound about growling and talking in the way only Huskies can. Mike could barely keep the dog in sight as Yukon raced for the cabin.

THIRTY-ONE

Miles away Ruth, Fred, and George were ready to begin their journey. Ruth had spent a lot of her time mending their traveling clothing over the past couple of weeks. A stitch here or a button there would make a big difference as to how the garments held up on the trail. Actually their clothing was in pretty good shape. Fred's old leather jacket was amazingly strong. If anything it just looked more broke in than ever. George still had his old wool bush coat intact. He had lost most of the original buttons but had fashioned replacements out of bone, painstakingly drilling holes in them with the awl on Ruth's Swiss army knife. Ruth had patched the elbows of her jean jacket and the knees of everyone's pants.

Her tools were simple. George had taken several different sized fishhooks and heated them on the fire. When they were hot enough he straitened them. He then filed the barbs off each one to fashion a needle. Darning needles were made from carved bone slivers. She scrounged whatever she could find for thread. At first it had been fishing line but when that got scarce she used sinew and even thin strands of copper wire.

For darning wool she sacrificed a couple of her designer sweaters. They were more suitable for showing off ones boobs than for providing warmth anyway. She unravelled the wool, rolled it into balls and used it to darn mainly socks, but even George's favourite jacket had a tiny pink patch in the elbow.

The last quarter of moose had been cut into strips and dried over the smoke fire in preparation for the trip. They collected fiddlehead fern sprouts and dried these as well.

They had long run out of matches. But George had found a couple of good sized chunks of quartz rock and had been teaching Fred the art of fire making the old way. He would strike the back of his big hunting knife with the rock. This would produce sparks that he would aim into a waiting pile of tinder. Eventually the sparks would ignite the tinder. He would get down on his elbows and blow gently onto the glowing tinder until it burst into flames, then feed the tiny flame with a bit of birch bark and finally small sticks.

"The secret," George said, "is finding the right tinder and then keeping it dry."

They each had a Ziplock plastic bag filled with their favourite mixture. It was finely shredded birch bark, ground dried spruce needles and cattail fluff. They carried their tinder in inside pockets of their jackets. Fred's jacket came equipped with a pocket. It was a simple matter for Ruth to add one to George's jacket.

Fred had found a pair of reading glasses in Mike's gear. He experimented focusing the sun's rays onto some of his tinder. Within a few minutes a tiny column of smoke rose from the tinder. With careful blowing he was able to nurture a flame from the tinder pile.

"Well, it works, but only on bright sunny days. Not much good when you really need a fire."

Still he figured it might be a useful tool. He put one of the lenses into his pocket and gave the other to George.

From the mosquito netting, Ruth fashioned bug hats that would fit over their existing hats to keep the bugs off their faces and necks. They had long run out of insect repellent. They would be traveling in the worst of blackfly season. In addition their route would lead them through miles of swampland infested with mosquitoes, horse-flies and deer flies.

"At least you can eat them big horse-flies," George said with a laugh.

Ruth and Fred shuddered at the thought.

Finally preparations were complete. Their best guess was that it was now mid-May. They would leave in the morning provided the weather cooperated. They readied their packs and set them by the door. All that was left to strap on were the sleeping bag and their blankets. Ruth added the fur parka to the pile as an afterthought. They could discard it along the way if it became too cumbersome, but it just might be handy before the trip was over.

In the morning they lingered over breakfast. As they were leaving they took one last look around. Their bear hide beds would have to stay. George had rolled them and tied them to the rafters. Their snowshoes also would stay behind. George latched the door and they all spent a few moments looking at their hut. They both loved and hated it after almost a year in the place. Without a word spoken, they shouldered their packs and left. Ruth turned a couple of times to look at the cabin as they walked down the trail around the little lake.

George led carrying the Henry rifle. He hoped to augment their meat supply along the way with the occasional grouse or rabbit. They were down to less than thirty rounds and had only one lonely bullet left for the pistol. They all agreed that, from here on, only crack shot George would do the hunting. Fred carried the axe and Ruth the bow saw.

The group moved steadily but almost silently down the trail. All three were wearing their homemade mukluks. George had rubbed bear grease and some of the airplanes motor oil into them to try to waterproof them shortly after Ruth had made them. It seemed to have done the trick as they had lasted nicely through the winter.

They walked steadily east for most of the morning staying high on the bedrock outcroppings as much as they could. Now a big swamp blocked their easterly path. They sat down for a rest.

"I know common sense says to go south from here," said George. "But I've covered most of the ground down there hunting many times, and I have never found a way through and I've traveled the edge for miles. I say we go north."

It was hard to argue with his logic.

Ruth got out her water bottle. The water bottle was really just one of Mike's old wine bottles with a carefully carved wooden stopper. That stopper had taken George most of an evening to make while sitting around the fireplace last winter. George had a similar wine bottle, while Fred carried the scotch bottle with the screw cap. They got their cups out and she poured each a measure of the boiled water. Then she got out their meat supply and doled out a piece of meat to each of them.

After their quick lunch, Fred got out the big airplane compass from his pack. He levelled off a piece of ground as best he could by eye and placed the compass on it. He took a bearing on north. He and George agreed that it looked like the swamp was running in a northeasterly direction.

For the rest of the afternoon they followed this direction trying to stay on the high ground so as to keep their footwear dry. Every hour or so, George would call a halt and he would head due east to see if they could cross yet. Each time he encountered the swamp. In late afternoon, after one of his unsuccessful forays, they decided to call a halt for the day and build a shelter for the night.

Fred suggested that George go on a hunting and scouting mission while Ruth and he built the shelter. George readily agreed. Without his heavy pack in tow he could travel much faster. While George was gone, Fred and Ruth went to work building a large spruce bough lean-to shelter. They found a couple of poplar trees with forks and used these as the basis of their structure. They cut a main pole and rested it into the forks. From here they laid out the rafter poles. They placed a layer of larger boughs over the poles. Next they got out the tube tents and Fred made an arbitrary decision to sacrifice them. They were pretty much shot anyway.

He got out his Swiss army knife and slit the top seams turning the tents into two big plastic tarps. They laid the tarps over the first layer of boughs and placed a second layer of boughs over the tarps to keep them down in case the wind came up. They cut smaller boughs for their bedding and laid out the blankets and sleeping bags. Once the shelter was complete, Fred went to work building a fire while Ruth went down to a nearby stream and filled the pot with water. She brought it back and then foraged around for food.

George arrived back from his scouting mission. He had found a little hill with a big spruce tree on the crest. He had been able to climb partway up the tree to get a better view of the area. From his vantage point, he could see a big lake directly to the east. It also looked to him that the swamp ended less than a couple of miles to the north.

"I think we should be able to get to that lake in a day maybe two," he said. "Maybe we could catch some fish."

Ruth smiled. "What I'd like to catch is a big plate of lasagna with garlic toast and a Caesar salad."

"With red wine," added Fred.

THIRTY-TWO

The Susan Lake cabin was surrounded by a junkyard. Joe had told Mike that, when he was a kid, the family was able to drive right to the cabin in the summer months. The forestry department had *deactivated* all the logging roads in the area in the late seventies by taking out the bridges. This cut off the vehicle access to the cabin.

"We tried going in by snowmobile. Had to fly them in in parts then put them back together." Joe had said. "But they break down too much. Finally I figured it was better to fly in with my dog."

Mike surveyed the yard. There were several old cars dating back to the mid-sixties and early seventies. A couple of old snowmobiles, a portable sawmill, and a couple of old rotten wooden boats lay strewn around the yard in no particular order. Behind the cabin, there was a dump of old cans and bottles. Litter was everywhere. Old rotten gloves and boots, pop cans, and whiskey bottles lay half covered in weeds.

There was an outhouse and a big woodshed. Mike decided to explore these later and headed for the cabin. Once inside, Mike noticed the state of the cabin was quite at odds with its surroundings. It was neat and tidy. He reasoned that probably the yard was such a mess because Joe spent very little time here in the summer. Besides that, without a road, how would one get rid of all this garbage? Joe wouldn't see how messy it was once the snow was on the ground.

As promised, there was a big antique white cook stove at one end of the cabin with some kitchen cupboards. There was also a small painted kitchen table and one wooden chair. Mike had seen two mates for that chair laying in the yard, badly in need of repair. At the other end of the cabin, in one of the corners, was a small airtight woodstove. There was no other furniture downstairs.

Upstairs there were two bedrooms. They had no doors. The bigger one had a slab of foam on a homemade bunk and a little dresser with a mirror. The other room was completely empty of furniture. Mike went back downstairs and started rummaging through cupboards and drawers. The first drawer that he opened sent him running back up the stairs.

He had found two boxes of 12-gauge shells, two boxes of .30-30 rifle shells and four boxes of .22 shells. Once inside the furnished bedroom, he dropped to his knees and peered under the bunk. Sure enough there were two gun scabbards under there. He pulled them out and opened the first one to find a classic model 94 Winchester .30-30 caliber lever action rifle. Mike had always loved the look of these guns. John Wayne, his childhood hero, always carried them in the movies. The second gun was a long doubled barrelled shotgun with two triggers. There was a lever at the back. He slid it sideways and the barrels hinged down so one could load it. He put the guns back into their hiding spot and went back downstairs.

In the same drawer that he found the ammunition, he also found some gun cleaning equipment, a half box of candles and two boxes of strike anywhere matches. He assumed the .22 shells he had found were for the little rifle he had lost in the fire. The other two drawers contained cooking and eating utensils and a selection of pots and pans.

The cupboards were crammed with food. It was mostly basic foods like dried beans, rice, macaroni, molasses, instant potatoes, pancake mix, yeast and baking soda. There were other staples like coffee, tea, salt, and pepper. There was other more specialty foods as well. There were canned soups, chilli, tomatoes and such. Mike's mouth watered at the sight. Beside the cupboard, there were four Rubbermaid tubs. Two were empty but one was almost full of flour. The last one was about three quarters full of dry dog food. When Mike took the lid off the dog food, Yukon came trotting over to mooch. He had been sound asleep by the door until that moment.

"No wonder you were so happy to get here," he said, filling Yukon's dish.

He built a fire in the woodstove and made dinner. After dinner Mike continued his search. He found a deck of cards on a shelf in the living room along with a couple of two-year-old magazines, one on snowmobiles and one on fishing. His hands were shaking he was so excited to have something to read.

Not now, he thought. *I have to keep exploring.*

He took them over and set them on the table to read later. There was a kerosene lantern half full of fuel on the shelf, so he took that down and put it on the table.

His downstairs search complete, he went back upstairs and checked out the dresser. It was almost bare. There was one pair of combination wool long john underwear, a pair of work socks with the heel worn out of both of them and a well-worn pull-over sweater. Mike held up the long underwear. They would fit him, but they couldn't have possibly have belonged to Joe. He sniffed them. They smelled clean. He put the clothes back into the dresser and went back downstairs. He found a pair of cut-off rubber boots by the back door. They were a couple of sizes too big for him, but he figured he could stuff them with something to make them work. They would be a lot cooler on his feet than the big felt pack boots he was wearing now.

Darkness was setting in. He would have to leave the exploration of the yard until morning. He lit the lantern and sat down at the kitchen table and began to flip through the magazines. Even with the help of the lantern, without his reading glasses, he couldn't read the print so he just looked at the pictures for a while. He played a couple of games of solitaire before hauling his sleeping bag up the stairs to the bunk and going to bed.

—

The ten miles that George guessed lay between them and the lake turned out to be more like twenty. They set out after breakfast. George was right when he said the swamp ended a couple of miles north. The problem was it drained into a deep stream. They followed the stream up for a couple more miles before they felt it was shallow enough to wade across. They all stripped down to their underwear, tying their pants and mukluks around their necks. The water was cold so they wasted no time getting across.

After getting dried off as best they could, they dressed and headed southeast according to the compass shot Fred had taken with the big compass. George figured they should intersect the lake at about this heading. By late afternoon, they still had not reached the lake, so they decided to make camp for the night. While Ruth and Fred collected firewood and built a shelter, George went hunting. When he returned, the couple had built a fine lean-to and had the fire going. The nightly soup pot was simmering by the fire.

They packed up in the up morning and again set off to the southeast. A few times they came upon game trails that seemed to run in the right direction. They stayed on these whenever they could, but most of the way was just plain bush whacking. By midday they came upon the lake. They sat down and had a rest and a piece of meat each for nourishment. George scouted around a bit after lunch and found a game trail that was heading south following the shoreline. They decided they might as well keep going for a few more hours. The weather was nice, and there was a breeze coming off the lake that was keeping the bugs away.

In late afternoon they found a nice looking natural campsite right beside the lake. There were several big spruce trees nearby so Fred and Ruth started to make camp while George got out his fishing rod and went down to the lake to try his hand at fishing. He tried several lures without any success. Finally he chose a big red and white spoon. On his second cast he got a hit. He reeled it in. He landed a pike that weighed at least ten pounds. He cleaned and scaled it at the shore then took it back up to show the others. They cut the big fish into pieces and roasted them over the fire on green sticks. They cooked and saved enough for a breakfast meal. Over dinner, they talked over their strategy. They would follow this lake to the south end and then turn east again to try to intersect the highway.

Fred awoke early the next morning with a toothache. The tooth had been bothering him off and on for the last month. Today however, the whole side of his face had swollen up to twice its normal size.

"I think you must have an abscess," said Ruth.

That was worrisome as they hadn't any antibiotic drugs to deal with anything like that. George didn't have any herbal solutions. Fred decided to tough it out and carry on. By nightfall the pain had not eased. He couldn't even think of eating. Ruth and George took turns looking into Fred's mouth trying to find the cause of his pain. They both agreed it was one particular molar that was the culprit.

"Can you pull it out?" asked Fred in desperation.

"I've never done anything like that in my life," replied George. "Let's see how it is in the morning."

In the morning, however, the situation was no better. Fred had not slept a wink all night and was pacing in agony down by the lake. George had a conference with Ruth and they decided the tooth should come out. George got the pliers from his tackle box and Ruth dipped them in boiling water a few times to sterilize them. George sat down on Fred's chest and clamped the pliers as hard as he could on the offending tooth.

"I sure hope it's the right one," he said.

He pulled and twisted with all his strength. Fred howled in pain and fainted. George came up with the bloodied tooth still clamped in the pliers. Fred came to after a few minutes and mumbled his thanks. He crawled into bed and slept until late afternoon under Ruth's watchful eye. When he awoke, the swelling was down and although the gum was extremely tender, the intense pain was gone. He had a big bruise on his cheek that lasted for a week thanks to George's rather rough dental technique.

"We're going to stay put for a couple of days," Ruth announced firmly the next morning. "I want to make sure Fred doesn't get that hole in his mouth infected before we take off again."

To her surprise George backed her up.

"I agree. We need all of us healthy if we're going to get out of here."

THIRTY-THREE

Mike awoke at dawn. He had to pee. He went outside, wearing his newly found cut off rubber boots. Once he was done with that, he started to roam the yard. He opened the doors of the various cars looking for treasure. He found a pair of very dirty coveralls in one and felt he had hit pay dirt. His old long underwear was in tatters at the knee. A quick bath for these coveralls and they would be fine. He took them down to the dock and scrubbed at them until he got the worst of the dirt out. He laid them out on the dock to dry and looked them over.

"Pretty styling wouldn't you say, Yukon?"

The big dog merely wagged his tail at the sound of his name.

Mike went over and checked out the woodshed. It was about half full of firewood. There was a chainsaw, an axe and a chopping maul lying against the wall. There was a five-gallon plastic gas can half full of gas. Mike opened it and sniffed the contents. It smelled like it might be this year's gas. There was also some chain oil in a plastic container.

A smaller shed beside it contained a variety of tools. Some serviceable work gloves and all sorts of chains, ropes, and come-along pulleys were strewn about the shed on benches and on the floor. He found a big blue tarp, rolled up and stuffed under one of the benches. *That might be handy later*, he thought.

The best thing was an old cedar strip and canvas canoe hanging from the rafters. It had been hauled up on two pulleys, one on each end. Mike untied the rope on one end then lowered the bow of the canoe to the floor. He went around to the other end and untied that rope and lowered the stern to the floor. It was obvious this thing had been tied up there for years. There was about an inch of dust on the inside. He was going to pull it outside for a better look, but hunger overcame him, and he went back up to the cabin for breakfast.

After he had eaten, Mike decided that the most important task of the day was a hot bath. He had found an old round galvanized tub hanging from the back of the cabin. He went down to the shed with the thought of getting the chainsaw to cut down a big green poplar tree. His idea was to cut two green poplar logs to support the tub above the ground. He would then be able to build a fire under the tub to heat water. He picked up the chainsaw and inspected it. He had absolutely no experience with one of these things. He quickly put it down and picked up the axe instead. Going outside he started work on felling the big poplar tree. It took a bit of effort but it finally crashed to the ground in about exactly the opposite direction Mike was planning it to fall.

He chopped off two lengths of the log and dragged them down close to the lake where he wanted to build the fire. He placed the tub on the top of the logs and with a bucket, began the slow process of filling the tub with water. Once it was full he built a fire under it. Mike spent the next hour nurturing that fire. Finally the water was getting warm. He went back up to the cabin and got the combination long johns underwear and a bar of soap.

Once the fire was blazing and the water was finally warm, he stripped down and lowered himself into the bath water. It was a small tub so he had to work at getting all parts of his body clean. After about a half hour, he was satisfied with the result. He got out and dressed himself into the combination underwear. He was about to start doing his laundry as well when he had a better look at the bath water.

"Wow, I must have lost five pounds in dirt after that bath, eh Yukon? Better start with fresh water."

He had lately got in the habit of talking to Yukon. He greatly missed his conversations with Joe and didn't want to go back to the silence that was his world before Joe and Yukon had arrived.

While the fresh water in the tub was heating again, Mike turned his attention to the canoe. He tipped it over and banged on the hull with his hands to loosen and release the dust. Once it was relatively clean he picked it up and carried it down to the dock. At the dock he was able to swish out any remaining dirt. Mike examined the little canoe. It was manufactured by the Walnut Canoe Company—one of the finest canoe companies around.

Once he had the inside rinsed out, he turned it over to examine the hull. Mike found a few small breaches in the canvas covering. The largest was a rip about three inches long close to the bow. Normally, if one were close to civilization, the answer would be simple. A fibreglass kit from the local hardware store would fix this in a heartbeat. Mike was not in civilization. As a matter of fact, with the map lost in the fire, Mike was not sure exactly where civilization was from here.

The water in the tub was beginning to steam. Mike went up and put all of his clothing into the tub excluding what he was wearing. He shaved off a few slivers from the bar of soap into the water, and stirred the whole works together with a piece of board he had found in the junk pile.

"Hell, there's room to spare, Yukon. Let's throw in the coveralls too."

While the laundry was soaking, Mike focused on the canoe. He tried to think of what he had at his disposal that he could use as a patch. Tar came to mind, but he didn't have any. He went down to the dock and stretched out in the sunshine to think about it. Soon he was fast asleep. Somewhere in his dreamlike state an idea hit him, and he awoke with a start. Asphalt shingles he thought. Asphalt shingles are made from tar. If he could melt one he could patch the hole.

He went up to the woodshed and ripped a couple of shingles from the eaves. After a few experiments he found that the easiest way to separate the tar from the shingles was simply to light the shingle on fire at one edge. Once it started to burn, the tar would melt and drip from the shingle and then he could drip the molten tar onto wherever it was needed and spread it with an old butter knife.

He worked on the canoe for an hour or so until he had patched all the rips in the canvas. There were a couple of old paddles in the shed. He selected the better of the two and carried it down to the dock.

"Come on, Yukon. Jump in!"

There was still a bit of ice on the main part of the lake, but the little bay in front of the cabin was open. It didn't give him a huge area to try out his new toy, but he had fun nonetheless. As he paddled around, he came to a decision. He would stay on here. He had food and he had shelter. He figure he had missed the deadline for Joe's plane to pickup, but they would return to look for him soon.

He didn't know that they had already found Joe's remains, and so no one really had any cause to check the Susan Lake cabin.

A few days later Ruth and George had a quick breakfast of the previous night's leftover fish before they packed up camp. Fred tried to eat some, but soon gave up. His mouth was getting better, but he didn't want to push it. He settled for spruce bough tea and some berries. They headed south along a well-worn game trail that followed the shore of the lake. George led, and Ruth and Fred wordlessly followed a couple of hundred yards behind him. Fred was happy to go slow, still weak from his lack of solid food. George was hunting for small game and asked them to keep back so they didn't scare off any animals.

Late in the afternoon they came across an old campsite with a lean-to shelter. The boughs were brown with age so it couldn't have been made recently. There was an old smoke rack beside the fire pit. George looked at the handiwork.

Mike?

He said nothing of his suspicions to the others. They decided to rebuild the shelter with fresh boughs and stay for the night. They awoke the next morning to a steady rain. Luckily they had spread the tarps over the roof of the shelter the night before. They were keeping the majority of the rain out, so they just stayed put. It rained most of the morning and finally let up around noon. George collected a few dry branches from the base of a big spruce tree and got a fire going to dry out their stuff.

Fred went down to the lake to fish while George took the rifle and went hunting. He came back an hour later with his pants soaking wet. He had a spruce grouse in his hand. Fred had managed to catch one little perch that would be considered undersized in all jurisdictions except this one. Ruth had collected some ferns and a few berries. She filled the pot with water from the lake, and put it beside the fire to heat. The men each cleaned their prizes and added them to the pot. The stew was tasty. They would have loved to have a little seasoning, but all their spices and herbs had long since disappeared over the winter.

The next morning they broke camp and again followed the trail south. Mid-morning they came across a stream that was too deep to cross so they were forced to follow it inland for an hour or so before they found a shallow spot.

Around noon they came across an obviously manmade trail. They followed it uphill from the lake. They were amazed to find a little cabin. The door was unlocked so they just went in.

"Oh," said Ruth when she saw the little woodstove. "Oh."

THIRTY-FOUR

Mike found a vintage fishing rod with a bait cast reel in the shed. He hunted up a few worms and put them into an old can that he picked up from the garbage pile at the back of the cabin and headed down to the lake. He got into the canoe and pushed off, leaving Yukon whining on shore. He baited the hook and let out some line.

He spent the next hour trolling around the confines of the cove. He had almost given up when he got his first bite. He reeled in steadily until the fish was right beside the boat. It was a walleye. With one hand holding the rod high, he deftly slipped two fingers into its gill and lifted it into the boat. Walleye have a very sharp dorsal fin that can cut like a knife. Mike whacked the thing a couple of times with the butt end of the paddle to make sure it was good and dead before he handled it. He paddled the canoe back to shore. If this were the species of fish in the lake, he would need a landing net of some fashion.

He filleted the fish on the dock. He gave the remainder of the fish to Yukon who waited patiently for his share. He took the fillets up to the cabin to cook later for his supper. The yard was full of dandelions. He collected a few to have with the fish. These weeds as most people called them were brought over by the early European settlers as a food source and had spread like wildfire across most of North America. Wherever humans settled it seemed the little yellow flowers would appear. Once a couple of plants were established, if left unchecked, the weeds would propagate an entire area. The good thing was that almost the entire plant was edible. Mike had tried a dandelion salad in a trendy restaurant in Toronto and remembered that it was surprisingly good.

With the landing net still on his mind, Mike went into the bush and hunted around until he found a little willow about as thick as his thumb. He cut it down and took it back to the shed. He found an old wooden pop case full of junk in the shed. He dumped it out and brought it outside to use as a seat. He went back into the shed and began a materials search. He found some nylon cord and a roll of black electrical tape He bent the willow branch to form the shape of the net frame and taped the ends together. For the rest of the afternoon he worked on his project, cutting and knotting the rope to form the netting. By suppertime, he had fashioned a crude, but functional landing net.

After dinner he went down to the lake and trolled around the little bay. He caught two more walleye and filleted them for the nest day's meals. At dusk he returned to the cabin, got out the cards and spent the rest of the evening playing solitaire.

The brace and bit he found in the shed had given him an idea. He had read somewhere that you could tap birch trees for their sap much like you could tap maple trees and that the sap could be boiled down to make birch syrup. Mike was up at first light eager to work on his project. He needed some tubing. He popped the hood of an old Oldsmobile station wagon and checked it out. There were a couple of choices that were obvious. There was a copper fuel line or there were two copper transmission fluid cooling lines. Mike decided the fuel line would be easier to clean.

He went up to the tool shed and found a hacksaw. Within minutes he had the gas line off. Now he cut it into six pieces each about six or seven inches long. He built a fire and heated the copper tubing until they turned green in the heat before he removed them. This should have removed any fuel residue he reasoned.

After breakfast, he cleaned out an equal number of pop bottles. Armed with the bottles, some wire, the copper tubing and the brace and bit, he set off in search of birch trees. He tapped six trees and pushed a piece of tubing into each hole. He wired a bottle onto each of the trees so that any sap that ran down the tubing would be caught. It was a slow process one drip at a time. It took four days to fill the bottles with sap. It took almost another full day of boiling the sap down in a pot on the stove before he had maybe eight ounces of syrup. It was well worth the effort. He made up a batch of pancakes to try the syrup on. The result was fantastic.

—

Ruth, Fred and George decided to move into the little cabin for a couple of days while they replenished their food supply. George insisted Ruth and Fred take the loft, but they gave him the foam mat in return. They searched through the cabin to see if they could find anything useful. The only food in the whole cabin consisted of one lonely tea bag of unknown vintage found hiding in a top cupboard. They found a part box of wooden matches and a half of candle in a drawer. In one of the cupboards they found a couple of pots and a cast iron frying pan. Another held two enamelled metal plates. In a drawer they found the usual selection of dinnerware and kitchen utensils. As simple as it was, these were the best accommodations they had found since their ordeal had began.

They awoke the next morning to a steady downpour. Ruth made a pot of tea with the tea bag. After breakfast, Fred got out the file and sharpening stone. He went to work putting a sharp edge on the axe as well as all of their knives. George sorted and cleaned his fishing tackle. Ruth braved the weather and went down to the lake to fill the largest of the pots with water. She heated it on the stove then took it up to the loft to have a warm sponge bath and wash her hair. It was heaven. Soon they were all out of make work projects. The rain continued to pour down for over a week.

To fill the time, Fred taught them a knife game he had learned as a child. He opened his pocketknife half way so the blade was perpendicular to the handle. He stuck the tip of the blade into the rough sawn floorboards. With a well practiced little flip of his fingers he spun the knife in the air. Points were awarded depending on how the knife landed. If the knife landed flat on the back of the handle with the blade in the air, one point was awarded. The big points came if one was able to flip the knife one complete rotation and stick the blade back into the wood. The space between the handle and the floor was measured by inserting fingers into the space. If one could fit three fingers into this space three points were awarded. Ruth of course having much more slender fingers than the men had a bit of advantage. Fred had years of practice on his side. In the end even with the odds against him, George won. He smiled secretly. George liked to win. The diversion helped them get through the days. Now that they had made their decision to walk out, any delay was frustrating.

After five days of rain, they decided that, rain or no rain, they had to forage for food or face starvation. When they awoke in the morning, the sky was grey and menacing, but the rain had slowed to a drizzle. Fred took the fishing rod and went down to the lake. George headed south along the lake on a scouting trip. He took along the little rifle as well as his big pistol with its lone bullet. Ruth stayed close to the cabin and searched for berries and greens.

George followed a fairly well marked game trail south. As he traveled, he looked for signs of game. Here and there the brush had been nipped off clean. This was the sign of a moose browsing. He found a few dried moose turds and slipped them into his breast pocket. They could help thicken up a soup. He would have to be sneaky so Ruth and Fred didn't see this addition to the pot. George found a few patches of blueberries. They were not quite ripe yet but he managed to find enough almost ripe ones to ease his hunger pains. He filled his other shirt pocket to add to the evening meal.

He was bent down, picking berries, when he heard a twig snap. He looked up into the face of a bull moose not twenty yards away. The moose sniffed at him trying to figure out what he was. George slipped the pistol out of his belt and eased off the safety. He aimed it at the bull's enormous chest and squeezed the trigger. The moose dropped to the ground. George sprinted over to get the little rifle where he had left it propped against a tree. As the moose struggled to get up he fired three more shots into it at point blank range. It lay still.

Both Ruth and Fred heard the shots. Ruth ran down to the lake and met up with Fred.

"He must of shot something big," said Fred. "That first shot was the pistol."

Fred had caught a couple of pike, so they decided to take them back up to the cabin first, get the axe and some rope, then go to find George. George had the big moose gutted by the time they found him. They cut the beast into quarters and spent the rest of the day hauling it back to the cabin. Now they were busy. They hung the meat in the woodshed and began building smoke racks.

By dusk they were exhausted. They discussed what they should do next. Ruth reasoned that, with all this meat and the berry season upon them, they should stay put for a while to smoke as much meat as they could and collect and preserve berries. It was now late June and the berries were starting to ripen. The long daylight hours in the north sped up the berry season. As hard as it was to stay put, they decided it would be the best plan.

Armed with pots, Ruth and Fred set out daily to hunt for blueberries in the rocky outcroppings above the cabin. Northern Ontario is a most interesting place to visit in the summer months. It is a land of extremes. There are thousands of lakes and swamps, but occasionally the Canadian Shield rises out of the ground. From swampland one can find oneself wandering on barren rocky hillsides that could stretch for miles. And then the land for some unexplainable reason would turn back into a swamp.

While Ruth and Fred picked berries, George tended the meat smoking fire and dried the berries. They collected as much other food as they could find. After about a week at the cabin, George made an announcement.

"As comfortable as this is," he said,"I think we should get ready to move on."

After some discussion, the other two agreed. They decided they would go back to their original plan. They would head south along the lake to the end then turn east to intersect the highway.

The following day they spent in preparation for the trip. Their packs were so heavily loaded with dried meat and berries that they had to help one another put them on. Even so they had wasted a lot of nourishing food. Bones that could have made many wonderful soups were thrown by the wayside. They replaced their original homemade utensils with ones from the cabin. Ruth had to admit that her two new pots were lighter than the old oil pan pot she was leaving behind.

THIRTY-FIVE

Mike decided to explore the area. He tore out a page from one of the magazines and wrapped a couple of fish fillets up in it and stuck them in his homemade creel. He loaded the rifle and put a few spare shells into a pocket. He picked up a dozen or so strike anywhere matches, his knife, and a can of steak and potato soup and added them to the creel.

He and Yukon left the cabin yard and followed an old skid road that must have been the way in at one time. Now the road had grown to the point where it was barely passable on foot. They followed the old trail for a couple of hours until they came to a more passable road. The road had obviously been a forestry road judging by the construction. It hadn't, however, been used for a few years. There were little poplar trees taking root here and there in the middle of the road.

Mike sat down on a rock outcropping at the edge of the road and took out the fish fillets he had packed for lunch. He shared them with the ever-hungry dog. While they rested, he made a decision. He would follow the road south for three or four hours. If he didn't find a way out in that time period, he would head back to the cabin. They trudged on south until mid-afternoon. He stopped to rest beside a little stream. Mike drank his fill then decided to head back to the security of the cabin. They arrived back at the cabin at dusk and, after a quick supper, Mike turned in early. He had done a lot of walking that day.

The next morning he and Yukon set out again—this time he was better prepared. He had taken his sleeping bag and into it rolled a pot, the axe and three days of rations, including some kibble for the dog. He got the tarp out of the shed and unrolled it in the yard. It was huge; he estimated it was about twenty feet wide by thirty feet long. He cut off piece that was about ten feet by twelve feet. He put his sleeping bag in the middle and folded the tarp around it. He tied it up with rope and slung it onto his back. He picked up the rifle and, with the big dog following, hit the now familiar trail. They followed the skid trail back to the road and again set out south. They traveled all day stopping only once for a quick lunch.

The road ended, disappointingly, in a big logging cut block. Mike could see open water through the trees at the edge of the clear cut. He bush whacked his way through and came out on the shore of a pretty little pothole lake. If there were fish in the lake he would never know, as he had not had the foresight to bring a hook and line. While he built a shelter, the dog went on a hunt. Mike didn't see him again until dusk. He knew just by looking at his bulging belly that the big dog had found a meal somewhere.

Mike awoke at dawn. He crawled out of his sleeping bag and went off to pee. When he came back, he built a fire, then made a meal. He decided to head east for the day to see if he could intersect the highway. The sun was his only way of judging direction. He was pretty sure he was traveling approximately east. He blazed a trail as he went so he could find his way back if need be. He had learned, by hard experience, how easy it was to lose your bearings in the bush.

Dusk found them at the edge of a huge swamp. The mosquitoes were intense. The dog's snout was swollen to twice its normal size. Mike turned and headed back as far as he could away from the swamp before he made camp for the night. Even with his bug dope, the night was almost unbearable. He finally bundled himself up in the sleeping bag so that just his nose was exposed.

His chemistry training kept him awake for another hour as he tried to remember just what was in this bug dope stuff.

In the morning he awoke. He sat up and took stock of the situation. With his supplies low, he decided to make his way back to the cabin. After breakfast he started picking his way back, hoping to intersect the logging road. Even with the blazes he had cut, his path was hard to follow. He found the road by mid-afternoon and turned north. Late in the day he stopped and made another shelter for the night. This one was pretty simple. He had found a large spruce tree with big overhanging branches. He hung the tarp from the branches to make a little tent. He collected some smaller branches for bedding and laid out his sleeping bag. All night it rained but the big spruce and the tarp kept him dry. He ventured out at dawn to relieve himself, then slept until mid-morning. When he did finally wake, he was ravenous. It was still raining, so there was little hope of getting a fire going. He got out his knife and opened a can of corn and ate it cold. He gave the dog the last of the dog food.

By noon, the rain had slowed to a drizzle. Mike decided to head back to the cabin. He walked at a steady pace all afternoon, stopping only at a few streams along the way for water. By late afternoon he had found the skid trail that led to the cabin. A steady rain had started. Soon he was soaked though to the skin.

He stumbled through the last part of the trip in the dark. Without any moonlight to help, the going was extremely difficult. He followed Yukon's lead. The dog seemed to sense Mike's difficulty and stayed close to him until finally they arrived back at the cabin. Once inside he fumbled around until he found a match. Once that was lit, he was able to find the lantern and get it going. He stripped off his wet clothes and went upstairs to get the dry long underwear from the dresser drawer. Soon he had a blazing fire going in the cook stove and put on a pot of water on to boil for tea. He lit the airtight stove as well and hung his clothes on a temporary clothesline to dry.

Exhausted, Mike wrapped himself in his sleeping bag, fed Yukon, ate some beans from a can and fell asleep in front of the stove. He awoke to a sunny morning.

Maybe this is a sign, he thought. *I should just stay here where it's safe and go fishing.*

By the end of the day, however, he'd decided that he needed to check the logging road to the north, arguing that, if south lead to a clearcut, then north had to be where the trucks had come from once upon a time. He spent two full days fishing and smoking and foraging what he could and set off early on the morning of the third day.

By early afternoon he'd reached river he could not cross. The road ended in a rough concrete abutment that had once held a bridge, and though the river at the bottom of the small gorge was probably no more than ten or fifteen yards across, it was fast and one glance told Mike that he wouldn't have a chance of crossing it.

Hell I'd probably break my neck just getting down to the water.

He walked downstream maybe a mile without seeing a more promising place to cross then walked back to the road and made camp there.

The next morning he decided to explore upstream. He and Yukon followed the river gorge upstream until, after a few hours, it broadened out into a vast swampy expanse that looked utterly impassable.

"Aww to hell with this, Yukon. Let's go back to the cabin. I'm done."

———

Ruth, Fred and George had been walking for a while and were now looking out over a glass calm stretch of open water.

"Could be wrong," said George. "But I think this is Big Buck Lake."

A fish jumped about thirty yards from shore.

"Oh yeah?" said Fred.

"Could be. Big whether it is or not."

Ruth said, "You think there could be another cabin on it?"

"Could be," said George. "If it's Big Buck there certainly is."

Their master plan of turning east was foiled when they ran into a big wide creek running south to north. George scouted around. Soon he was back.

"I found a blazed trail," he said. "I followed it for a bit, it looks like it runs pretty much south. I think we should follow it."

The others agreed. The thought of trying to swim the big creek was not appealing. Worse would be getting their heavy packs across. They set up camp for the night.

After breakfast the next morning, Ruth handed each of the men a slice of dried meat for trail rations. She put a piece into her jacket pocket herself. They shouldered their packs and trudged on down the trail. George had been right. This definitely was a manmade trail. Trees were blazed and here and there were saw cut logs that had once fallen across the trail and had sections removed for ease of passage.

The mid-morning silence was unexpectedly dispelled by the roar of an airplane engine. It took them all completely by surprise. Fred managed a feeble wave before it was gone.

"I wonder why he is flying so low," he said.

"Maybe he's dropping someone at the cabin we just left," said Ruth sounding uncharacteristically desperate.

George thought for a moment before he spoke.

"Nah, I'm pretty sure that was a trapper's line cabin. There would have been a boat or a canoe if it was used for fishing. This ain't trapping season."

A few minutes later they heard the plane again. This time it was flying south at about the same altitude but a few miles west of them.

"They are searching for something."

Late in the day, the trail they had been following ended on the shore of a long skinny lake. As was their routine, Ruth and Fred built the shelter while George foraged for food. He came back to report that the big creek they had found at the end of the last lake was unfortunately connected to this lake.

"Without a boat, there is no way to get all this stuff across."

Fred got out the big airplane compass. The lake, he discovered lay almost directly north to south.

"I say we follow this river south," said Fred. "As long as we are going either south or east sooner or later we're going to hit a road."

PART 6

SUMMER

THIRTY-SIX

Over the course of the early summer, Mike had seen a few planes in the distance. Once when he had been out hunting, he saw one fly directly over the lake but had not been close enough to signal it. He spent most days either hunting, fishing or picking berries. The darn dog ate almost as much as he did, so it was a full time job putting food on the table so to speak.

One morning, in what he believed was early July, Mike awoke to a huge din outside the cabin. He quickly went downstairs and grabbed the rifle, stuffing shells into the breach as he headed for the door. The dog had treed a black bear. Mike took careful aim and fired. The bear dropped out of the tree dead. The dog was on it in an instant ripping and tearing. It took all Mike's strength to pull the big malamute off. He got a piece of rope and tied the dog up to a tree so that it didn't mutilate the bear carcass while he was having breakfast.

He spent the morning skinning out the bear and butchering it—hacking it into smaller pieces was more like it. He smiled to himself thinking of the bear George had killed early on after the plane crash. Back then he was too queasy to even watch, let alone help.

"How things have changed, Yukon," he said over his shoulder.

By noon he had the job about complete. He went down to the dock and washed himself and his coveralls. He went back up and set up smoke racks, built a big smoky fire under them and began drying the meat. Once he had that underway, he dragged the rest of the carcass up the old road and into the bush for the birds to scavenge.

Mike fried up two big bear steaks for dinner. One was for him and one—the larger of the two—for Yukon for his part bagging the bear. He spent the rest of the evening slicing up bear meat into thin pieces to make the drying process easier. That night, he stored the partially smoked meat in the back of an old station wagon so it was safe from night raiders.

In the morning, he built up the smoke fires again and loaded the rack with strips of meat. His plan for the day was to build a cold room like the one Ruth had designed at the pothole lake cabin. The Susan Lake cabin had a wood floor. It would be too much work to rip up a section of floor so that he could dig the food well. He decided to dig it in the tool shed instead. He cleared the junk from one corner of the dirt floor in the shed and went to work on the hole. The only tools he had were a short handled spade and his axe. Every half an hour or so, he had to stop digging and tend to his smoke fires. When he did this, he would also turn the meat strips. The jays were collected in the yard watching his every move. If he let the fire burn down too low the bold ones would swoop in and steal some of his precious meat.

By the end of the day, he had a sizeable pit dug. It was about four feet square and five feet deep. Tomorrow he would make a cover for it. He collected the meat off the drying racks and took it back to the wagon for safekeeping. He judged that one more day on the racks between the smoke and the sun and the meat should be dry enough to store.

Mike spent all of the next day drying the meat. Between feeding the fire and flipping the meat, he scrounged enough lumber from around the yard to build a secure cover for his food well. He found another wooden pop case in the shed and took them both down to the dock to work on. He used water and sand from the lake bottom to rub into the wood to clean the boxes. He made some crude but effective lids for the boxes out of the wood scraps from the yard. Once the boxes were clean, he filled them with dried meat and lowered them into his food well. He put the covers on each to keep the flies out.

—

The other three survivors were making their way down this new lake. It was a beautiful July day. There was a bit of a breeze coming off the lake to give them some relief from the bugs. The black flies had thinned out in the last couple of weeks, but the horseflies and the deer flies had replaced them. The horse-flies were big and slow and easy to kill, but the deer flies could drive one insane. They had to keep their jackets and hats on even in the heat of the day because of them.

Around mid-afternoon they came across a well marked manmade trail heading uphill from the lake. Without hesitation, George turned and followed it. The trail led to a clearing. What once had been two buildings were now two separate piles of ashes. They studied the scene for a few moments. George broke the silence.

"It's weird. It's like someone sifted through all these ashes looking for something."

He pointed out several metal objects piled neatly beside the building ashes. There were the remains of a gun, a stove, some traps and several kitchen items stacked at one end of the bigger buildings ruins. The only building still standing was the out-house. Ruth walked over and opened the door hoping against all odds that there was toilet paper in there. She was disappointed to find nothing of value.

They decided to build a shelter down by the lake, as the bugs were too bad up in the clearing. George went hunting. Ruth was going to pick berries. Fred decided to go for a swim. He stripped down once the others left and waded into the lake. He was float-ing on his back enjoying the sunshine when he heard a little splash behind him and turned sharply in the water. Ruth had snuck back and had stripped down to join him. She had always loved skinny-dipping as a kid.

George arrived back at the camp a couple of hours later. He had shot a grouse to add to the nightly stew. Ruth cleaned it and added it to the pot. George also had a pocketful of what he called wild cranberries that were a welcome change. She cubed a couple of pieces of dried moose meat along with a few wild mushrooms and added them to the mix.

"This is going to be a great meal," she said as she busied herself cutting up the moose meat.

She had her back to the men. George winked at Fred and threw some secret ingredients into the pot. He had diced up a few big grubs before he got home. At dinner she raved about the flavour the cranberries had given their meal.

They followed the lake shore all the next day. Late in the afternoon they reached the end of the lake. They decided to camp for the night. George went scouting. An hour later he came back from his mission.

"I found another trail," he said. "This one has fresh blazes on it."

"How fresh?" asked Fred.

"I think this year. Come take a look"

While the men were gone Ruth made the evening meal. They arrived back just as it was ready. "I agree with George," said Fred. "Those blazes can't be more than a couple of months old. There was still sap oozing from them."

The more the men talked the more they were convinced they were close to civilization. Ruth was not so sure. She thought they had to go a lot more to the east or a lot more south from here before they found any permanent settlements. In any case she agreed it was worth a try. Her main concern was that the trail seemed to be heading southwest instead of southeast.

In the morning they filled their water bottles with boiled water in preparation for the trip. They headed inland following the blazes. By late afternoon the trail led them to a clearing with a small lean-to hut. The door had a peg in the hasp so they knew it was vacant. Someone had been there fairly recently. There was a little stove inside and some spruce boughs that had been used as bedding. The spruce boughs were dry but still green.

Ruth picked up one of the boughs and the needles fell like rain. Using a fresh cut bough Ruth swept the cabin clean and built a fire in the stove to cook dinner.

"It feels like a storm is coming," said George. "I think we found this shack just in time. Come on, Fred, we better get some firewood. Looks like we may be here for a while."

There were big black clouds building to the north. The sound of distant thunder made everyone pick up the pace. They stashed as much dry wood as they could under the bunk and made another pile under the eaves covering it with the tube tent tarps.

The storm hit with a vengeance. Lightning flashed and thunder crashed. They all feared that the lightning would start a forest fire. George opened the door a few times to have a look. The rain poured down so hard at times that they had to shout at each other to be heard. The little cabin was watertight. Not a drop got in. As fast as the thunderstorm arrived it left.

George banked up the coals in the stove and lay down on his bed. Soon he could hear the others softly snoring. He could not sleep for hours. He started thinking about his wife, kids and grandkids. He wondered how they were making out without him. Obviously they thought he was dead. He longed to be able to get a message to them to let them know he was fine.

They woke to a steady rain. There would be no traveling today. Ruth had put a pot under the eaves to collect rainwater the night before. Fred brought it in full to the brim. They lazed around the hut all day with nothing to do. Ruth longed for a good book she could curl up with. The men both took an afternoon nap. George awoke in the middle of the afternoon. The rain had slowed to a drizzle. He put on his jacket and went outside to collect the rainwater pot. As he bent to pick up the pot he heard a little rustle in the brush behind him. Keeping perfectly still he listened. He heard it again. He took a couple of careful steps toward the sound. It was a ruffed grouse. He stepped back quietly and slid back into the cabin to get his gun.

When he came back the bird was still in the same area. It saw him and froze trying to blend into the surrounding brush. George took careful aim at its head and squeezed the trigger. The grouse fell over and frantically beat its wings for a few seconds before it died. Grouse was, as always, a welcome change to the normal moose meat diet.

George went to work cleaning the grouse. Tonight they would waste little. The breast and the legs were plucked of feathers. He also added the heart, the liver and the gizzard to the pot. While George worked on the grouse, Fred brought in some dry firewood from under the tarp and built up the fire. Ruth foraged close to the cabin and was able to collect a cupful of various berries and a handful of what she thought were edible mushrooms. She showed the mushrooms to George before she cut them up for the stew.

George nodded. "Yes, those are good."

Ruth decided that the one little grouse wasn't nearly enough meat for the three of them. She got out a couple of pieces of their dried moose and cubed them up to add to the pot. They let the stew simmer for a couple of hours while they sat and talked. The rain had let up so they made plans to leave in the morning. When the dinner stew was finally ready, it was a masterpiece. They all agreed it was one of their best. A potato and an onion would have been the only thing it could be missing.

The next day was dull, but it wasn't raining. George got up early and went on a scouting mission. George came back his jeans soaked through.

"The bush is really wet," he said. "It looks like the sun might burn through the clouds. I saw a patch or two of blue sky."

They decided to wait a couple of hours before they left. While on his scouting mission, George had found a trail with a few old blazes on it.

Around mid-morning they decided to take to the trail. No one wanted to spend another day sitting around the little hut. They shouldered their packs and left the little clearing. All morning they tramped through the still wet bush trail picking fiddlehead shoots as they went. By noon the sun came out. They stopped in a clearing with a big rock outcropping to rest a bit. Taking off their packs they lay down on the warm rock and felt the sun and the rock dry their clothes. After an hour or so of dozing in the sunshine, George got up and put on his pack.

"Time to move on," he said.

George led the troupe. He had the little rifle and kept a careful watch for game. They were just talking about making camp for the night when George saw a patch of blue through the trees ahead. They hurried forward to the shore. They were surprised to find that there was an old campsite on the shore with a fire pit and the remains of a lean-to shelter.

"This was made this year," said George.

"How do you know that?" asked Fred.

"The needles are brown but have not fallen off," said George. "Also if it were made last fall the snow would have collapsed it."

Fred nodded slowly in agreement. They all automatically set about their chores. George began collecting the firewood for the night while Ruth and Fred cut boughs and began rebuilding the shelter. Fred went down to the lake to try his luck at fishing. He fished until he was called for dinner with no luck at all.

George chuckled when Fred arrived back to the fire empty handed.

"After dinner, I'll show you how to fish, my friend."

They ate their dinner and while Ruth was making her rosebud tea George and Fred went down to the lake. Fred gave the master the fishing rod while he threw out a still line. Ruth came down a while later with a cup of hot tea for each of them. By dusk George had four walleye landed. Fred was still skunked. George made a wire stringer and sunk the fish under water with rocks. He didn't want to lose his catch to some marauding bear in the night.

In the morning they had a fine feed of walleye fillets. Ruth had planned on saving some for later but the men were so hungry she just let them go to it. This would be lunch as well she decided. They set out after breakfast along the lakeshore. George was in the lead as usual. Small game was scarce today it seemed. They saw lots of moose sign but not much else.

Late in the afternoon they found an old fire pit. There was a big spruce tree with overhanging branches and a spruce bough bed under the tree. It was obvious that whoever made this fire had spent the night under the tree. They decided to do the same and set to work cutting fresh boughs.

George walked down to the lake to try his hand at fishing to see if he could add a little fresh protein to the pot. He tried every lure he had, but the fish either were elsewhere or just not biting. When he came back empty handed, Ruth cubed up a couple of slices of the dried moose meat for the dinner pot. The moose rations were getting low. If they didn't find fresh game soon, they would be out of meat in a couple of days.

THIRTY-SEVEN

Mike decided to use one of the summer's rainy days to further explore the interiors of the old vehicles scattered about the yard, to see if they contained any other treasures. His first attempt at salvage had been rather hasty. The closest vehicle was a big Oldsmobile station wagon. He crossed quickly from the cabin door to the car so as not to get too wet. He opened the door and slid in behind the wheel. The car was huge. It was probably early seventies vintage. He popped open the glove box and emptied the contents onto the passenger's seat.

The first treasure was an Ontario road map. He unfolded it and studied it for a while. There wasn't enough detail to pinpoint his exact location. But he was able to get a general overview of the area. It confirmed that the main highway number 105 was the only major road in the area. Still he thought, this labyrinth of logging roads around here must be connected to the main highway. He carefully folded the map and put it on the seat. The only other items of value in the glove box were a couple of pens and a pack of paper matches from the Voyageur Motel in Thunder Bay.

Under the seat he found a couple of empty coke bottles and a ratty old ball cap. The crest on the cap read "Northern Truck Stop Matheson." He put the hat onto the seat with the rest of his treasures and climbed into the back seat. There wasn't much to be found. In the very back of the wagon was a compartment for the spare tire. He got out of the car and opened the back window and then the tailgate. He opened the spare tire compartment and set the lid on the ground. In the compartment was the spare tire, but he also he found a pair of serviceable work gloves. The work gloves were the canvas back kind with the leather palms and fingers. The last item was a thick nylon towrope. Mike thought this might be handy. He walked around to the front passenger's door and added the towrope and gloves to the treasures on the front seat. His gaze settled on the seat. It was in pretty good condition.

"This would make a pretty good couch," he said but then realized that Yukon was off hunting. *I'll come back for you when it quits raining.*

Mike was on a roll. He ran through the pouring rain to the next vehicle. This one was a late sixties Chevrolet station wagon. It looked like it had a few rough bush miles on it. There wasn't a straight panel on the whole car. He opened the driver's door and hopped in behind the wheel. The first thing he opened was the glove compartment. Peeking out from the remains of an old mouse nest he found a half bottle of liquid insect repellent and a pack of spearmint gum.

Digging further turned up a partial box of band aids and two half used match books. On a roll now he started to feel around under the seat. The first thing he found made him yell out.

"Yes!"

A long forgotten bottle of Canadian rye whiskey—three quarters full.

Mike twisted off the cap and smelled it. It smelled like whiskey. He stuck a finger in and wetted it. It tasted like whiskey. He took a careful pull from the bottle. By God, it was whiskey!

This, decided Mike, was the best find of the day so far. He put the bottle carefully on the front seat. He went on exploring under the seat. He found a pair of stiff dirty work socks. He pulled them out and added them to the pile on the seat.

The rest of the station wagon was disappointedly empty except for the spare tire and the jack.

Mike was getting hungry, so he collected his treasures and headed back to the cabin to make himself a late breakfast of oatmeal and tea. Afterward he braved the elements again to go down to the lake for pail of water and to haul in some firewood. By this time he was soaked through to the skin. He changed into his long underwear and filled a pot of water to heat on the stove. The hat and socks got a darn good scrub in the hot water.

That night, still in his long underwear but with the stylish addition of the hat and socks, Mike got gloriously drunk. He didn't set out to get drunk. It just happened. After dinner Mike put the kettle on to boil. Once the water had boiled, he got himself a cup and poured a generous shot of the rye whiskey into it. He added a bit of sugar and filled the cup with hot water. He sat down at the table and started playing cards. Before he knew it the cup was empty. He made himself another and played a few more hands of solitaire. Soon he was humming songs. Then he was singing. By the end of the evening, he was dancing around the cabin shouting out every song he knew, wishing he had his harmonica. Yukon howled along with him.

The more the dog howled, the more Mike laughed and sang. He passed out in the chair late in the evening. He awoke in the middle of the night freezing cold and nauseated. He quickly slipped into his rubber boots and ran outside gagging. He made it just to the corner of the cabin before he lost his dinner. He stumbled back to the cabin and crawled up the stairs to bed.

Mike dragged himself out of bed sometime mid-morning. His head pounded and his throat was dry. He dressed and went downstairs. He needed water, and he needed to pee but in that order. He got a cup and dipped it into the water bucket and drained it. He filled it again and drank that one down too. Then he went outside. Mike desperately wanted to go back to bed and sleep, but he forced himself to get active. He went on a hunt for bait. He found a few worms, got his fishing rod, and went down to the dock to fish.

Yukon followed behind.

He didn't have the energy to paddle the canoe, so he simply baited the hook and dangled it over the end of the dock. His head pounded, so he lay down on the dock and closed his eyes. He slept for a good hour. When he awoke the big dog was curled up at his feet. Yukon had also had a late night. Mike finally gave up. He reeled in the line, put the rod away and went back up to the cabin to bed. When he awoke late in the afternoon, he felt a lot better. He was even hungry. He swore off drinking whiskey—which was a good thing seeing as he had emptied the bottle the night before.

The next day, Mike walked down to the dock before breakfast, fishing rod in hand. He would spend the day fishing, and collecting berries. He cast the bait out from dock a few times with no luck, so he decided to try trolling with the canoe. Within an hour, he had his first walleye and added three more in quick succession. This was enough food for the day, so he headed back to shore to fillet them. He kept the fillets and the heads and tails and gave the rest to the dog.

He got another pot for berry picking. He daubed a little of his liquid fly dope behind his ears and onto the back of his neck. He found the newly washed hat and put it on. It still had a few grease stains on the brim, but it looked good. He got the rifle down and loaded it. As a precaution, he put a few extra rounds of ammunition in his pocket. Mike had seen a lot of bear scat around some of those berry patches. He didn't want to take any chances. Calling Yukon, he headed off.

Mike and Yukon spent the morning picking berries. Yukon was good at sniffing out the berry patches. Mike just had to watch him and then race over to where he found the berries before Yukon could eat them all. They worked their way south along the lake where Mike knew there were some good blueberry patches. Yukon found a big choke cherry bush, so Mike grabbed some of those as well. They were really sour, but he thought they would make an interesting addition to stews.

By early afternoon, his pot was nearly full, so he started working back toward the cabin filling the rest of the pot as he went. He was just coming into the clearing when some movement caught his eye. He looked and saw a cow moose stepping into the clearing, with a calf right behind her.

Mike slowly set the pot of berries on the ground. Yukon had gone off on an adventure of his own so wasn't there to frighten off the game. Mike levered a shell into the chamber as quietly as he could. The sound spooked the mother and she turned back quickly towards the bush. The calf was not as fast and Mike managed to squeeze off a shot. The calf dropped but then struggled to its feet. Mike fired again. This time when it fell, it lay still. He ran down to where it lay and checked it. It was dead. Mike left the calf where it lay and took his gun and the berries up to the cabin. He dropped them off and collected up some butchering tools. This was the part of the job he hated, but at least he had a bit of experience now.

The moose was a young bull. It was this year's calf, so it wasn't very big. He went to work gutting it. Yukon had shown up after the sound of the gunshots and was at his side, patiently waiting for the castoffs.

—

Ruth woke first in the morning. She crawled out of bed and walked down to the lake. She went down the shore a little ways until she found a nice place where the rock sloped gently into the lake. She stripped down and dove in. Floating around, she dreamed of a hot bath with scented soap, shampoo and candle light.

At least I can swim, she thought.

Ruth loved being in the water, and the long winter with no way to immerse herself was hard to get through. After her swim, she dressed and made her way back up to the camp. George was up and was busy making a fire when she got back. Fred was still dozing in his bed.

"Want some tea?" she asked.

"Sure that would be good."

At the sound of their voices, Fred sat up and began putting on his boots.

"Good morning, Folks."

The other two waved in response.

They had their morning tea and started packing up their gear.

"I hope to make a lot of progress today," said George. "It's going to be a good travelling day."

They picked up the blazed trail again and started off. George was setting a pretty good pace, so they walked in silence, saving their breath. Around midday George called a halt for lunch. They ate their dried moose meat slowly, well aware of how little they had left. They had been looking for signs of game all along the trail but hadn't seen a thing.

"We'd better get going again," said George. "Still lots of daylight left."

They had been walking for about two hours when George suddenly stopped. "There's fresh moose tracks just ahead. Why don't you guys hang back here while I see if I can track it."

Ruth and Fred were just setting down their packs when a rifle shot rang out followed by a second shot a few seconds later.

Poachers, thought George but said nothing.

It could also be treaty Indians who had a right to hunt year round. The sound of the gunfire had been close but not that close.

"We had better be careful," said George. "You guys stay well behind me."

He cocked the little rifle and slid the safety on.

—

Mike began the process of gutting the moose. There was no easy way around it. He slit open the belly of the moose, rolled up his sleeves and stuck his hands and forearms into the cavity and started hauling out the guts. Once he had all the innards out onto the ground, he separated out the heart and the liver for his own use. Between the dog and the birds the rest would be soon gone. Once the messy part was over, he went down to the lake and washed up as best he could. He went up to the cabin and got the bucket and washed out the cavity of the little moose with a couple of buckets of water.

He had just finished cutting off the creature's head when the dog whined. Mike looked up expecting that the dog was looking for a handout. Yukon was staring at the edge of the clearing. Mike was amazed to see three humans walk out of the bush. Yukon charged toward them barking furiously.

THIRTY-EIGHT

"Don't move," George called back quietly to Fred and Ruth. He slipped the safety off and raised the rifle into position as a precaution. "There's a man coming this way too."

Mike ran after Yukon calling him to stop. As he got closer Mike recognized the three.

"George," he shouted. "Don't shoot! He won't hurt you."

At the sound of his name, George lowered the rifle and stared at this strange man who seemed to know him. George didn't have a clue who this fellow was. The stranger was tall and skinny with long hair and a beard.

"It's me," he said. "Mike."

George was trying to think of the Mikes he knew. It was Fred who finally recognized him and laughing, hurried forward to give him a huge bear hug.

"Hi Doc," he said. "How are you?"

Now the other two realized who this strange man was and came running forward. Ruth wrapped her arms around him.

"I'm so glad you're alive."

"Me too," said Mike with a grin.

George was next in line. He shook his hand for a long time. "Sorry I didn't recognize you, Mike," he said. "You've lost a bit of weight."

"Bush life can do that to a guy," said Mike. "You look like you've lost a bit yourself."

Mike told them about the moose he had just shot, so they dropped their packs and went over to check it over. Without hesitation the men grabbed butchering tools and went to work. While the butchering was going on, Ruth first made friends with the big dog and then walked around the yard checking it out. Yukon, who normally would have stayed close to the fresh kill, followed her around at a distance at first, slowly getting closer until he was happily walking by her side.

Ruth picked some berries at the edge of the clearing. She offered a few to the dog who took them gently. She scratched his ears. He really liked that. She found a few mushrooms and added these to her berry collection. As she wandered, she discovered a long forgotten garden. Onions had gone to seed years before and had taken over the little plot of ground. She gently pulled one out. The bulb was still quite small, but it sure tasted good. She collected enough for two onions each for tonight's meal. Carrying her version of treasure, she went to check on the butchering progress.

The boys had quartered the moose and were getting ready to carry it up to the cabin. Mike suggested storing it in the back of one of the old station wagons for the night, safe from bears. Tomorrow they could start drying it. They were going to have the moose heart for dinner tonight.

"Mind if I take over cooking, Mike?" Ruth asked.

"Please," said Mike. "That would be wonderful. Wait till you see what's in the cabin. It's almost like civilization!"

Ruth took the moose heart up to the cabin. When she opened the door, she almost dropped it in surprise. The yard was so messy she was expecting the same in the cabin. Instead she saw a gleaming, welcoming cabin complete with a wood cook stove. She lit the stove and began warming up the oven. Her grandmother had a stove exactly like this when she was growing up, so she knew how it worked.

While the oven came up to temperature, Ruth snooped through the cupboards, a big grin on her face. She found a roast pan and, after looking it over like it was a rare gem, put the meat into it. She looked through the cupboards some more and found a bit of salt and pepper for seasoning. Ruth almost felt like crying she was so happy to be there. She arranged the onions and mushrooms around the roast. There were plenty of options for side dishes. She decided on a package of instant potatoes, giggling to herself as she read the package instructions, more for the thrill of reading than because she didn't know how to make them.

The men came in after they had washed up. Mike gave them the grand tour. Ruth had already snooped everywhere but followed along, excited to share the wonder of it with Fred and George.

"It's pretty darn nice, Doc," said Fred. "But I can see you weren't expecting company. There's only one chair."

"Don't worry," said Mike. "I have a plan. I was just waiting for the right day to get around to it. This sure as hell is the right day!"

Within a half an hour they had salvaged two car seats and set them up on blocks of wood so that they were proper table height. Now things were starting to feel home like.

Ruth had a big grin on her face. "Now if only we had some pictures to hang."

They devoured the meal until there wasn't a scrap left. Ruth made a pot of tea. This was real tea, not the spruce tea they had been drinking for the last year. There was a lot of contented sighing around the dinner table. After dinner was over and the dishes were cleared, George leaned back on his car seat.

"So how come you're not dead, Mike? And where did that dog come from?"

Fred and Ruth leaned forward eagerly. There was a long silence while Mike wondered what to say.

"I *should* be dead." he said. "I would have been if I hadn't stumbled onto a trapper's cabin. I decided to stay put for the winter. Then I met Joe. It was his cabin."

"I know, Joe," George said excitedly. "Where is he? Why didn't you leave with him?"

"He's dead," said Mike, his voice breaking. This was the first time he had talked about it. "He fell through the ice when he was collecting his beaver traps. By the time I found him he was already dead. Yukon was his dog."

The others didn't say anything. Then George said, "So this isn't the cabin you found when you met Joe?"

"No, it was one of his line cabins. Joe had come through checking his traps and found me there. I don't think I would have made it if it wasn't for him. All that time being alone. When Joe came, I knew I would make it. We were going to walk out to this cabin and meet his plane ride out. It was supposed to come mid-April and pick him up. But he died before that. I tried to find the cabin on my own so I could meet the plane but couldn't. I came back to the line cabin. I had left Joe's frozen body boarded up in the woodshed. I didn't know what else to do with it. Then the cabin burnt to the ground and took the woodshed with it. Joe was cremated."

"We found that cabin," said Ruth slowly. "We wondered what had happened there. It looked like someone had sifted through the ashes, sorting things out. Things were stacked in a neat pile. We didn't see any human remains though."

"That's strange," said Mike. "I didn't do that."

"Someone must have come looking for Joe and found the cabin," said Fred. "They would have taken his remains away."

Another long silence, all four thinking of the lost rescue opportunity.

"Anyway, after it burnt down, I had to leave. I made it to a line shack and stayed there a bit until I got enough food together to try and find this place. It took a bit, but Yukon led me to it." He gave the dog's ears an affectionate scratch. "I've been here maybe a month now. Enough about me! How did you guys end up here?"

"Just lucky!" all three said at once, laughing.

"We're walking out." said Fred.

"Well, I found an Ontario road map. Maybe we can figure out where we are now."

Mike got it out and spread it on the table. There wasn't much detail, but some of the bigger lakes were marked. Fred studied the map for a long time. His years of flying over this area had taught him well. He went over to the window ledge and got the stub of a pencil.

"Do you have any paper, Doc?"

"Afraid not, but there are a couple of magazines over on the shelf."

"How about a can label, will that work?" asked Ruth.

"That would be fine," said Fred. Ruth got up took out a can of creamed corn out of the cupboard. With the blade of her Swiss army knife she slit the label off the can and brought it back to the table.

Using the road marked distances, Fred was able to determine a scale.

"Do you have some string or a thread, Doc?"

Mike handed him some string and peered over his shoulder. Laying the string out he used the pencil to mark off five mile increments. That was the best accuracy that the map could realistically provide. He used the string to check other mileage markings. Once his scale was calibrated, he began using the string to measure distances between lakes all the while trying to remember actual distances from his flying days. Fred worked away on the map for at least a half an hour while the others talked quietly around the airtight stove. Finally he spoke.

"I think I know where we are," he said. The others leaned over the map on the kitchen table. Using the pencil stub he circled one of the unnamed lakes.

"It looks like it's about thirty to forty kilometres as the crow flies to the main highway."

George spoke up. "There has to be a road from here," he said. "Otherwise they couldn't have got all those cars here. If there is a road, we can walk out in two or three days."

"It's not quite that easy," said Mike. "There's a road alright. But south it leads to a clearcut that backs onto a swamp, and to north that first missing bridge is a doozy."

"What do you mean *missing bridge?*" asked Ruth.

George said, "When the lumber companies are done in an area they pull up their big culverts and bridges to use them elsewhere. They lift them out with cranes and drop them on the back of flatbeds."

"Still the roads are the key to getting out of here," said Fred. "Granted those roads'll be all over the map, so to speak, but they eventually lead back to civilization. I think we should try it. By now, everyone in the outside world thinks we are long dead. And it looks like they know Joe is dead too. We can't possibly expect anyone to be still looking for us. Even if it takes us a month to hike out, it's better than spending another winter out here."

"I'm sure as hell not spending another winter, not when there's no good reason," George said. "We all have folks to get back to I reckon, I know I do. I mean to see my family again."

"Me too," said Ruth and Fred put his arm around her shoulder.

"Amen," said Mike.

"Right," said George. "We have the little moose that Mike just shot. We can start drying that tomorrow.

"Well," said Mike, "and I have quite a bit of dried bear meat in my cold well."

George looked over at Mike with a stunned look on his face. *Boy, I have underestimated this guy.*

They figured it to be now sometime in mid-July. It would take them a week or so to dry the moose. In the meantime they could collect as much other food as possible. They reasoned that, if they left soon, there would still be food to be found along the way to augment their diet. They all agreed to the plan. Tomorrow they would begin preparations.In ten days they would leave, weather permitting of course.

THIRTY-NINE

Ruth woke up in the morning after a good night's sleep. Mike had given them the room with the bed and had moved his sleeping bag into the other room with George. Even though the bed was small, she and Fred snuggled in under the sleeping bag. She got up in the morning and went out to the outhouse.

This thing could use a scrub she thought. This would be her afternoon chore. At least there was still some real toilet paper left. She folded up a wad and squirrelled it away in her back pocket for future emergencies. She went down to the lake for a wash before heading back up to the cabin to prepare breakfast.

George was already up and in the kitchen when she got back. He had a fire going on the woodstove with the coffee pot on the top. He was busy cutting up moose liver into a frying pan. He had added some fat so that it wouldn't burn. The smell of the liver gave Ruth an idea. She went back out and walked over to the old garden. She selected a couple of onions and brought them back up to the kitchen.

"Let's fry these with the liver."

"Great idea," said George.

The other two sleepy heads woke up to the smell of liver and onions with fresh coffee. The smell lured them out of their beds. They both went down to the old dock to wash up. When they returned, the two chefs served a gourmet meal. Ruth made a sauce out of some the blueberries and chokecherries that Mike had collected the day before. Again there were no leftovers. The poor dog had to settle for an offered moose leg bone. He carried it off into the bush—they wouldn't see him again until nightfall.

After breakfast, the men got the moose meat out of the back of the old station wagon and began the smoking process. George was elected chief butcher, while the other two kept the fire going. The racks Mike built to dry the bear meat were perfectly serviceable, so they carried them over to the fire pit.

   While George butchered the moose, Mike and Fred collected firewood and turned the strips. Ruth rendered down the berries they had collected, then packed the mush into cakes. She spread these out onto the hood of one of the old cars to dry. She took the pot and began collecting more berries and mushrooms all within sight of the drying berries. She went back several times during the day to systematically turn each and every berry cake.

   In the afternoon, Ruth boiled some water and gave the out-house a long awaited cleansing. Once the butchering of the moose was completed, George and Mike left Fred in charge of the smoke fire while they went fishing. They carried the little canoe down to the water's edge. Mike took the stern because, with his inferior bait cast rod, all he would be able to do was troll. They paddled over to the mouth of a little creek and trolled up and down twenty or thirty feet off shore in front of the creek.

   Once they hit into a school of walleye, George got six and Mike got five all within ten minutes. Then the fish were gone. Satisfied with their catch, they paddled back to the dock. With both men filleting they made short work of the job. They decided to add the fillets to the smoke rack. Ruth cut some choice pieces of flesh from the remaining carcasses to make a fish soup for dinner. The dog got the rest.

Their routine for the rest of the week was pretty much the same. They spent the daylight hours collecting and drying food. They ate three hearty meals a day to build themselves up for the trip.

Ruth and Yukon spent their days in the nearby woods collecting berries, dandelions and mushrooms. Yukon was quite smitten with Ruth. He followed her everywhere. If she sat down to work on a project, he would lay his big snout on her foot and go to sleep. That way if she moved he would know.

Mike and George went fishing every morning and again in the evening. They were learning the lake and now had several productive fishing holes. Fred tended the smoke fires while the other men were fishing. Once they were back, he would hand over those duties. He would take the little rifle and hunt small game to augment their diet. Most of what Fred shot went into the daily food pot. Some days he would combine things and accompany Ruth on her berry picking expeditions. With both the gun and the dog along, they felt more comfortable expanding their horizons into new territory. On one such day, Fred left Ruth in Yukon's care in the middle of a large berry patch while he pushed on further hunting game.

Ruth was engrossed in her chore when suddenly Yukon rose and charged into the brush barking frantically. A huge black bear came flying out of the brush at him snarling and swiping at the dog with his claws. This was this bear's berry patch, and he was going to defend it. Ruth backed up slowly away from the fight until she was safely behind a big spruce tree and only then peeked out to see what would happen next.

Yukon circled carefully. He was fully aware of his opponent's deadly claws. The bear charged again but Yukon was much too fast for him. He faked a move, then as the bear went by, bit it hard low on one of its back legs. The bear reeled around but the dog was already gone. Yukon worked the big bruin over for almost half an hour before it broke off, leaped into a tree and climbed out of the dog's reach. Now Yukon had him at his mercy. He lay down at the base of the tree waiting. Fred arrived back to the clearing an hour or so later. He didn't see Ruth who still thought it wise not to leave the security of the tree. He saw Yukon and followed the dog's gaze up the tree until he saw the bear.

"Ruth?"

"Over here," called Ruth softly.

The sound of human voices sent the bear scrambling even further up the tree. The poplar swayed under his weight, but he hung on desperately. Fred didn't want to aggravate the situation by shooting at it with the little Henry rifle. He walked over to where Ruth was.

"Let's slowly make for the edge of the bush over there," he said. "Then you call the dog off."

At first the dog ignored her calls. This game was quite fun if you were winning. Finally when her tone changed, he relinquished his control of the bear and headed to the authority of his new master. Ruth dropped to one knee and gave the dog a big hug.

"Oh, you're such a brave big boy."

Ruth had pretty much been skunked for the day in the berry picking business, but Fred had shot two grouse, a rabbit and a squirrel. That night they feasted on a medley of meats for dinner with a side of rice. Ruth made sure that Yukon received a secret portion as a reward for his bravery.

The next day Ruth took a break from her berry picking chores. The plan was to leave the next day, so she wanted to make sure all the food preparations were in order. She laid out the packaged goods first in order to make a good mental inventory of what they had.

One box of salt, half a bag of sugar, forty tea bags, twenty pounds of flour, five pounds of white beans, five pounds of oatmeal, three pounds of rice, four packages of onion soup mix, a can of tomatoes, a can of chilli, a can of cream corn, and a can of potatoes.

Not bad, she thought. *Not bad at all.*

She went out to the garden and pulled all of the onions. She had a total of twenty-seven of various sizes. They had several large bags of dried berries, about a hundred pounds of dried moose meat twenty pounds or so of dried bear meat, forty dried fish fillets. A big bag of dried and chopped mushrooms and another of cattail root. There was also about twenty pounds of dog food left.

Ruth had taken the remains of Mike's blanket poncho and sewn it into a pack for him. She found a couple of old towels and made a couple of small packs for Yukon, one for each side. They looked like saddlebags. They had two straps that went below his belly. She filled the bags with dog food and called the dog in for a test fit. At first he resisted having the packs on him until he turned and sniffed them. Once he smelled his own dog food, he seemed all right.

They spent the rest of the day making preparations to leave. They would take both rifles, but had decided the big shotgun was redundant so they would leave that behind. Mike got out the rest of the tarp and laid it out in the yard. The piece he had cut off of it previously would be sufficient for a shelter roof. He cut the remaining piece into four to wrap their sleeping bags and blankets in.

They decided one axe was enough, so George spent an hour on it making sure it was sharp. While he was at it, he put an edge on everyone's knives. Fred drained some oil from one of the cars. He collected up the mukluks and rubbed motor oil into the leather to help waterproof them. Mike made a decision to take his winter boots along. He could always throw them out. He added them to the pile. He had found enough work gloves around the place to make up four pairs of gloves with one odd glove left over. Everyone was issued a pair. All day the pile by the door grew. Rope, matches, a pot, cups and spoons were added. Mike added the combination underwear to his pile.

They were out of toilet paper, so they threw the two magazines in with their gear. Once dinner was over and the dishes were washed, they split up the load and began packing their packs in preparation for the trip ahead. The men took some of Ruth's share and split it between them.

PART 7

FALL

FORTY

They were up at first light. Ruth made a fire and boiled water for tea. She laid out some dried berries and a couple of strips of dried moose meat for each of them. This would have to do until dinner. They each had a full water bottle with them. After a quick cup of tea, they hoisted their packs and headed off down the trail. Mike, who knew this part of the route, carried the big rifle and led the way. George followed him carrying the small game gun. Ruth was next, followed by her faithful companion Yukon. Fred brought up the rear carrying the axe.

At midday they stopped for a rest, mainly to give their backs a rest from their heavy packs. They ate their trail rations washed down with swigs of water from the water bottle. After lunch they resumed their journey. They tramped for another four hours or so, calling a halt for a few minutes every hour or to relieve their shoulders of the heavy packs. Late in the afternoon, they arrived at the missing bridge Mike had told them about. They dropped their packs and walked back and forth on the bank assessing the situation. Although the gap was narrow the stream looked fast and deep.

"Too dangerous," said George.

The others quickly agreed. They had not all struggled so long and so hard to take any crazy life threatening risks. Since Mike had already explored upstream from there, they hoisted up their packs and headed downstream. They hiked downstream for another hour still not finding a safe place to cross. George called a halt and suggested they make camp. With their shoulders aching from the heavy packs, they were more than happy to quit for the day. They went to work like beavers building a shelter, collecting firewood and water.

Ruth got a fire going and set to work preparing the evening meal. Tonight they were having a stew based around a can of potatoes. She wanted to use up the canned food first as it was heavy. She chopped some moose meat and added two chopped onions, some dried mushrooms and a handful of dried berries. While the stew simmered, Mike and George took one of the rifles and hiked further down the river. They walked for over a half an hour, until they came to a big spruce tree on the bank of the stream. An idea hit both of them at the same time.

"We could chop that tree down and drop it across the river," said George. "I could go across first with the axe and trim off the branches as I go. The rest of you could crawl over behind me."

Mike liked the idea. They hurried back to tell the others. They met up with Fred on the trail back. He had been collecting more firewood. George told him of the plan. Suddenly Mike's eyes darkened.

"No, hang on, that won't work," he said. "The dog won't go across that log, and he is way too big to carry."

"Leave him behind," said George. "He eats too much anyway."

Mike started to boil. Fred quickly diffused the situation.

"Come on, you guys," he said taking a step between the other two. "Let's talk about this over dinner. I'm starving."

Mike cooled off on the walk back.

After dinner George again proposed the plan.

"The problem is the dog," said Mike. "He won't walk across that log even if you had a pound of bacon waiting for him on the other side."

"He can swim across," said George.

"He can't swim worth a darn," replied Mike. "I threw him off the shore once to give him a bath and he almost drowned. He's got way too much hair."

Now Ruth jumped into the fight.

"I will not leave that sweet dog behind to starve to death," she said her voice rising. George had never seen Ruth angry before, so he didn't dare argue back. Her face was red with rage.

Now it was Mike's turn to be the diplomat.

"How about this," he said. "George and I will cross on the log. Fred you take Ruth and the dog back to the cabin. When we get out we will send a plane in to get you."

It all made sense. Ruth made a pot of tea and they sat around the fire discussing the new plan.

George proposed that he and Mike travel light. They would take the little rifle so that they could shoot small game along the way. To be safe they thought they should take a week's rations of the food. They opened their packs and redistributed the gear. Ruth counted out fifty pieces of the dried moose, and ten pieces of bear meat. That would be plenty agreed the men. That would give each man three slices a day for a week with a few to spare. They took a few of the fish fillets and some of the berries patties. Berry picking would slow them down too much. George said no to the mushrooms and cattail root, for he could find these easy enough.

She cleaned out the potato can and filled it with flour. Mike cut a piece of tarp and wired it over the top of the can. They took ten of the tea bags and a bit of sugar also tied up in a bit of tarp. Ruth wrapped up some salt for them and added it to their gear. They wrapped some rice up in a piece of tarp and tied it off with wire as well. They put the can of chilli, the can of cream corn, and two packs of onion soup mix onto the pile. Mike counted out seven onions and added them to the food.

At that point George called a halt to the food collection. He wanted them to travel as light as they could. They took the big tarp and one smaller one, the axe, the big compass, the map and some matches. They would take the pot and their personal eating utensils and cups. Each man had his knife. They added a coil of rope and a few pieces of snare wire to the pile of gear. George had his fishing rod and a little plastic tackle box with the basics in it.

In the morning, they had a quick breakfast of dried moose meat and berries. Ruth and Fred wanted to make sure their friends got across the river safely but they didn't want to carry their heavy packs with them, so they hauled the packs up on a large overhanging branch with a rope and tied the rope off so that the packs were out of reach of any bear that happened along. They hiked down along the edge of the stream until they came to the big tree. The men took turns chopping at the tree. George directed the axe blows, as neither Fred nor Mike had ever attempted to fall anything of this size before. George started by cutting a large notch out of the tree in the direction he wanted it to fall. He handed the axe to Fred who chopped away at the backside under George's direction until his arms tired, then he handed the axe to Mike. Mike chopped until the tree wavered. George ordered them all to stand clear while he personally delivered the final blows. The tree landed with a mighty crash exactly where he had planned it to land.

A good third of the tree had landed on the opposite bank but it was the skinny third. George was cautious.

"Stay here until I get right over on the other side," he said. "I don't want too much weight on this thing at once. Mike nodded in agreement. George dismantled the little survival rifle. The rifle was built to easily come apart without any tools. A nut held the barrel in place. Once this was loosened the barrel came off and was ready to be stowed. The breech was again locked into place by a hand-tightened key. Once the butt plate was removed, there was a spot for the barrel, the breach and a spare clip inside the plastic handle. With the butt plate reinstalled the rifle was now a compact little package. The manufacturer claimed that in this configuration it would even float. He put the rifle into his pack.

"That reminds me, Fred, I left that pistol of mine at the cabin. Can you bring it out for me when you come on the plane?"

"You bet," replied Fred.

George gave Fred a hearty handshake then went over to give a big bear hug to Ruth.

"See you soon," he said.

With that he shouldered his pack and picked up the axe. He worked his way slowly across the log, chopping off branches as he went. The further across the log he went, the easier the job became, as the branches were getting thinner. It was very uncomfortable work but within the hour he was on the far bank.

Now it was Mike's turn to cross the makeshift bridge. He didn't like heights, and the twenty feet to the water looked like a hundred once he was out on the log. He concentrated on looking straight ahead and not down as he inched his way across. He made it in less than fifteen minutes, but it seemed like a full hour to him. With a wave, both parties set back downstream each on opposite banks. Occasionally they caught sight of each other as they traveled.

FORTY-ONE

Ruth and Fred retrieved their packs. They were really heavy now as they had all the gear that George and Mike didn't want. They made frequent stops to rest. There was no sense rushing, for they wouldn't make it back to the cabin that night anyway. Late in the afternoon, they made camp, and in the morning they ate a bit of the rations before hitting the trail. Again they paced themselves taking frequent breaks. They saw several grouse along the way, but Fred did not want to waste the big gun's ammunition on them. They arrived back at the cabin mid-afternoon, and Fred collected firewood while Ruth unpacked the gear and put it all away.

After dinner, they couldn't help but talk about the future. It seemed now only a matter of time before they were rescued, and suddenly the prospect of returning to their lives made them both a little breathless. That and the time alone together lent the evening a heady air of intimacy.

"Y'know Ruth, when we get back there will be a lot of people who are going to be very happy to see us, and some of them will have been torn apart over the last year and a half. It's going to be a crazy time."

"Oh sure," she said. "I am expecting a lot of tears. I can't even imagine how my parents have held up."

It was a sobering thought, and she looked a little sad. Yukon, as if sensing this, padded up and put his head in her lap.

"The world will have moved on without us," Fred said. "It's hard to predict what we're going to come back to."

"That's true."

"I'm not sure what is going to lie ahead for me, I really don't," he said. "But there is one thing I *do* know."

"What's that, Fred?"

He reached into his pocket and produced a silvery ring.

"Fred what—"

"I know that, whatever I face, I want to do it with you, as my wife," he said. "If you'll have me."

She gave him a stunned look that only slowly gave way to a broad sweet smile.

"Yes," she said. "I'll have you. Of course, I will."

"Give me your hand," he said. "God, I hope this fits."

He slipped the ring on her finger and leaned in to kiss her. When she threw her arm around Fred, Yukon made a little snort and then stood up and walked off.

When she came up for air she held the ring up in the dim light of the cabin.

"I've never seen this before. Where'd—"

"I made it," he said. "From a toonie. Tapping out the edges with rocks whenever I had time alone. The core popped out on its own after a while. I was only able to finish it properly when we first got here though because there was a chainsaw file in the shed, and I used that to finish out the inside. I hope it's not too rough."

"I love you," she said, amazed. "It's perfect. But I don't know when you found the time."

"I had plenty of time while my leg was healing up. You three were scurrying around a lot leaving me to hold down the fort. I did most of the rough work before the Doc took off."

Ruth was stunned.

"You mean you've been waiting to ask me for over a year now?"

"No," he said. "Not exactly, but I knew I might want to ask you before all was said and done. And I knew *that* almost right away."

"Kiss me again."

Fred did.

That night they made love for the first time. They didn't intentionally plan to make love. It was just that they had the place to themselves and well, one thing just led to another. Later in the afterglow of events they both agreed that they would wait until they were back in civilization before making love again. Ruth figured that they were probably safe that one time but didn't want to push their luck. Kids she wanted—and Fred was glad to hear it.

"...but unless you want to be the one the help deliver them, maybe we should be a hundred percent sure we can have them in a hospital."

"Agreed," said Fred.

Fred walked around the place with a spring in his step all the next day. Ruth had a warm fuzzy feeling herself. She couldn't help cuddling up to him whenever he was near. They talked about the situation and decided to be really careful until rescue was sure.

———

The day they crossed the fallen tree, Mike and George had walked back upstream until they found the logging road again. They rested for a few minutes and chewed a slice of the dried moose each for lunch. During their break, George reassembled the gun. They shouldered their packs and headed due east down the old logging road. Sometime in the mid-afternoon, Mike caught sight of a movement at the edge of the road. There were three grouse in a spruce tree. He whistled at George and silently pointed them out. George loaded a shell into the rifle and took careful aim. One fell flapping to the ground, a second one flew off but the third tried to play the invisible game. George bagged him as well. They cleaned the birds saving only the breasts.

They figured it was August now, but it felt colder than it should be for the time of year. The days were nice, but as soon as the sun went down it was darn chilly. Mike was wearing everything he owned which wasn't much. He had his old ratty underwear bottoms plus the combination wool underwear, a tee shirt, his housecoat bomber jacket and the coveralls. He wore two pairs of socks, mainly because his rubber boots were so big. He also had his ball cap and his work gloves. His felt pack boots hung from his pack. Tomorrow, he decided he would wear the felt packs. The rubber boots were giving him a blister, and his feet were almost always cold first thing in the morning.

George had on his long underwear bottoms, work pants, a tee shirt, a work shirt, his well-worn sweater, his homemade down vest and his wool bush jacket. He was wearing his mukluks. He had one pair of socks that he was wearing and a spare pair of almost worn out ones in his pack. He also had an old ball cap he had found in the woodshed and a pair of work gloves.

In late afternoon they decided to make camp. They worked quickly and soon had the frame for a shelter set up. They pulled the tarp over the frame and weighed it down with a few evergreen boughs. While George made dinner, Mike cut boughs for their beds. After dinner they made a pot of tea and built up the fire. It was cold. Mike got his felt lined boots out and tried them on. They were big but they were warm. He was going to just leave the rubber cut off boots behind, but George tried one on over his mukluk and it seemed to fit perfectly. He pulled the other one on. This would save the soles he thought. The next day he would try walking on them for a while.

They awoke to a thick layer of frost covering everything. Groaning, Mike got out of bed and pulled on his coveralls. He made a fire and put a pot of water on to boil for tea. He used the last of the water from their water bottles. They would have to find a stream today to refill them. He got out the meat rations and took two pieces for each of them from the bag, and put the rest back in the pack. They drank the tea and chewed on the meat in silence. They each saved a piece for lunch. Finally George spoke.

"Time to go."

They shouldered their packs and continued their journey.

George liked the new rubber boot addition for a while, and then his feet started to hurt where blisters were forming. He took off the rubber boots in disgust and threw them into the ditch at the side of the road. Mike had a little package of band-aids that he offered to George. He patched up his feet and hobbled painfully on for the rest of the day. Around mid-morning they came to a big stream where another bridge had been taken out. They assessed the situation and decided that again the river was two deep to cross. Mike climbed down the bank and filled both their water bottles. They decided to follow the river south to see if they could find a place that was safe to cross. All afternoon they followed the river without a hope of crossing it. They finally stopped to make camp.

In the morning they made tea and had a piece of dried fish each for breakfast before setting out. They followed the river until they reached a big swamp. They had no choice but to head west to try to find a way around it. The swamp was huge. They skirted it all day. Finally they decided to make camp for the night. They found some high ground and built a shelter for the night. While Mike made dinner, George scouted the area. He found a little hill and climbed it so he could get the lay of the land. It was not good news he had to report. The swamp covered the land to the south as far as he could see. He could see a big lake about five miles south of here. Everything else was a swamp wasteland.

After dinner they made tea with that morning's tea bag. They sat around the fire discussing the situation. Finally they decided they would hike back to the road and try the north route. They retraced their steps the next day back to where they had camped the night before. Setting up camp was a simple matter of stretching the tarp across the existing frame. The bedding limbs were still quite fine.

The next morning after tea and the usual ration of dried moose meat, they headed north again along the river. They paused for a few minutes when they reached the road for a quick lunch. They had only traveled for a little more than a half of mile when Mike stepped between two logs and fell headlong, twisting his ankle in the process. He tried to stand up but his right ankle was on fire. He swore loudly and sat back down quickly.

George turned and ran back when he heard Mike curse.

"What happened?" he asked.

"I wrecked my ankle," said Mike.

"Let me see."

"Goddammit, what a jackass move. I can't believe—"

"Hell you didn't mean to do it. Cut yourself some slack."

George carefully removed Mike's boot and slid off the sock. He pushed and prodded the ankle for a couple of minutes. Mike flinched in pain but said nothing. He looked both grieved and terrified.

"I think it may be just a bad sprain," George said. "You won't be going anywhere for at least a couple of days."

He helped Mike over to sit under a big spruce tree. He took the smaller tarp off his sleeping bag and spread it out for Mike to sit on.

FORTY-TWO

A week had gone by, and still there was no sign of rescue. Ruth and Fred started to worry.

"We shouldn't have split up," said Ruth. "George didn't say so, but I could tell he thought we were nuts to stay behind."

"Well, he was certainly more..." Fred struggled for the right word. "Let's say *pragmatic* when it came to Yukon, it's true."

Yukon, upon hearing his name, looked up at them as though trying to piece together what they were saying. Ruth reached down and scratched the ruff of his neck.

"I just couldn't have lived with myself if we'd abandoned him. But now we don't know what's happened to them. Dammit, Fred, I just want to get on with our lives."

"I know, Ruth," he said. "We have to have some faith. George is very capable, and God knows there's more to Doc than meets the eye."

Ruth's fears and self-recriminations were never far from her these days.

Fred had taken the shotgun out from under the bunk and had begun hunting small game to stretch out their food supply. He also set a still line set off the end of the dock in hope of catching some of the little perch that liked to use the dock for shade and protection during the day. Ruth checked the lines several times per day. She quite often was rewarded with a fish.

Days went by. Fall was in the air. Fred decided he should get busy and put up some firewood just in case. He went to the shed to get the chainsaw. He opened the gas can that was sitting beside the saw. He sniffed it, and it smelled relatively fresh, so he filled the saw's fuel tank. He dripped some into the saw's air breather. The choke set on full closed, he pulled the saw over with the pull start. On about the tenth pull it fired, then started. Yukon barked and came running from the cabin to see what all the ruckus was about, then he went back to find Ruth.

Fred warmed it up for a while before he tried a cut into one of the logs. The chain was really dull, he decided. He shut the engine down and went over to the shed for the rattail file he'd used to finish Ruth's ring.An hour later, he was satisfied with his attempts. The chain was about as sharp as he could make it with his skill level. Now he needed chain lubrication oil. He found a can and crawled under one of the old cars with a wrench and opened the drain to the oil pan. He filled the can and replaced the oil plug. He crawled back out from under the car and filled the chain lubrication compartment of the saw. Now he was ready to cut wood.

All day he worked cutting firewood, mostly the easy deadfall. He wasn't too selective. Whatever was easiest to find, he cut. Whether it was spruce, pine, poplar or birch if it was down and dry, he bucked it up. Ruth came out to help. While he cut, she carried. By dinnertime, they were out of fuel for the saw but they had a sizeable pile of wood stacked by the woodshed ready to be split.

"Tomorrow," he said. "I am going to start hunting for moose."

Ruth nodded her head in agreement. It had now been over two weeks since they last saw George and Mike. To help allay her nerves, she pulled their supplies out of the cupboards and laid them out on the table so that she could get a sense for what they had to work with.

There were fifteen pounds of dog food, five pounds of flour, ten tea bags, two cups of rice, two cups of white sugar, a cup of oatmeal, half a box of salt, two cups of dried berries, and three small onions.

Plus, she knew that they had quite a bit of the moose and bear left over. Ruth felt they could survive for quite a while, but she was worried about not having enough berries or greens to keep them healthy. If help didn't arrive soon, they would have to collect food to survive yet another winter, and because the berry season was over and the pickings would be slim.

Fred was up at dawn and off hunting. He had made a rope sling for the shotgun and had it hung over his back. He carried the big lever action rifle at the ready in his arms. The shotgun was for small game and the rifle was for big game.

Ruth spent the morning in the nearby woods collecting twigs and bark in the duffle bag. She filled the bag several times making trips back to stow the fuel into the woodshed to be used for future kindling. In the afternoon she got the axe and began splitting firewood. She wasn't as good as Fred at this, and she knew if he were here he would have taken over the chore. Still, in a couple of hours, she had quite a sizeable pile of firewood split and stacked in the woodshed. Yukon followed her around all day while she worked.

Ruth and Fred both agreed that they would not count on a sure rescue. They would use these last warm days of Indian summer collecting winter provisions. The thought of spending the winter here alone didn't scare either of them. They were a lot better prepared than they had been for last winter. They were more concerned for George and Mike. The fact that a rescue plane had not arrived could only mean one thing. George and Mike were still out there in the bush.

Fred came home late one afternoon having shot four ruffed grouse. They cleaned them all. They saved the breasts for another day. Ruth used the legs, gizzards and organs as the base for the night's meal. She added a bit of salt, a few berries, and a bit of rice to the mix. It seemed a bit thin, so she stirred in two spoonfuls of flour. She had been scouring the woods while picking up kindling, collecting all the berries and edible greens she could find.

After dinner they made a pot of spruce tea, choosing to save the real tea for later. They treated themselves by adding a pinch of sugar to the brew. Fred told Ruth how he had come across some fresh moose tracks near the swamp at the end of the lake and how tomorrow he planned to go back there at first light to see if he could get a shot at one.

———

That first day, while Mike rested his ankle, George went looking for worms or grubs. He wanted to see if that river had any trout in it. He found a couple of small worms under a rock and went down to try his luck. By mid-afternoon, he had four trout. Mike had sat under the tree, in pain but patiently waiting for George to return. When he did come back, George checked Mike's ankle. It had swollen to twice its normal size and was extremely tender to the touch. They decided to camp right where they were for the night. George got busy and built a little shelter for them and laid out their sleeping bags. He built a fire then let it die down. He then cooked the trout slowly over the coals. They had one fish each for dinner and kept the other two in reserve for the next day.

When darkness came Mike hobbled over from the fire and crawled into his sleeping bag. George was already curled up and snoring in his. Because of his throbbing ankle, sleep eluded Mike until the wee hours of the morning. When he awoke, George was already up and had a fire going. Mike pulled on his coveralls and painfully tried to put on his boots. He couldn't get a boot onto his injured foot so he was forced to hobbled out to pee with one boot on and a socked foot on the other. Afterwards when he made his way back over to the fire, George handed him a steaming cup of spruce tea. George then warmed one of the fish over the fire and they shared it for breakfast. The other one he split with Mike for later.

"I think I'm gonna go on a scouting mission today. See what I can see. Since you can't travel, I'm going to leave you here with the gear."

Beside the half share of fish, George took the rifle and a box of shells as well as a package of paper matches. He took Mike's smaller pack and wrapped his water bottle in the small blue tarp. He counted out four strips of moose meat and one of the dried fish fillets and added those to the pack as well.

"If I'm not back tonight, don't panic. I would like to find a place to cross this damn river."

Mike gave his friend a steady look.

"Don't worry about me," he said. "I can look after myself. You just be careful out there."

George grinned and picked up the rifle. "See you later," he said. "Sit tight."

FORTY-THREE

George followed the river all morning with no luck finding a way across. He stopped mid-afternoon to eat the rest of the fish, washing it down with a couple of swigs of water. The ground was getting swampy now. He headed what he thought must be west until he came to a bit of dry ground and then turned north again. He came across a little hill, so he climbed up to get the lay of the land. To the east he could make out the river again. It looked like it opened up into a small lake. George guessed it was probably a beaver pond. He pushed on trying to find a way through. When he was abreast of the pond, he headed east struggling through the brush. Finally he came out on the bank of the thing. The sun was setting so he knew he wouldn't make it back to Mike's camp tonight. He built a little lean-to using his knife to hack the branches off. He collected as much wood as possible for the fire. Once the fire was going, George got out his water bottle and a strip of the moose meat. He warmed the meat over the fire and had his dinner.

With the darkness came the cold. George was no stranger to being exposed to the elements. He wrapped the tarp around his shoulders and squatted on the boughs in the shelter. The fire reflected some heat into the little lean-to. As long as the fire burned, he was warm. George dozed all night waking every once in a while to feed the fire. By dawn he had run out of firewood and the fire was now just hot coals. George got up and danced around trying to get the circulation back into his legs and arms. He went into the bush and found some more wood and built the fire back up. He took a piece of dried moose meat and ate it for breakfast. He drank down the last of his fresh water.

He packed up his gear and headed north again. Around noon he came upon a little spring bubbling out of the ground. He rinsed out his water bottle as well as he could in the little pool below the spring before he refilled it. He chewed down some of his moose rations before he moved on. He was near the end of the pond now. He found where the river left it and headed north. It was still too deep to wade, but George found a spot that was only maybe ten feet across. An idea came to him. They could throw their gear across here, then swim the scant few feet. It might be difficult for Mike to climb the steep bank, but if necessary, he could go first and throw him down a rope and help pull him up the bank.

George turned and retraced his steps. He would have to hustle if he wanted to get back to his camp by dark. George arrived back at his little camp by the shore of the beaver pond late in the afternoon. He had shot a little red squirrel on the way, so that would be dinner for tonight. He collected up the night's firewood. Once he had a fire going, he went about cleaning and skinning the squirrel. He roasted it slowly over the coals skewered onto a green stick. There wasn't much meat on this thing. George was tempted to eat his last piece of dried moose as well. He decided to forgo that idea and filled up on water from his water bottle instead. He spent another cold night with only his campfire to keep him warm. In the morning, he ate the last of his moose meat rations and headed back south to find Mike.

—

After George left, Mike hobbled around the camp for the rest of the morning feeling sorry for himself. Around noon he felt hungry, so he ate the half of fish George had left for him that morning. His ankle felt a little better, and he was able to put a tiny bit of weight on it. He struggled to put a boot on it, but when he finally did he was able to limp around the immediate area in the afternoon collecting what firewood he could. At dark George wasn't back, but Mike didn't worry. There weren't many men savvier in the bush than George. He went off to the shelter and crawled into his sleeping bag. It took a couple of minutes to find a comfortable position for his ankle. Soon he was fast asleep.

The sun was well up when he finally awoke. He got up and painfully pulled on a boot over he still swollen ankle. He then slowly hobbled down to the river for water. His ankle was getting stronger all the time. He could put some weight on it now but it still caused him to limp. George didn't arrive back that day either.

Now Mike was a bit concerned.

He'll be all right.

Mike was getting sick of moose ration. There just wasn't enough to fill him up. After his evening meal of weak tea and moose, he got George's fishing rod and tackle box and went down to the river to try to catch some fish. He caught three little trout within an hour. He cleaned them and roasted them over the fire. He saved two for the next day and devoured one then and there.

Mike got up the next morning and tested his ankle. It was quite strong now. He decided to give George until noon before he went looking for him. At noon he packed up the camp. He stuffed everything into the duffle bag except the sleeping bags and the axe. He rolled the sleeping bags up and tied them with cord. One he tied onto the top of the pack. The other he decided he would carry under his arm. He picked up the axe with his other hand and headed north along the river.

The two men met late in the afternoon by the riverbank. They talked for a bit then decided to make camp there for the night. After dinner, they made a pot of tea, and George outlined his plan. Obviously Mike was well enough to travel.

They left at sun up. Mike still had a bit of a limp, so the going was slower than when George was traveling alone. In addition, they had their gear to pack. By late afternoon they had only made as far as George's beaver pond camp. Since the shelter was already built, George left Mike in charge of collecting firewood while he went hunting. Mike wished him well. He relished anything but dried moose meat at this point.

George was back in less than an hour. He had bagged a snowshoe hare. He cleaned and skinned it. He made a spit out of green wood and began the slow process of roasting it over the coals. Mike used the last of the flour to make a couple of twisty breads as he called them. Bread dough wrapped around green sticks and roasted over the fire was what they really were.

It was feast or famine out here. Chicken one day and feathers the next. After their big meal the night before, they awoke to dried moose meat rations again. They packed up camp and headed north again towards where the river narrowed. They arrived at the spot late in the morning. George took the survival rifle apart again. This time he wrapped it in his sleeping bag. He threw the sleeping bag over to the opposite bag. Then he threw Mike's sleeping bag over. Next went the axe and his pack. They stripped down to their underwear and stuffed their clothes into Mike's pack. Mike threw the pack over to the other shore. George waded in first. The water was over his head but he was across in just a few strokes. "How is it?" asked Mike. "Actually it's not that bad," said George as he hauled himself out. Mike slid in. He spent an extra couple of minutes rinsing out his hair before he climbed out.

George hustled around getting wood for a fire. As soon as he dropped off the first batch of kindling, Mike went to work building it. He stripped out of his long john bottoms and pulled on his combination long johns. He was warm almost immediately. Once the blaze was going they hung their respective underwear near so they would dry. They decided they might as well make camp here. George took the rifle and went off to see if he could find anything for dinner while Mike built a shelter.

Mike put a pot of water on the fire late in the afternoon to boil. He had found a few cattails and had collected their roots. He put them into the pot to simmer adding a pinch of salt. George came back empty handed, so Mike chopped up three pieces of moose meat and an onion and added them to the pot.

They awoke the following day to the steady drum of rain on the tarp roof. There would be no traveling today. Worse there would be no hunting. It rained steady all day. Finally, late in the afternoon, it stopped. Mike and George were able to secure enough dry wood to get a fire going. It took two more days of bushwhacking before they arrived back at the road. They had only managed to shoot one grouse along the way to augment the moose diet. They were, for the most part, out of food.

They left in the morning after a quick cup of tea. Each man took a side of the road and walked slowly looking for game. They walked slowly and quietly for about an hour. Mike heard a rustle in the leaves on his side of the road. He whistled softly at George who came quietly back. They listened for a bit. There was the distinctive clucking of a nervous grouse. George stepped quietly off the road into the brush. He flushed up three of them. One flew for quite a ways while the other two just flew up out of reach into nearby trees. It was child's play for George to pick them off. They stopped right there for brunch. While George cleaned and plucked the birds, Mike got a fire going. They roasted the breasts over the fire. The legs, and organs they saved for that evening's soup pot.

They packed back up after lunch and carried on down the road, searching for food as they went. Late in the afternoon, they came to another breach in the roadway. This one was where forestry had taken out a large culvert. The creek was fast but it was only a few inches deep. It was a simple matter to get across. They decided to make camp here for the night, as the creek was a good source of fresh water. George set up camp while Mike got a fire going and began preparing the evening meal. They were convinced they would hit the highway tomorrow. So after dinner they celebrated with a pot of tea.

In the morning they made tea with the previous night's tea bag. Mike filled their water bottles and they hit the road on empty stomachs. The day promised to be warm and sunny.

"It's Indian summer," joked George.

Again they hunted for food but found nothing but a few dried-up berries. They stopped at midday to boil some water for spruce tea. At least it made them feel better. After the tea they carried on until they came to yet another bridge outage. This one was too deep to cross so they decided to follow it north looking for a better place to cross. As usual the creek led into a swampy area. They stayed on dry ground trying to keep the creek in sight. Finally it opened into a beaver pond. There was a dam at the far end so they headed down that way to see if it was possible to cross on it. It was a big substantial dam so crossing was no problem. They got to the other side and Mike started heading south.

"Hold on," said George. "Let's just take our stuff up on that higher ground. I've got an idea."

He ditched his pack and got Mike to stay down out of sight.

George again used his old trick. He took the axe and went back down to the dam. He chopped and pulled at a spot in the middle of the dam until he had caused a breach in it. Water was gushing out of the hole. Now he simply loaded the gun and hid himself on shore and waited. He didn't have to wait long. Within ten minutes a couple of ripples appeared on the surface of the water. Two heads appeared. George waited until one of them cautiously pulled himself right up onto the dam before he fired. The big beaver dropped dead. Its mate slapped its tail in alarm and disappeared under the water.

George motioned to Mike who walked quickly down the hill to help. George handed Mike the rifle and the axe to carry while he went out onto the dam to retrieve the dead beaver. George picked up the beaver and hefted it. Forty pounds he guessed. He carried it over to the edge of the water to begin gutting and skinning it. Mike went up the hill to where the gear was stashed and began building the night's shelter.

George had the beaver skinned out and was cutting meat into strips when Mike arrived back down. At George's request, he started collecting wood for a drying rack. That night they dined on the beaver tail. It was very rich and fatty, but that was what both of their bodies craved at that point. They dried the meat until dark over the fire then put it all into Mike's pack and hoisted it up on a rope suspending it out of reach of any bear that happened to chance by.

In the morning they lowered the meat and spread it out onto the smoke racks and resumed the drying process. They decided they would remain where they were for a day and work on preserving the meat. George left Mike in charge of the fires and went foraging for other food. He shot a mallard duck that made the mistake of landing on the pond. He waited until the duck swam close to shore before he fired. He was able to get a pole and drag it the rest of the way to shore, so he didn't have to get wet. He took it back to camp, and Mike volunteered to clean it and ready it for dinner. George found a few cattails for the pot. He also found some wild hazelnuts still hanging in their pods on top of the leafless bushes. The nuts would make good trail food.

They roasted the duck on a spit over the coals of the smoke fire. When it was golden brown, George removed it from the fire, and they ate all the meat they could stuff into themselves. The bones were thrown into the pot with the cattails and the ducks organs and a few dried berries that George produced from his jacket pocket. This would be a breakfast soup for tomorrow, so they put it back beside the fire to simmer.

In the morning, they warmed up their soup and drank down every drop of the nutritious broth. They packed up the camp after breakfast and started heading back south towards the logging road. They reached the logging road by mid-afternoon. They made a quick stop while they filled their water bottles from the river and ate some smoked beaver before heading down the road. They walked until sundown and made a quick camp. The next day they headed out again, eager to keep going. By mid-morning they came upon a new dilemma.

The road they had been following teed into a wider logging road. This road seemed to run directly north and south. George checked the road for signs of travel. There were definitely tire tracks but they were old. How old he could only guess. Mike got out the map and spread it out in the middle of the road and weighed it down with a couple of rocks. He squinted at the map. George guiltily took Mike's reading lens out of his tinder bag, wiped it on his sleeve and handed it to Mike. Mike took it and used it like a magnifying glass to scan the map. This road wasn't on the map either. He handed the glass back to George.

"Keep it," said George with a straight face. "They're yours."

They discussed it for a while then decided on south. Logically south or east brought them closer to civilization.

FORTY-FOUR

Airborne. As he cleared the trees that hemmed in Duck Lake, Danny Gallagher banked left, intending to fulfill a promise.

That morning, by the time the sun had taken the frost from the wings of his Cessna, he had been ready to take to the air. The afternoon before he'd flown in to Duck Lake with four hundred pounds of non-perishable supplies for a trapper by the name of Norman Larose. Larose was not there yet—Danny was set to fly him, his dogs, more gear and some perishable food items in the following week—and so, once he had taxied up to the small dock by the Duck Lake cabin, it had been up to Danny to unload the supplies. And when he was done he'd spent the night at the cabin as he'd arranged.

He had promised Bud that, on the way back the next day, he'd keep an eye open for "Fred and those folks" even though they'd gone missing almost a year and a half ago and were almost surely dead. Danny and a number of other local bush pilots had taken part in the search and rescue effort last year but had come up empty. It had pained him to give up on Fred, but he had eventually. One of the hard realities of being a bush pilot is that you risk going down, dying either in the crash or later, and being lost to the wilderness, disappearing as sure as a ship being forever swallowed up by the sea.Bud has never given up on Fred, and Danny certainly wasn't going to fault him for that. What had sustained Bud initially was the capability of both Fred and George, the guide for Trout Lake Lodge (not that such capabilities do you much good if you die in a plane crash). But more recently it was the strange matter of Joe River's death. Investigators still could not quite piece it together, but one thing was clear—there was at least one other person involved, and *that* person was still at large.

Well, it was *something*. There was no arguing that. And so Danny decided that he would give the area a quick once over on his way back to Kenora. He had no other pressing deadline. His next booked flight was not for three days.

His first destination was Big Buck Lake. He buzzed the cabin there, but there was nothing to suggest there was anyone there, no conspicuous signals laid out on the shore, no smoke rising from where he knew the cabin stood. From Big Buck he made a cursory pass over Long Lake—where Joe's remains had been found in a burnt-out shed in April. But again, nothing caught his eye. He pulled back up to a comfortable altitude of two thousand feet and set a course for Susan Lake which was to have been Joe's extraction point had some cruel fate not intervened.

The trip took less than a half an hour. He easily spotted the lake and pulled back on the throttle to begin a slow descent. He dropped to a couple of hundred feet above the surface of the lake and as he passed abeam the cabin he looked for signs of life but saw none.

Sorry Bud, he thought. *Nothing this time.*

He glanced down at the chart strapped to his thigh and, unsure where else to check, decided to head back to Kenora.

———

Fred woke up at dawn. He'd planned to go hunting, so he dressed quietly and kissed Ruth softly on the lips. She awoke and stretched.

"Good morning, dear. You're up early."

"I know. Go back to sleep, I just wanted to let you know I've gone hunting."

His plan was to take both guns. He would hunt for moose for a couple of hours. If he didn't have any luck with the moose, he might be able to bag a grouse or two on the way home. He walked quietly along the old logging road in the gathering light looking for fresh tracks. He had the shotgun slung across his back with a homemade rope sling. He carried the big rifle out front ready for action. He walked slowly along like this for an hour and a bit. He saw a couple of grouse along the way, but refrained from shooting least he scare off the big prize. Finally his stomach told him it was time to head home.

Ruth had gotten up soon after Fred left. She went down to the dock with the old fishing rod and threw a line in. By the time Fred emerged from the bush, she had landed four nice walleye. Fred hadn't got his moose, but he had three grouse and a rabbit on the way home. At least this would keep them going for two or three more days. Ruth went up to the cabin to get the sharp knife while Fred began cleaning the grouse. She brought down a pot and they began tossing bits in for tonight's soup. The fish heads went in as well as the little grouse legs. In went the livers hearts and emptied gizzards from the birds. The breasts would be another meal. Fred expertly filleted the fish.

Once the fillets were piled up on the dock, Ruth took each fish carcass and trimmed any morsels of meat she could before handing them to the dog. Yukon took the offerings into the bush a few feet away. He didn't eat any of them until he was sure Ruth wasn't going to offer him anymore. Only then did he return to his cache to eat.

Ruth carried the pot, and Fred took the fillets and the meat back up to the cabin. She was going to get a fire going in the stove and get the soup pot simmering with the evening meal. They decided they would have a fillet each for lunch.

"I'll call you when it's ready," she said. "Why don't you relax a bit? It'll take a while for the stove to heat up."

"Alright, I'm going to go down to the dock to try fishing again while lunch is cooking. This afternoon I'll go hunting again."

Fred walked back down to the dock. He baited the hook and tossed the line off the end of the dock. It was a beautiful Indian summer day. He stretched out on the dock in the sun and dozed off.

Ruth busied herself in the cabin. She added a spoonful of the precious rice, a few dried berries and a pinch of salt to the soup. She went outside to collect wood to start the wood stove.

Today would be perfect for drying the fish, she thought, as she headed over to the woodshed for an armload of firewood.

Fred was now sound asleep on the dock. He was having a dream about rescue. He could hear the rescue plane getting nearer and nearer. Suddenly, his eyes snapped open. This was no dream. He jumped to his feet. He could make out a floatplane flying low over the water heading in their direction. Ruth heard it too and dropped her firewood and ran down towards the dock.

———

It was only out of the corner of his eye that he caught it. Even still Danny was unsure that he'd seen anything at all.

Was that movement on the dock?

He pulled up and made a big sweeping turn. He turned onto his final leg and lined up on the lake again this time with the intent on landing. He dropped to within a few feet of the water and cruised down towards the south end where the cabin was. He touched down and turned in toward the dock and could scarcely believe his eyes.

———

Fred had been jumping so high, arms waving wildly, that he thought he might collapse the dock. Ruth was screaming and waving as she ran. When the plane banked they both let out long hoots of joy that brought Yukon running. The big dog howled as Fred and Ruth embraced. Fred could hardly believe it. Ruth was openly weeping. She gave him a huge kiss on the lips and he lifted her off her feet and spun her around almost putting them both into the lake.

It was Danny's little Cessna. As it taxied up to the dock, Fred shook his head and smiled. *Son of a bitch.*

Fred waited until the prop had completely stopped. Then he expertly grabbed the strut and steered the plane down the edge of the dock. The door opened and out stepped Danny Gallagher.

"My God is that you, Fred? Christ I almost didn't recognize you."

"Holy shit, Danny. How the hell are you?" Fred clapped him hard on the shoulder.

"Great," he said shaking his head in disbelief. He looked over at the woman standing behind Fred. "Well, you must be, uh..."

"Ruth," she said still crying tears of joy.

"Kevin and Anne's daughter, right." He took her hand. "They are going to be glad to see you."

"Me too," she said. "You have no idea."

Yukon came onto the dock wagging his tail.

"So where are the other two?" Danny said.

The smile on Fred's face faltered, and he looked at Ruth.

"Oh," said Danny, "I'm sorry, did they not—"

"You mean they weren't the one who told you where to find us?" asked Ruth, suddenly grave.

"No ma'am," he said. "I swung by here again as a favour to Bud, you see... hey isn't that Joe Harper's dog?"

"Yes."

"Klondike," he said.

"Yukon," she said.

Fred said, "No look, George and Mike tried to walk out from here two weeks ago along the old logging roads. They were going to send folks here once they got out."

"Well now it's you two who'll be sending folks out for them I guess," he said. "Let's get you back to civilization."

"But they should have been at the highway a long time ago," said Ruth. "Something must be wrong."

"Look if they're still alive..." Danny said and instantly regretted it as Fred shot him a look. Danny took a deep breath. "What I *mean* to say I'm sure they're fine. If they're on the old roads they won't be hard to find. When we get back we'll send folks up the 105, and if they don't find them there, all them old roads are still mapped out. You'll see."

"They were reasonably prepared," said Fred. "They had a little rifle, and good sleeping bags."

"They must be out of food by now," said Ruth.

"George is never out of food," said Fred.

"You got that right," said Danny. "What about that city guy? I heard he was a bit of a pill."

"Not anymore," replied Fred. "Not any more."

Still in shock, Fred and Ruth staggered back to the cabin to collect, as Danny had put it, "whatever gear you want to bring with you."

There wouldn't be much to collect. Fred grabbed George's gun and gathered up his sleeping bag and the bearskin. Truth be told it was hard to concentrate. He and Ruth were both of the mind to leave most stuff behind in case anyone else found themselves lost up here.

"I have the only thing I need to bring back with me on my finger," she said.

And the reality of a new life with Ruth hit Fred like a bolt from the blue. Ruth put out the fire in the stove, and the two of them stepped back out into dazzling sunlight.

I'll have Danny fly me back out here in a week or so and close up properly, Fred thought.

Back on the dock Danny was all smiles.

"There will be some happy folks back in Kenora," he said.

She had her hand around Fred's hip and was looking at Danny with a big sweet smile. Danny blushed and was momentarily tongue tied."Now look folks I was up here dropping off a skid of supplies, and so I don't have the backseats in, which means—"

"Shotgun," said Ruth.

Fred smiled and tossed the sleeping bag and bearskin in the back of the plane.

"Looks like it's you and me in the back, Yukon.""Oh Jeez, I forgot," said Danny.

"What?"

"This here dog is fussy about getting into the plane. Joe and I used to have to tie a rope to his collar and really manhandle him."

"I can go back to the cabin and find some rope," said Fred.

"No I got rope. It's a matter of which one of us're going to attach it to his collar. He can be pretty ornery."

Meanwhile Ruth had climbed into the back of the plane.

"Here, Yukon!"

At the sound of her voice, Yukon barked once, leapt up into the plane and curled up on the bearskin beside her.

Danny laughed out loud.

"By God, even Joe couldn't get him to do that."

"Guess that means I got shotgun," said Fred.

Ruth's heart leapt as soon as the plane lifted off. She scratched Yukon's head, and the big dog looked at her with soulful amber eyes.

I guess I'm coming back from the dead with a dog and a man. Not a bad deal.

Fred and Danny chatted over the intercom all the way home.

"It feels great to be back in the air," Fred said. "I have never been grounded that long." *Not even close in fact.*

"Think you can still remember how to fly one of these things?"

"You bet I can. Just try me." Fred laughed, happier than he had been for a long time.

Danny took his hands off the controls.

"It's all yours, buddy."

Fred took the controls, a bit nervous at first. But as soon as he had the yoke in his hand and he felt connected to the plane it all came back to him. Fred had often wondered if he would want to fly again since the day of his crash into the bush. Now having control of Danny's plane made him realize that flying was in his blood.

"You better take 'er back, Danny," he said after a moment. "I got something in my eyes."

FORTY-FIVE

Danny sailed up to the dock at Morgan Air. They all watched with anticipation and amusement as Bud hobbled down the stairs to greet them. Danny shut down the engine and let the plane drift in to the edge of the dock. Bud tied off the pontoon while Danny climbed out. Fred purposely had his back to Bud when he climbed out.

When Bud looked up, a strange man was helping a young woman out of the plane. Bud recognized Ruth immediately and his eyes bulged almost out of their sockets. Fred turned to face him and Bud finally realized who this bearded stranger was. It was a race to see who could hug who first. Bud had tears running down his face, but he had a huge smile on his face.

While they were all hugging one another, Danny coaxed Yukon out of the plane. The big dog emptied his bladder all over the dock as soon as he could and then went to stand obediently at Ruth's side.

"Let's go see Mary," Bud finally choked out.

They grabbed their gear and climbed the stairs to the lodge. As soon as Mary saw Fred she squealed with delight. She ran across the living room and threw herself into his waiting arms. After a few moments, she broke free and grabbed Ruth in a big bear hug.

"You go phone your mother," she said, sobbing and pointing at the office.

"Oh God," said Ruth then let out a small sob.

When she passed through the office door, she had to steady herself.

A half hour later, once he got the phone, Bud had brought every one up to speed on what was going on. Bud brought Fred up to speed.

"So have you called Mavis yet?" asked Fred.

"Yes, I called her myself. On my cell phone. She sounded hopeful but said she wasn't going to tell the kids yet. Said they've been through too much already and she doesn't want to get their hopes up. I told her that if they are on the roads they are close. Real close. Maybe today. Maybe tomorrow. Who knows."

God don't go making promises, Bud, Fred thought.

"When I told Mavis that they had gear and a rifle as recent as three weeks ago she thought about that then said 'Well then they should arrive anytime now.' Just as no nonsense as that."

"What about Mike's folks?" Fred asked. "His wife back in Toronto or wherever."

"Mary will try to call her once Ruth is off the phone.

Cathy's her name. She was here last spring for a week just after you folks went down. A real nice lady, Mrs. Cleveland. She had a hard time with the waiting and not knowing."

Ruth dialled the satellite phone number for the lodge with shaky fingers. After a few rings her father answered.

"*Hello?*"

Ruth took a deep breath trying to figure out what to say. Finally, she just blurted it out.

"Dad, it's me, Ruth. I'm alive."

There was no answer, but she could hear him breathing hard over the phone. She had a fleeting notion that he was having a heart attack. Then she heard him sobbing hard. She could hear her mother in the background asking him what the matter was. The sound of a phone changing hands. Her mother's voice, sharp and suspicious.

"Hello, who is this?"

"Mom, it's me," she said, then though she couldn't have said why, "I'm so so sorry. For putting you—"

A gasp that almost sounded like the yelp of a dog. Sobbing in the background

"Oh my sweet baby. Oh my god. Oh Ruth. Oh my god..."

FORTY-SIX

It was a cool night, but not as cold as it had been recently. Mike and George were sitting around the fire more exhausted than they had been for a very long time. They had pushed hard for the past couple of days, making only the flimsiest of shelters and not spending time hunting or gathering. Opting instead to put miles beneath their aching feet. They had just about finished the beaver meat and there were no more berries of any kind. Still both of them felt good about what they'd accomplished over the past forty-eight hours and neither had needed to coax the other further along the old logging road. They stopped when they had to and not before. Thankfully the weather had cooperated.

George stretched and gave a loud yawn and Mike reached into his pants pocket.

"Hey that reminds me," he said apropos of nothing almost delirious with exhaustion. "I was saving this for, well, actually I don't know what I was saving it for."

He held something out to George.

"What is it?"

"Gum. You want some?"

"Where'd you get it."

"Glove compartment of that dead Chevy station wagon back at Susan Lake."

"Nice."

"You want some?"

"Hell yeah."

The gum was hard as rock but softened up pretty quickly and tasted sweet and fruity. They both sat there chewing with amused relish.

"You know, Mike," George said, with a twinkle in his eye, "when I get out of here I just might give up smoking."

Mike started to laugh, unsure of why he even found that so funny. George joined in, and soon they were slapping themselves on the back laughing like drunken sailors.

In the morning they awoke to yet another clear day. They made a pot of spruce tea to warm themselves before they left. They arrived at a tee intersection around noon. Mike got the last of the beaver meat out of his pack and split it as close to fifty–fifty as he could.

"This is it, buddy," he said. "Either you shoot something or we are out of food."

"I'll keep that in mind," he said. "We'll stop earlier today, so I can bag something."

But they ended up following the road north until late after-noon when they came across a small stream and decided to camp for the night. Mike wondered if they might go the night without dinner. If so they would likely delay departure tomorrow while George hunted and he fished.

Mike started making a shelter, though there was no hint of imminent rain. He was hungry. Though they had both meant to stop earlier, it was hard to stop when the highway and rescue might be less than a mile away. Carrying nothing but the rifle, George stalked off to look for dinner. When he was done with the shelter, Mike started on a fire. He had just got it going when he heard the distant crack of the rifle.

Twenty minutes later, there was George with a grouse in his hand.

"I never doubted you for a moment, George."

They stewed as much of the grouse as they could. Still it wasn't much of a meal. They drank the broth as a tea after dinner. Both men went to bed still hungry.

In the morning Mike woke with a giddy flutter in his stomach, and it took him a minute to trace it, but he did eventually.

"Was I dreaming or did I hear a trucks last night at some point? I don't think I was dreaming."

"No," said George with a smile, "I thought I heard them too. We have to be close."

They brewed a spruce tea while they packed up camp. There was no talk of breakfast or lunch. If they'd heard a truck, the highway was waiting for them, and neither of them was going to waste another minute foraging or moving quietly in hopes of bagging their next meal.

This was it.

While they weren't ready to drop their gear, both men felt sure that they would not be unpacking it again and somehow that made it seem lighter than it had before. George contented himself with thoughts of Mavis' cooking and the smell of her hair and the weight of his grandkids whom he liked to carry on his back and how much they'd have grown and all he had missed and the joy at being part of his small world once more.

Mike joy at the thought of seeing his family again was tempered with the gnawing anxiety that they had moved on with their lives—not so much his kids of course, but Cathy. The thought of her with someone else made his legs feel weak.

It'll be great just to see her, to hold her again. We'll just deal with anything else that we have to deal with after I get back.

They walked down the road for no more than a kilometre before they came across not the highway but an active logging road. Fresh tracks probably from the trucks they had heard in the early morning were evident in the roadbed. They turned east on the main logging road and within an hour they met the main highway.

"I almost can't believe it," Mike said.

"I know what you mean," said George. "Let's just keep walking. I think if I waited here I might go crazy."

Mike nodded and readjusted his gear.

"I know what you mean. Standing here feels almost eerie and unreal. How does that Tragically Hip lyric go? The one about stepping out of the wilderness."

"No idea."

The first car they saw was a gleaming red chevy heading south. A young man driving it. A deep booming bass thumping from the sound system. And when they tried to flag it down, it simply sped up.

Both men swore bitterly, but then Mike thought about it.

"I can't blame him I suppose. What would you do if you in that guy's place?"

"I'd pick us up."

"Look at me, George. I'm dressed like a lunatic and carrying an axe."

Mike tossed the axe in the ditch then glanced back at his travelling companion. George nodded, then spit on the asphalt and began disassembling the rifle.

"Polite society, George."

They trudged on for another couple of hours. Along the way they passed a little stream and they filled their water bottles. They saw two cars heading north but nothing more came south. An airplane passed fairly low overhead at one point, but they didn't even bother trying to wave it down.

I've given up on planes, thought Mike. *Who needs 'em?*

About twenty minutes later, however, a police cruiser appeared heading north. They waved at him, trying to flag him down. He passed them then flicked on his lights, turned around and pulled up behind them.

Mike was trying to figure out what to say when the officer got out and gave them both a quick once over.

"My understanding," the young officer said with a big smile on his face, "is that you two will be looking for a lift."

FORTY-SEVEN

Highway 105 rushed by in a blur, and the drone of the engine threatened to put Mike to sleep. He and George had stripped off their outer layers and crammed them, along with their gear, in the trunk while Officer Carnes radioed in with the good news. The cruiser was heated, and the backseat felt like heaven.

My god, do all cars feel this good? Mike thought.

Fred and Ruth had been picked up by a bush pilot the day before and flown back to Morgan's Bay, the same pilot who'd found Joe Harper's remains in the spring, and Mike would need to give a statement by the way when the dust had settled. All this according to Officer Carnes. That same pilot had also flown Ruth's folks in from Trout lake that evening and Bud had picked up Cathy at the airport first thing this morning.

"A nice lady, met her this morning before I headed out," said Carnes. "She is sure looking forward to seeing you, I can tell you what."

"And my kids?" Mike said feeling breathless at the thought of Cathy waiting for him.

"I gather she hasn't said anything to them yet, wants to surprise 'em I guess."

But he knew Cathy better than that. *She doesn't want to get their hopes up.*

George was sitting up front. Apparently Carnes knew George's oldest and supposed that by the time they hit Kenora, Mavis would be waiting for him.

When Mike thought about Cathy, he wanted to ask Officer Carnes to stop somewhere so that he could freshen up, but he couldn't bring himself to. He couldn't ask George to wait. And some part of him knew that Cathy wouldn't care what he looked like.

"Sorry about the smell by the way," Mike said from the back seat. "Can't remember the last time I had a proper bath."

"Hell, this is a police cruiser. You two aren't even the worse smelling folks I've picked up this month."

When they pulled into the lot at Morgan's Bay, Carnes had the lights flashing and gave the siren a short woop. It felt dream-like to Mike. He could see Fred with his arm around Ruth and a woman he guessed was Mavis walking towards the car. And then there was Cathy on the stairs.

George threw open his door and got out.

"Hey girl. Sorry I'm late," he said his voice thick with emotion. Then something sounded like, "We ran into some weather."

Cathy was running down the stairs.

Mike felt like he was moving underwater. He tried to open his door but it wouldn't open. Then he realized he was in the back of a cruiser, and would have to be let out. There was a click as Officer Carnes disengaged the lock.

"Sorry about that, Mr. Cleveland. Go get her."

When he opened the door she was right there. He practically leapt from the cruiser and threw his arms around her.

"My god," she said. "I missed you so much."

Some time later, still in the parking lot, Yukon bounded over to him. Mike was weeping by this point and stooped to pet the big Malamute. Then Fred was there and Ruth. Mike stood up and smiled.

"You couldn't have waited another couple of days and let me and George be heroes, huh?"

Fred laughed and clapped him on the shoulder. "Sorry Doc."

He was about to introduce Cathy but then realized that they'd already met.

"So what did I miss at the lake," he said. "Other than rescue, of course."

"Well, we're engaged," said Ruth. "Does that count?"

Mike didn't know what to say to that. George introduced Mavis and then congratulated Fred and Ruth.

"Guess we were cramping their style, huh Mike?"

"No kidding," said Mike. "No telling what they got up to while we were busting our humps."

Ruth blushed and looked away. Mike glanced back at Cathy and started crying again.

"Come on," she said. "We'll call the kids together. They are going to want to talk to their dad again."

That night in the hotel room Mike held Cathy firmly in his arms. He broke apart for a moment and exposed his now very firm bare bum to her.

"I need to have a tattoo of a float plane *right here.*" Cathy started to giggle. It became an uncontrollable laugh! "Why not?" she sputtered.